MW00426069

INTO A CANYON DEEP

A CHRIS BLACK ADVENTURE

The Chris Black Adventure Series

By James Lindholm

———

INTO A CANYON DEEP

A CHRIS BLACK ADVENTURE

JAMES LINDHOLM

CamCat Publishing, LLC
Brentwood, Tennessee 37027
camcatpublishing.com

This is a work of fiction. Names, characters, places, and incidents are either products of the author's imagination or are used fictitiously.

© 2020 by James Lindholm
All rights reserved. Printed in the United States of America. No part of this book may be used or reproduced in any manner whatsoever without written permission except in the case of brief quotations embodied in critical articles and reviews. For information, address 101 Creekside Crossing Suite 280 Brentwood, TN 37027.

Hardcover ISBN 9781931540360
Paperback ISBN 9780744301298
Large-Print Paperback ISBN 9780744300321
eBook ISBN 9780744300871
Audiobook ISBN 9780744303056

Library of Congress Control Number: 2020937715

Cover design by Jerry Todd. Book design by Maryann Appel.

5   3   1   2   4

For Gran

Your encouragement (and early reading suggestions)
launched me on a lifetime of adventure.

Author's Note

Though Dr. Chris Black and his CMEx team do not exist outside of the printed page, the process they follow to conduct scientific research in the deep subtidal is very much based in reality, including the use of remotely operated vehicles (ROVs) for working deep below the effective depth of SCUBA divers. Faculty, staff, and students working at institutions around the world regularly confront challenges of sampling in a marine environment that frequently doesn't cooperate. I hope that *Into a Canyon Deep* will give you some insight into the endeavor of marine exploration. It is also interesting to note that fact often mirrors fiction. While the main plotline for Chris Black's first adventure is entirely fictional, not long after I completed the story it was reported in the local news that a similar discovery was made on land. You can look it up once you've finished the story.

Life-threatening violence aside, the southern Monterey Bay area that is depicted in these pages is definitely worth a visit when you have the opportunity. In my role as a practicing research scientist I regularly refer to the Bay as the greatest 'living laboratory' in the world for the study of temperate ecosystems. We have tide pools, kelp forests, deep canyons, all accessible from shore, along with the invertebrates, fishes and marine mammals that live in those environments. It is, in a very real sense, the "Blue Serengeti," a term that my colleague Dr. Barbara Block first coined.

1

Spinning into the wake of the receding fishing vessel *Lizzie J*, Joe Rothberg's many wounds bled steadily. A blue, bioluminescent aura enveloped him as the movement of his sinking body agitated thousands of small planktonic organisms.

Only minutes before he'd watched the sleeves of his favorite sweatshirt slowly wick saltwater up his partially submerged arms as he'd dangled from a half-inch nylon line on the boat's bow. Hanging by his broken right leg, Joe's head was only inches from the cool ocean's surface.

He knew it was supposed to be pretty deep out there above the Carmel Canyon. The captain had said more than two *thousand* feet—two thousand feet. He saw and smelled the beach close by, even in the pitch black of the moonless spring night.

Maybe if I yell, he hoped, someone will help. Maybe someone will call the police or the Coast Guard.

Joe had tried to focus beyond the steady drum of the pulse beating in his ears, tried to remember the tricks his counselor had taught him when he was a kid, tricks to control the jumble of random ideas bouncing around in his head. "Identify what I'm feeling, identify what I'm feeling, identify what I'm—fuck! What am I doing out here?" The dark waters didn't respond.

He kept coming back to the fact that he'd been helping dump toxic waste into the ocean. Sarah is going to kill me if she finds out, he thought. *Not* cool.

Joe had felt the disappointment of Sarah, his parents, even his old counselor, Margaret Black, more intensely than the growing strain on his broken leg. His high school glory days were long gone. At least that was what he had realized when two weeks earlier he'd come home to find Kevin O'Grady, wearing camouflage pants, an expensive suede jacket, and what looked like military boots, sitting in the living room talking with Sarah. The baby was resting in the bouncy seat beside the couch.

They'd been sitting on the *same* couch, not across from each other as Joe would've if he'd been visiting someone else's wife. He knew that Sarah and Kevin had dated back in high school. In fact, there'd been rumors that Kevin was the father of Sarah's first baby, the one she aborted.

What hurt Joe most was what he'd seen in the first seconds after he came in the front door. Sarah had been smiling. There was a light in her eyes that he hadn't noticed in years. What he wouldn't give to see that light again and to be the reason for it. Instead, he saw the light go out when he entered.

O'Grady's size—the living room appeared to shrink in size with him in it—and the fact that he was seriously mean, kept Joe's pain and irritation at bay. Even if Joe had wanted to make some kind of point that day, to assert his husbandly authority, to try to earn back some respect from his wife, he knew it wouldn't have mattered. O'Grady could beat the shit out of him, no problem.

The next surprise came when O'Grady had turned to Joe that day and offered *him* a job. Sure, most of the spiel had been total crap offered up for Sarah's benefit. O'Grady had made up some story about a business partner needing help at night in a new warehouse in neighboring Seaside.

The job had brought Joe offshore for the eighth time in the past two weeks. He'd been supervising the disposal of toxic waste. Not so much supervising as standing around, actually. Joe's primary responsibility had been to match each barrel with a list O'Grady had given him and to make sure that each one made it over the side before the boat headed back in. O'Grady's boss apparently wanted a white man overseeing the dumping operations, even if that white man had far less experience with this type of work everyone else on board. Though O'Grady's business partner, if that's what he was, hired dozens of Mexican, Asian, and African American workers, down deep, Joe had figured, he was still just a racist dick.

Joe's regrets about working for a guy like that, and dumping waste into the ocean to boot, had grown with each trip down from Monterey. Two nights ago, on his seventh trip, he realized that he had to do something. He couldn't quit, he needed the money too badly. And he didn't want to call the cops, since he didn't want to get arrested. And anyway, he'd overheard O'Grady talking about the fact that his boss owned the cops. So that was a dead end. But he could try to alert someone to what was going on out there.

After some contemplation, a solution had come to him. Earlier in the evening he had stopped at the FedEx store in Monterey before coming down to the dock. He felt much better about everything after that stop. He would take his money from tonight and be done with it. He would never have to think about Kevin O'Grady again.

Tonight was perfectly calm, which Joe knew was unusual for this time of year as strong northwesterly winds tended to blow hard day and night. So instead of supervising, he'd spent much of the time leaning on the rail, enjoying the lights shimmering on the glassy ocean's surface as cars went speeding down California Highway 1. Below him little bursts of blue light formed and then exploded just under the surface like fireworks. Bio-lumi-something or other, he was told.

An accidental cough from one of the Vietnamese crewmen as they approached him, coming at him from the stern alerted him. Joe noted that all the evening's barrels had been dumped. And then he realized that the five crewmen were carrying clubs. Oh shit! Had they figured out that he had betrayed them?

Not waiting for an answer, Joe moved as fast as his fat ass allowed him, climbing out onto the narrow rail that surrounded the boat and shimmying along the outside of the wheelhouse as he moved toward the bow. His chubby, sweaty fingers moved quickly along the wooden trim while his old Converse high tops kept pace below them. The lifeboat mounted on the bow might be his chance to escape.

The relief Joe experienced upon reaching the bow ahead of his pursuers was short-lived. O'Grady, whom Joe hadn't realized was on board tonight, came forward from the other side of the wheelhouse carrying his aluminum baseball bat.

"End of the line, Joey boy," O'Grady said. "No loose ends."

At that point Joe, still panting from his exertion, had given in to the inevitable. There was no way he was going to get out of this. No way. His shoulders slumped and he made no effort to dodge either the incoming bat or the kick that followed.

O'Grady had obviously not waited to hear the splash, nor had he looked over the side. Had he done so, he'd have seen Joe's body snagged on a line that was running from the bow of the fishing boat to the stern.

Joe felt the boat's powerful engines come to life through the barnacle-encrusted hull before he heard them. Could he make it all the way back to port in this position, he wondered? Maybe he could sneak away once the boat was tied up back at the fish pier.

As the boat began the return trip to Monterey, the bow lifted and then dipped into the oncoming swells. The first swell to brush the hull grabbed Joe from the line and swept him aft toward the stern of the boat.

The chill of the fifty-five-degree water barely registered as Joe was briefly free of the boat. The surge of adrenaline accompanying his release had armored him against the pain of being dragged along the weathered hull. Joe had had just enough time to consider his situation before he'd been drawn under the boat as he approached the stern.

Within seconds he was sucked into the portside propeller, which had been moving at full throttle. The propeller had ripped open Joe's left thigh, nearly severed his right arm, and sliced deeply into his scalp.

Adrift and sinking fast, the last synapse of Joe's dying brain fired in an expression of hope that Chris Black, someone he'd not spoken to in over twenty years, would know what to do with the package Joe had sent him.

2

Chris Black was not thinking about packages. Not thinking about work. Not thinking about much at all, other than his dad. For each of the past five years, Chris had come to this rocky promontory at the northwestern edge of Point Lobos State Nature Reserve to privately acknowledge the anniversary of his father's death.

Point Lobos, named by Spanish explorers after the abundant California sea lions, or "wolves of the sea," found there, served as the southern boundary of Carmel Bay. Looking to the west across the windblown swells of the Pacific from his perch on the rocks, the sheer vastness of the Earth's largest ocean quieted Chris's overworked brain. He knew that the only thing between him and the Chinese mainland was twelve-thousand-odd miles of deep blue sea; more than half of the circumference of the globe. But looking at it on a map didn't do that distance justice; one had to see it firsthand.

With a research cruise starting in two days, there were plenty of things that Chris, the chief scientist for the cruise, knew he should be thinking about. But tradition dictated that he be at this place on this day regardless of what was else was happening in life. Wearing jeans, a fleece-lined jacket, and a university baseball hat, neither the strong northwest wind nor the periodically cascading foam from the crashing surf below bothered him much.

In his late thirties, Chris had the physique of athlete, toned by action rather than gym workouts. Though at six foot two Chris wasn't huge, a certain energy was emanating from him that made him seem bigger than he actually was. The lines on his face and the grey streaks in his otherwise dark hair only added to his overall character, or so he'd been told on a couple of occasions. He'd also been told that he looked like Agent Mulder on *The X-Files*, but the only agent from that TV show he cared about was Scully.

Chris was a native of nearby Carmel-by-the-Sea. His family had been stable and, though not particularly wealthy for the area, they didn't want for much. His father, first a military fighter pilot, then a commercial airline pilot, and ultimately an executive for United Airlines, had been a largely stern but fair influence on Chris's life.

Dad. Normally memories of his father were conflicted, a complicated mosaic of memories both bad and good. Andrew Black had instilled in Chris, at an early age, a strong notion of right and wrong that clearly derived from a world view shaped by war. That instillation had come at a cost, however, with countless holidays marred by barking orders instead of kind words, homework sessions more appropriate for boot camp than third grade, and generally unpredictable grumpiness that always kept the family on edge.

On the other hand, by teaching Chris to swim and, later, to SCUBA dive even before formal certification agencies were doing so, Andrew had inadvertently solidified Chris's career trajectory before Chris was ten years old. In later years, when reporters or interested students pressed for an explanation as to why Chris spent so much time in the water, or why his interest in marine biology endured over the years, his memory returned like a reflex to his earliest childhood.

He remembered many early June days like this one, when no one in their right mind would enter the cold water of southern Monterey

Bay without a wetsuit, except Chris and his dad. They'd spent hours over the years frolicking in the surf in their bathing suits, clinging to an inflatable raft while pretending to be castaways from a pirate ship. Chris could remember being so cold that his fingers had stopped working and he couldn't feel his feet, but at the same time he hadn't wanted to be anywhere else in the world.

Movement down to his left alerted him to a man and a young boy climbing along the rocks close to the water. Probably tourists, Chris figured. The red-faced man carried a gut that was seriously taxing a bright red Carmel T-shirt that no self-respecting local would be caught dead wearing. His jeans weren't faring much better. And he was wearing flip flops. It was no small hike to make it all the way out to the point with a child that was probably only five or six years old. The poor guy's discomfort from the exertion was palpable even at a distance, and wearing flip flops would not have helped anything. Chris was surprised the flip flops had made it as far as they had.

The blonde child, wearing a blue T-shirt emblazoned with a *Superman* logo and red shorts, leapt from rock to rock with more facility than the man. Not every step was surefooted, and there were quite a few loud warnings from the man, who was likely the kid's father, but the indomitable spirit of childhood won out. Chris smiled at the thought that the kid was probably very good at video games and other digital challenges but was nevertheless fearless out in the world of real physical dangers.

Chris returned his gaze to the open ocean and wanted to re-focus his mind on his own dad. But the father-son dynamic playing out in the present won out over re-hashing those of the past.

He looked back down to see the boy was now several feet ahead of the man frenetically moving over the rocks just above the high tide line without watching the water. If he wasn't careful, one of the coming swells was going to take him out.

Come on kid, Chris urged silently as he felt his own muscles tense, turn around. *Never* turn your back on the ocean.

"Hey, kid!" Chris yelled as he stood up, hoping at least to get the father's attention. "Watch out for that swell!"

Too late. The next swell rolled in, an amorphous blue-green predator stalking its prey. It reached the boy and effortlessly lifted him off the rocks, drawing him back into the water. He quickly disappeared below the surface.

The father screamed, but Chris couldn't hear what he said.

Chris removed his smartphone and wallet, placing them safely in a crack in the rock behind him. The kid was going to be history if someone didn't get to him very soon. He turned to and prepared to make the ten-foot drop to the water, waiting for the next surge of water and trying to keep his eyes on the boy, who was back at the surface for the moment and struggling.

The next swell came, and Chris leapt, feet first and shoes on. There were too many dangers beneath the surface to enter head first, and though shoes would make swimming more difficult, against the rocks they would be invaluable.

He hit the water and immediately opened his arms into a "T" position to halt his momentum and to keep himself at the surface. The frigid water instantly closed around his chest, drawing away his breath.

Chris knew that the fifty-five-degree water was not the most immediate problem. Though water wicked away body heat at more than thirty-two times faster than air, he planned to be out of the water well before hypothermia had a chance to set in. The real threat came from being right in the impact zone as the swells from the north Pacific came crashing in against the barnacle-encrusted rocks.

Two quick overhand strokes carried Chris over to the boy. The boy's eyes were wide with panic and his lips were already turning blue. Chris grabbed him with his left arm while trying to get purchase on the rocks with his right.

"It's okay, big guy. I've got you. Let's get you out of here."

The boy was surprisingly light. Chris realized that he might be able to swing him up to the father if the ocean cooperated. No sooner had that thought crossed his mind than the swell receded. Chris held on briefly but realizing that the water level was dropping too fast and too low, he released his grip and let the current take them with it.

The boy screamed, probably thinking that they were going to be sucked out to sea.

"It's alright," Chris said, "We'll be out of here... NO!" Chris was preparing to ride the next swell up high enough to pass the kid back to his father, when he realized that he was jumping off the rocks, apparently to try and save them.

The father hit the water awkwardly, arms flailing, just as the next swell came in, and he dropped like a rock. Chris held fast to the boy and squared his feet against the rocks. As the wave swept in, Chris used his leg strength to keep them off the rocks while leaning back to create less resistance against the oncoming water, pulling the boy briefly underwater. He could feel the boy struggling but held firm.

Popping his head back above the surface, Chris scanned the area for the father. The man was floating at the surface a few feet away. He wasn't moving and he was bleeding from a gash across the forehead.

Chris realized that his range of good options was rapidly shrinking. The rock wall was steep and high as far as he could see in either direction, offering no obvious point to climb out of the water.

He decided to get the boy out before returning for the father. If he tried to rescue them both simultaneously, all three of them would surely die.

Side-stroking toward the lowest point on the cliff a few feet away, keeping the boy's head above water, Chris spotted two men climbing down toward the water's edge. The two men formed a human chain, placing the lower of the two just within reach of Chris.

Chris once again timed his approach with the swell and rode the surging water up the face of the cliff. Using his feet to climb as high as possible, he grabbed the boy with both hands and thrust him upward to the waiting arms of the passerby.

Seeing the man grab the boy, Chris launched himself off the rock with his feet and began to search for the father. Fewer than ten minutes had passed, but he could feel the cold water zapping him of energy. He had to find the father fast before they were both crushed against the rocks.

Chris shivered uncontrollably as he backtracked to where he had seen the father last. He was starting to feel pain from cuts on his arms that he must've sustained earlier without realizing it. He leaned back and tread water for a minute to collect himself for one final push. He judged the probability of success to be very low, and he was beginning to wonder if he'd get out himself.

And then something bumped him from behind. Chris spun around to find the father floating behind him, face down and not breathing.

Chris flipped him over and supported his head out of the water. He gave two short rescue breaths but struggled to keep the man's face above the surface while doing so. He needed floatation.

His cold-addled mind drifting, Chris looked around him to see what, if any, options he had remaining. The swells kept coming in, but he and the father were now far enough away from the rocks that being crushed was not an immediate concern. He twice looked past a large yellow jacket floating next to him. The third time he looked at it he also heard the men yelling down to him from the rocks above.

They were yelling something like, "Grab the jacket!" which Chris found interesting since there was a jacket right next to him.

11

He looked at it more closely. It looked like someone had tied off the sleeves, neck and waist to make a rudimentary floatation device. Brilliant.

A large swell pushed Chris and the man toward the rocks. When Chris's left shoulder slammed into the barnacle encrusted rock wall the pain electrified him long enough to break his stupor.

He turned the man to the right, grabbing the yellow jacket and placing it underneath the man's torso. Chris then began to kick as fast as he could. With shoes on, he found the flutter kick normally used by breast "strokers" to be the most efficient means of propulsion. He swam in thirty-second increments, stopping only to give the man two rescue breaths before proceeding onward.

Later, in the relative comfort of the nearby Ranger station, the two men who'd been on the cliff above described to Chris how amazed they were that he managed the ten-minute swim around the corner and into the only protected inlet within hundreds of yards. Chris listened as he warmed up with a detached interest, for he remembered none of it.

To hear the two men tell it, Chris had rescued the father and his son from certain death. Both were on their way to the hospital, cold and bruised, but alive. Chris could only smile and wonder if his own father had been watching from somewhere out there.

3

"We're going to need a bigger boat." Dr. Chris Black smiled as he recalled Chief Brody's timeless words from *Jaws*.

It was two days later, and he'd slipped back into his role of chief scientist aboard the research vessel *MacGreggor*. A large male white shark swam slowly off screen. Its ominous black eye had briefly looked right into the camera, but the shark appeared to be unaffected by the presence of the *Seaview*, a remotely operated vehicle, or ROV.

Chris leaned back to turn down the volume on the smartphone speakers behind his head. He was once again wearing jeans and a dark blue fleece emblazoned with the university's logo.

"*That* was a big white shark."

"Farewell and adieu to my dear Spanish ladies," hummed Robert "Mac" Johnson, the pilot of the ROV, sticking with the *Jaws* theme. He was wearing a spotless, one-piece blue work suit with "ROV Team" stenciled across the back, complemented by a well-loved khaki baseball cap with a badly frayed bill. Nodding toward Chris, Mac added, "Farewell and adieu my ladies of Spain. We've got something else on sonar, large, directly ahead, about fifteen meters out. Nap time's over."

"I haven't napped since you made us watch *Waterworld* again," Chris replied, still thinking about the shark. This was deeper than he had seen white sharks before this close to shore, and it was still pretty early for them to begin arriving on the Central Coast. "We've definitely got to bring more movies out with us on these cruises."

"*Waterworld* was epic, way ahead of its time," Mac said as he maneuvered the ROV into position in front of a huge piled boulder reef located halfway up the Carmel Canyon, six hundred feet below the *MacGreggor.* "Filming at sea like that was hard core."

The three graduate students—Matt, Travis, and Marisa—sitting behind Mac and Chris looked at each other incredulously. Though it was sunny outside, the group was confined to the *MacGreggor's* ROV lab, or "mission control," a darkened, fourteen-by-eight-foot windowless room in the interior of the state-of-the-art ship. While windows would've been appreciated by anyone stuck in there, solar glare made watching video difficult, so no windows were provided. When the ROV was in the water, the only illumination in the room came from the six large flat panel screens arrayed on one wall from the ceiling to the top of the control console. Each displayed the output from one of the *Seaview's* cameras or sonar.

It was an often-overwhelming view for the uninitiated. Watching six large screens, each capturing one of the ROV's cameras moving over the seafloor six hundred feet below at different angles, could be six times more nauseating than a typical boat ride. This was frequently compounded by the fact that the ship itself, subject to swell and wave conditions back up at the surface, would rock in yet another direction altogether. Many a student had come to sea on the *MacGreggor* with a desire to master mission control only to find that the room quickly mastered them, sending them out to the deck rail after just seconds inside.

Immediately in front of the screens sat the large, intricate control panel used to operate the ROV. The ROV pilot and the chief scientist sat in comfortable bucket seats with easy access to redundant sets of all controls, including the joysticks used to fly the ROV. Both wore wireless headsets for communicating with the ship's captain on the bridge and with the deck crew at the stern responsible for launch and recovery of the ROV.

Behind the pilot and chief scientist, additional scientists, graduate students, and other observers sat in the four, slightly less comfortable chairs. This was by design. If the chairs were too comfortable, the alluring relief of sleep would win out every time.

"Yeah, hard core." Chris raised his eyebrows as he looked towards the students. "Don't let Mac near the movies tonight."

Marisa laughed.

"What was that?" Mac asked.

A large pile of boulders loomed in front of the *Seaview*. Each boulder was car-sized and covered with tall vase sponges and large, multi-colored anemones. Interestingly, the lack of light at great depths didn't prevent the sea life from displaying frequently remarkable coloration, rivaling coral reefs for pure beauty. Science had yet to explain precisely why animals are so vividly colored at a depth where colors are not visible, but the phenomenon has been documented worldwide. Above the reef swam a massive aggregation of fishes, so dense at points that the reef disappeared behind them.

Mac used the joystick control to slow the ROV's approach and gradually began to fly up the side of one of the boulders, keeping the ROV a half meter above the boulder's surface.

"Let's capture all this on video," Chris instructed, nodding to Travis, the graduate student immediately behind him and to his right.

Chris Black had made a career out of exploring life beneath the waves, including the notable discovery of prehistoric fishes long-since believed to have been extinct, and most recently, the discovery that great white sharks, long believed to be a coastal species, in fact spent much of their time in the open ocean, often swimming to great depths.

His close friend Mac Johnson was a physical and temperamental counterpoint. He wore his hair a bit longer, in a small pirate-like ponytail, which usually poked out from under one of his many baseball caps. Chris was tall and long-limbed, but Mac was a compact five foot nine and a dense one hundred ninety pounds. His ponytail and perpetual smirk gave him the appearance of youth, though he was the same age as Chris. And where Chris was quick to start up a discussion with a stranger, Mac was far less conversational, often even when among friends.

It was also common for Mac to play the role of naysayer to Chris's can-do optimist. Where Chris's upbringing had been a picture of stability, Mac's parents had divorced when he was eight years old, leaving Mac the "man of the house" at an early age. Absent a paternal authority figure, Mac had found his own way to stability, and this had, in his own words, left him grumpy most of the time.

Mac and Chris had grown up surfing, swimming, and climbing together as well as pursuing a few less-than-productive activities. Following an interminable four years in high school, Chris took off for college and graduate school on the East Coast. Meanwhile, Mac joined the Navy. He took rapidly to his work and earned a coveted spot with the SEALs before an injury brought a premature end to his military career.

After a two-year post-doctoral fellowship at the Woods Hole Oceanographic Institution in Massachusetts, Chris returned to the Monterey Peninsula around the same time that Mac finished an electrical engineering degree down south in San Luis Obispo. When a new research center was built on the campus of the university's marine lab in Monterey, Chris and Mac had come together again.

Chris Black had been hired by Dr. Peter Lloyd, director of the marine lab and now of the university's new Center for Marine Exploration (CMEx) as well, to lead a team of faculty, staff, and students conducting research on the pressing ecological questions of the day. As many of those questions required diving deeper than the one hundred twenty feet that conventional SCUBA diving allowed, Chris immediately introduced Peter to Mac and initiated a discussion about bringing an ROV program to CMEx. Never one to vacillate, Peter had instantly seen the utility of the proposal and had hired Mac shortly thereafter.

Now, five years later, the CMEx was flourishing, even in a tough economic climate. The Research Vessel, or RV, *MacGreggor*, and the ROV *Seaview*, formed the foundation of a multi-million-dollar research program second to none; and students flocked to the program from all over the world to experience the challenges of working underwater firsthand.

There was a growing mythology among CMEx students surrounding Chris and Mac's extracurricular exploits. True or not, the legends made Chris and Mac more intriguing than their academic achievements, drawing even more students to work with them.

Four hours later, having transected the main branch of the Carmel Canyon, the *Seaview* came to the surface just offshore of Monastery Beach in southern Carmel. Out of the dark lab and into the noon-day sun of the upper deck, the group watched as Mac used a remote console to "fly" the ROV along the surface back toward the crane at the stern of the boat. Against a backdrop of white sands, cypress trees, and the monastery that gave the beach its name, the ROV was lifted from the water and placed gently on the deck.

Chris slapped Mac on the back as music blared in the background. "Cheated death once again, old friend!"

"Yeah, yeah, yeah. Just happy to be here," Mac grumbled. "I wasn't happy with the port thruster at the end of the dive, and the HD camera needs to be reoriented a bit. I'll need about forty-five minutes to get things rolling before we dive again."

"Sounds good." Chris didn't give in to his friend's grumpy mood. "I'm catching a ride back to shore to give that 'dog and pony show' this afternoon over in Pebble Beach. Gretchen will swap out with me and join you on the next dive. She'll keep Matt and Travis in line."

"I hope she brings chocolate. It's going to be a long afternoon without chocolate," Mac said, sure that this particular point needed no clarification.

4

"This doesn't look too fuckin' good. Not too fuckin' good at all," Kevin O'Grady remarked. "We might be totally screwed here."

A black SUV and a black truck were parked side by side facing the ocean in the dirt parking lot at southern Monastery Beach overlooking Carmel Bay. The smattering of other cars in the lot belonged to recreational SCUBA divers who had come to test themselves against the world-renowned surf entry. Dubbed "Mortuary Beach" by the local newspapers, the signs throughout the parking lot depicting recent drownings didn't even merit a glance from the enthusiastic masses.

Kevin O'Grady sat behind the wheel of his new truck watching the ROV recovery through high-powered binoculars. He'd been watching the *MacGreggor* for more than three hours and knew this was going to piss off his boss.

"I'm gonna call this in," he noted aloud, receiving a grunt from the occupant to his right, who was working at emptying a bag of nacho cheese chips.

"See that orange shit all over your fingers? Don't get any of that on the seat or anything else. And turn down the fucking radio," Kevin said without taking his eyes off the *MacGreggor*.

His large fingers punched away at his smartphone and waited. His current boss picked up on the first ring. "What?"

"I'm watching them recover the robot, or whatever they call that thing, right now," Kevin explained. "They've been underwater for more than three hours, and it looks like they're right where we made our delivery last week."

There was a deep, uncomfortable pause on the other end of the line, so Kevin continued. "I can see Black standing at the rail, and his friend Johnson is there, too. He's supposed to be some kind of tough guy. Former SEAL or some shit like that. The others must be students. And a small boat just pulled up with some chick on board. They must have come from Stillwater. Looks like Black is getting in. He has something in a yellow case that he's taking with him. What do you want us to do?"

"Who do you have there with you?"

"Not exactly the A team, but they should do," Kevin replied, looking over at his colleague who was now tilting the bag of chips up at a forty-five-degree angle to empty the last remaining crumbs into his mouth.

"Okay," the boss said slowly. "Send a couple of guys over to Stillwater and tell them to follow Black. Discretely. You come back out here. We have some things to discuss."

"Will do. I'll be back shortly." Kevin rolled down the passenger side window of the truck and motioned for the two guys in the SUV to do the same. "Boss wants the two of you to go over to Stillwater and follow Black wherever he goes after the boat comes in. Think you can handle that?"

"We're on it." The driver fired up the SUV's engine. He dumped a breakfast sandwich wrapper out the window.

"Don't fuck this up. Follow him and call me. Do nothing else. Understand?"

Both nodded as the SUV backed up and merged into the northbound traffic on Highway 1, using the turn signal Kevin noted. That pissed

20

Kevin off. First chips all over his seat, and now they're using turn signals. Fuckin' amateurs.

Kevin started up the truck and cranked the radio. He slammed into reverse, directing the truck right into the southbound lane facing directly into a line of cars travelling about fifty to sixty miles per hour. Tires screeched and bumpers crunched on impact as three cars crashed into one another.

"God damned tourists," he offered as he accelerated, without turn signals, into the northbound lane, causing three more cars to veer off the road.

5

Gretchen Clark pulled up alongside the *MacGreggor* in one of the CMEx's twenty-seven-foot Boston Whalers, and she did indeed bring chocolate—lots of it. She knew from experience that chocolate kept field teams happy in a way that little else could.

Chris noted that the Whaler was being piloted by Alex Smith, one of several capable CMEx technicians. He was a strapping youngster, and Chris wondered from the rail above if Alex's obvious interest in Gretchen had been picked up on by the recipient of his attention. Hard to tell since Gretchen kept her cards close to her vest.

Gretchen was twenty-nine and about five foot six. She was Chris's right hand at the CMEx. He said frequently that Gretchen held together the entire house of cards, from supplying chocolate to administering grants and analyzing complex ecological data. It was a complicated job description that had only become more intricate over the years.

Chris had hired Gretchen right out of college at Dartmouth, while he was back in Woods Hole, to work on a short-term project. When he got the faculty position at the university and headed back to California, she came, too. Now in her eighth year on the team, Gretchen had more field experience than many scientists twice her age, and yet she still had the nicest, calmest disposition of anyone Chris had ever met.

This latter fact served the CMEx team quite well when gauging a problem's seriousness. One swear word from Gretchen meant it was panic time.

Stepping onto the deck of the *MacGreggor*, saltwater dripping off the bright yellow, waterproof CMEx jacket and pants she wore on the ride out, Gretchen pointed methodically at Mac, then Chris, as she stepped on board. "Hi, everyone! Mac, I brought lots of chocolate. Chris, here is your transportation. But I need to talk to you for five minutes before you go if you don't mind."

Gretchen passed the chocolate to Matt and Marisa, who handled the bags with serious attention as if they were valuable specimens. Mac quickly swooped in and snagged a bag of M&M's before they disappeared. "Hang on! I'm taking these before the frenzy begins," he said to no one in particular. "Everyone, watch your fingers."

"That's optimal foraging for you. Grumpy, yes, but still optimal," Chris replied, referring to the well-known ecological theory that suggests organisms will forage for food in a way that maximizes their energy intake, while minimizing the energy expended to find and consume that food. Then he turned to Gretchen. "What's up, Gretchen?"

"I don't want to bother you, but I have just a couple of signatures and some other things on my list. Are you heading back to campus this afternoon?" Gretchen stepped into the adjacent stateroom and Chris followed. She pulled several pieces of paper out of a waterproof Pelican case and laid them out on the desk.

"I can if necessary. I don't know how long the donor meeting is going to last."

"It's a bummer that you have to get off the boat in the middle of a cruise to meet with donors. You might miss some exciting stuff."

"No doubt that I will. But this isn't like the old days when we were at sea more than we were on land. At least not for me. Working with

Peter to keep CMEx funded is my responsibility now. I actually think it's pretty interesting. Talking with non-scientists is refreshing. And talking with non-scientists who are interested in funding us is even more so."

"Right. So, moving on it would be great if you could sign these." She slid the forms toward Chris.

"Alright. That's it," Gretchen said as Chris passed back the forms, signed. "You can hit the, er, road, as it were."

"Aye, aye. On my way," Chris replied, slipping on his own waterproof jacket in preparation for the ride.

They walked back out onto the deck. Before stepping down into the whaler from the *MacGreggor's* stern dive platform, Chris looked back to Gretchen and quickly fired off a few more thoughts.

"Looks like the wind is coming up. Text me later with your progress, and I'll check in after the dog and pony show with the donors."

Gretchen smiled and saluted. From behind the ROV, Mac said something that sounded like, "Better you than me."

"I think we can all agree on that. I'll handle the smooth-talking." Chris put on a hat and nodded to Alex to shove off.

Alex rapidly brought the whaler's duel outboard motors up to full speed, and the boat barely touched the water as it flew across Carmel Bay. Chris's laptop computer, smartphone, and other valuables sat safely in a Pelican case under his seat, so he sat back and watched Carmel pass by through the spray.

They passed Carmel River Beach, where the Carmel River entered the southern part of the Bay. Its steep white sands and crystal blue water evoked images of a tropical paradise

As they rounded Carmel Point, Chris recognized the familiar "butterfly house" and the "copper roof house," both built right down to the water, and the latter designed by Frank Lloyd Wright. Carloads of tourists could be seen meandering around the point on Scenic Drive, trying valiantly to understand the protocol for driving with seas of bikers and walkers on a single lane road barely a car-length wide.

Carmel Beach proper came into view next, where dog owners, literally from around the world came to frolic with their pets. As a dog owner himself, and given the increasingly small number of places one could take a dog these days, Chris had to begrudgingly admit that it was nice to have access to such beautiful beach where dogs could run free. His own dog certainly enjoyed every opportunity to frolic in the sand and roll around in the smelly piles of kelp lining the beach. But Chris had stepped in just enough unbagged dog crap and chased off just enough wild pets and their owners to avoid buying into the madness of complete dog supremacy.

As the whaler crossed over to Pebble Beach and into Stillwater Cove, Chris noticed a Coast Guard vessel tied up at the small pier next to a boat from the Monterey County Sheriff's Office. The pier was packed with emergency vehicles of various sorts, and many uniformed people were mulling around.

Stillwater Cove was just over the line between Carmel-by-the-Sea and the private Pebble Beach development. It was a small harbor with little boat activity, save the handful of sailboats that moored just off the beach each summer. Activity like this was something one didn't see frequently down here.

"What's up, I wonder?" Alex asked as he maneuvered the whaler into the small floating pier ahead of the official vessels. "We saw these guys in the area when I brought Gretchen out, but there's a lot more happening now."

Nodding back toward the officers standing near the sheriff's boat, Alex added, "I know a couple of those guys. If you can wait a minute, I'll check it out."

Chris was running on a fairly tight schedule, but the jarring presence of all this emergency personnel in an otherwise tranquil area intrigued him, so he took his time collecting his things.

"They found a body over in the rocks," Alex reported when he returned. "No I.D. It looks like he'd been in the water for more than a week."

"Huh. Another tourist washed out at Monastery? I haven't heard about anyone going missing," Chris said, recalling his own near miss only two days before. There had been several incidents over the past few years in which unsuspecting tourists had been washed out to sea while walking along Carmel's beaches too close to the surf line. Most people repeatedly underestimated the power of the ocean.

"No, actually this looks like a boating-related accident. Remember that I did that marine mammal rescue internship last year? I saw a lot of propeller marks on dead animals. This guy looks just like those animals did. *Not* a good way to go."

"I'm not sure there is a *good* way to go. I'm outta here. Thanks for the ride in. I'm not sure yet if I'll be heading back out tomorrow. Gotta check with Peter first. I'll give you a call."

"Cool. I think I'll see if I can learn anything more about the body. I'll have my cellphone with me, so give me a call if you need a ride back out, or anything else. Later."

6

Chris grabbed his Pelican case and began the wobbly walk up the ramp from the floating dock to the parking lot. After a couple of days on the boat he could feel his body trying to re-adjust to life on solid ground. While most people who came out with them to sea had trouble getting their sea legs, Chris always found it much more uncomfortable to return to land. He preferred the feel of the Pacific's undulating swells underneath him to the unforgiving concrete on land.

He dug out his keys and threw his case into the back of his vintage 1964 Land Rover 109 Safari Wagon. His father had cared for the forest green vehicle meticulously when he was alive and left it to Chris after he died. The elaborate roof rack and the hood-mounted spare tire gave the impression that a safari was imminent. Though Chris generally kept the front two-thirds of his truck immaculate in homage to his father, the rear compartment was frequently cluttered with a wide variety of stuff, so he'd have to move a bit of gear around in the back to accommodate the case.

Leaving the yacht club parking lot, he cruised slowly through the Pebble Beach golf course, avoiding errant balls, golf carts, and uptight golfers. After turning right onto Seventeen-Mile Drive, he punched it and headed for the Pebble Beach/Carmel Gate.

The Seventeen-Mile Drive was world famous for its breathtaking views of the rocky California coastline. Transitioning from field mode to fundraising mode, Chris's attention was elsewhere, and he didn't think anything of the black GMC truck that followed him into the moderate traffic a couple of cars back. There were always maintenance crews and landscapers driving around both Pebble Beach and Carmel.

Having grown up in Carmel-by-the-Sea, Chris had known these streets well for most of his life. He'd spent much of the late 1970s and early '80s with his friends Mac and Jase glued to his bike, riding like a madman through every street, secret path, and back yard the small city offered.

He left New England and returned to the area at the height of the recent real estate bubble when property values were ridiculously high. The modest inheritance that he'd received at his father's passing had enabled him to buy a small, modern house on a street off the "Golden Rectangle," home to some of the most desirable real estate in the area. The extremely private street hadn't even showed up on Google Maps.

The two-bedroom, two-and-half bath, eighteen-hundred-square-foot house sat back among the evergreens against one of Carmel's many small canyons. The furnishings were largely IKEA, which Mac enjoyed pointing out every time he came by. "Hmmm," he'd muse, "should I sit on the Chairnoldson or the Couchinglerden? I guess it depends on whether we eat at the Fjallnas or the Tableingsdottir."

The walls were generally spare, with selected photos and art works from various interesting locations around the world mixed with framed movie posters from some of the classics—*Batman* (1989), *The Sound of Music* (1965), and *Re-Animator* (1985), an eclectic mix that kept his guests on their toes.

It was a comfortable home, neither cluttered nor too Spartan. Around one corner one might find a few SCUBA tanks, around another a road bike. But there weren't any clothes on the floor or dirty dishes in the sink. It wasn't a bachelor pad per se, but also clearly not yet a family home.

A small out-building served as a locker and housed the usual array of important outdoor accoutrement, including road and mountain bikes, a kayak, long and short surfboards, and an odd assortment of SCUBA gear that for one reason or another wasn't at the CMEx's dive locker; all standard gear for the quintessential California boy. His time in New England had ultimately been interesting and productive, but for the ten years he'd lived there he woke up nearly every day knowing he would return to California someday.

Less than an hour after stepping off the *MacGreggor*, Chris opened his stainless-steel front door and dropped to his knees to prepare for the furry onslaught he knew would be coming. The attack was first detectable by the distinctive sound of toenails desperately trying to get purchase on the redwood floor. Rounding the bend at full speed, his dog, Thigmotaxis, leapt at Chris with tongue fully deployed.

"Gooooood girl, Thig. Such a good girl," Chris said while receiving a slobbery tongue to his left eye. Thig, named for an ecological concept that described an animal's attraction to its habitat, was a four-year-old Soft Coated Wheaten that Chris had rescued from obscurity a couple years earlier at the animal shelter. She was the second dog he'd owned in his life, and he was hopeful that she would be around for a while. "Goooooood girl. I missed you."

They ate together at the bar in the kitchen while Chris looked through emails. Chris had a frozen fruit smoothie, since he kept no fresh food in the house while at sea. Thig dined right next to him on kibble with a bit of brown rice.

There was a note on the table from Mary, the neighbor who'd fed Thig while Chris was away, indicating that all was well. She was a friend of his mother's, and he'd known her for years. He picked up the phone and gave her a quick call.

"Glad you're back, Chris. How was your trip on the boat? We saw you out there during our morning walks the past couple of days. Any exciting discoveries?" Mary was part of a group that walked the entirety of Scenic Way every morning like clockwork. At sixty-five she looked great, so the miles must be paying off.

"Ah, you know. Some ups, some downs. About what you'd expect for the first week of a cruise. Everything okay with my furry pal here?"

"No problems at all. She and Josie get along famously, and both joined us each morning." Josie was Mary's Jack Russell terrier. "Oh, there was, you know, it's probably nothing."

"What's that?"

"Well, several times I noticed a couple of men coming by your place in a black truck. They would just pull off the road in front of your house, look to see if you were around, and they'd back up, then drive away. The third time it happened I walked out my front door pretending to be working in the yard so that they knew someone was watching. You know, in case they were casing the joint."

Chris laughed. "Casing the joint. Been reading more detective novels on your new Kindle?"

"You know, I can't put that thing down! It's so much fun."

"I'm not sure I'm ready for that yet. I still like the heft of a book in my hand, the crinkle of the plastic cover from the library."

"What a romantic! You're going to make some woman happy one day."

Chris laughed again. "Oh yeah, they're lining up around the block. And you're starting to sound like my mom. But seriously, thanks for your help with Thig. I'm pretty sure that I won't be back out on the boat for a couple days. Are you around later in the week in case I head back out again?"

"Not going anywhere. Why go anywhere when I live in paradise already?"

"Can't argue with that. And thanks for the heads up on the guys in the truck. I'm sure it's nothing, but it helps to have attentive eyes around."

He was about to hang up when Mary added, "Oh, Chris. Speaking of your mother, have you met Mr. Mysterio yet?"

"I wasn't aware that there's a Mr. Mysterio around. What's his story?"

"Well, I don't know much," Mary clearly reveled in the opportunity to be the first to gossip about Margaret's new friend with Margaret's own son. "All I know is that he's a doctor and that they've had dinner together a couple of times around town."

"Hmmm. I'm sure I'll get to meet him at some point," Chris said, with no enthusiasm. It wasn't that he had any problem with his mom seeking companionship. That was entirely up to her. And Chris would be happy for her if she found someone with whom she could spend some time. The issue was that Margaret's first foray into the dating scene after his father had passed hadn't gone very well. Against his mom's wishes, Chris had confronted the man and, in no uncertain terms, requested more chivalrous behavior. In vain.

"When you do meet him, Chris, try to be nice this time. We don't want to send another one running for the hills because he's afraid of you."

"I'm working on my people skills. I checked out some old Tony Robbins tapes from the library, and the exercises are going well. Her new beau will never know what hit him."

"That's what I'm afraid of! Talk to you later."

He clicked off, then listened to his voicemail messages. Not surprisingly, the first call was from his mom, Dr. Margaret Black. She was a child psychiatrist who lived a few blocks away and had a practice

31

in a small office down at the Crossroads Mall off Highway 1. As per her standard protocol, she left no message. Marvelous. At least she didn't invite him to dinner with Mr. Mysterio.

The second call was from Chris's boss at the CMEx, Peter Lloyd. "Call me if you can before the Pebble Beach thing. We should talk about last minute strategies before you go."

Chris looked at his dive watch. About an hour before show time. No time to call Peter now. He took a quick shower, shaved, and dressed in a blazer, tie, and a clean pair of jeans. Brown suede shoes completed the picture. Nice, but not too nice—scientist chic, though he would never admit to thinking that as he looked at himself in the mirror.

He filled Thig's water bowl and gave her a kiss and a few tummy scratches, grabbed the Pelican case, and headed out the door. His landline was ringing as he walked to his car. He'd have to recover the message from voicemail later.

———

Access to the exclusive development of Pebble Beach was achieved through one of four guarded gates. The guard waved him through after he explained that he was giving a presentation at the Lodge.

He arrived at the Pebble Beach Lodge with ten minutes to spare, so he had some time to breathe and consider the purpose of this particular donor meeting.

The role of a research scientist had evolved significantly in recent years to require nearly as much fundraising as actual research. Much of this fundraising involved the traditional scientific pastime of writing grant proposals to agencies like the National Science Foundation or Sea Grant. This aspect of the job hadn't changed much. Proposals were still submitted annually, though with the recent tightening of state and federal budgets, the competition for a shrinking number of grant dollars was growing.

The ever-changing funding climate also required that scientists broaden their fundraising efforts to include private donors and foundations. Here the goal was to woo would-be donors for support that ranged from the low thousands to the millions of dollars, and most of the time came without the terms and conditions associated with traditional grant sources.

Frequently, this type of private money came as the result of presentations to small groups or individuals, the proverbial "dog and pony show." Presentations such as these required a different set of skills than proposal writing, so not all scientists thrived in both.

Chris was aware of entire research institutes that had been endowed by a single individual after only a couple of casual conversations. A spontaneous poolside conversation in Palm Springs, with the right person, could lead to million-dollar research budgets. A few minutes in the frequent flyer's lounge at any major airport could lead to a new science building.

Knowing this, Chris made a point of taking advantage of every opportunity to speak to donors, even those opportunities that interrupted a research cruise. Of course, even if he hadn't been so motivated himself, Peter, who had demonstrated unparalleled skills at parting the wealthy from their dollars, would've had him doing these things anyway. So resistance, as they say, was futile.

This afternoon's challenge was to sit at a table with three or four potential donors from around the Peninsula and infuse them with the excitement of marine biological research, while at the same time conveying how important their donations would be to advancing this research. One had to simultaneously give the impression of having one's act together, but at this same time convey a poignant sense of need. A delicate balance.

It was always helpful to have "just stepped off the boat" when attending these types of functions. The no-bullshit image of a field scientist appealed to many donors, probably because they had no other experience with field research than these interactions. Ideally, Chris would've loved to meet the donors at the dock as he literally stepped off the boat, though actually taking them out to sea was a gamble. A seasick donor could easily lose the motivation to give. Chris had seen it happen more than once.

He left the Land Rover and found his way to the Lodge entrance, bringing "the field" with him in the form of the weather-beaten Pelican case at his side. Nothing said tough-guy like a worn plastic case with strategically placed stickers. Through the entryway, he walked out on the main terrace where he quickly spotted Michelle Tierney, a representative from the university's Development Office. Development reps were the gatekeepers between donors and faculty. Meetings like this weren't allowed to happen without a representative present. While the presence of an intermediary was frequently frustrating, Chris had worked with Michelle before and he actually enjoyed their combined approach. Further, it was Michelle who had single-handedly pulled these donors together today, so he was happy to have her there.

"Hi, Michelle." Chris nodded to a woman and two men seated at the table. Without catching Michelle's eye for fear that one of them would crack a smile, he added, "I'm sorry if I'm a bit late; I just got off the boat." He received enthusiastic nods from all three donors for that.

"In fact, if you turn and look out to the left, you'll see our research vessel working as we speak just over there off Point Lobos." He pointed, and indeed there was the *MacGreggor*, on site and within view as planned. "While you can't see it from here, we have our diving robot in the water right now about one thousand feet down in Carmel Canyon." He couldn't have choreographed that better.

34

But before Chris could say another word, a tough-looking gentleman in his sixties queried, "Dr. Black, if you're here with us, who the hell's running the show on the research vessel?"

7

"We followed him to his house. He was there for about forty-five minutes before he took off again. He just walked into the Lodge over here in Pebble Beach. He's carrying that yellow case. He sat at a table with three old people who look like some kind of big shots, and a younger chick. Right before we stepped outside, he pointed out to where the boat is working right now and said something, but I couldn't hear what it was."

"Shit. This is bad. We need to know who he's meeting and who he's talking with," Kevin O'Grady made no attempt to hide his impatience with his henchmen on the other end of the line.

"Well, we can't very well sit down at the table with him."

"Figure out what he's doing and DON'T GET SPOTTED!" Kevin yelled into the phone.

This last bit was intended for his boss' ears. After leaving Monastery Beach, Kevin had driven straight out to the property in Carmel Valley where his current boss lived. The Valley extended inland from Carmel-by-the-Sea, perpendicular to Highway 1. Carmel Valley Road meandered through farmland and small housing tracks, hugging the hills along the north side of the valley. About fourteen miles out, after passing through Carmel Valley Village, the road narrowed as it wound up into the hills.

The Valley had several redeeming qualities, chief among them an abundance of sun when compared with Carmel-by-the-Sea and relative isolation, particularly the farther into the valley one went. In fact, the isolation was so profound this far from the coast that it was equally likely to encounter a wealthy land baron or meth lab operator.

Kevin hung up the phone and turned to his boss to give a report but didn't get a chance to open his mouth, much less form words.

"I don't like the way this is going," his boss said. "I don't like it at all."

The man swung around in his desk chair and looked out the window at the oak trees dotting the landscape. "We've got to get control of this cluster fuck before our friends find out about it."

"I don't know nothing about 'our friends' other than what you've told me. What's their story?" The moment the words left his mouth, Kevin regretted it.

The boss stared at Kevin from behind his desk. He had the look of a predator sizing up potential prey, calculating the benefits of consuming the prey against the expenditure of energy required to capture it.

"Their story is nothing you want to know about," the boss said at last, apparently having decided not to pounce on Kevin that day. "You think I'm dangerous? These guys make me look like a pussy. And they don't like problems. So, let's not give them any."

8

"Very good question, but I am sure Dr. Black has left very capable staff in charge on the *MacGreggor*," Michelle interjected quickly. "But allow me to offer some quick introductions before Dr. Black begins. Chris, I'd like to introduce you to Stuart and Nancy Dean. And I think you may have already met Dr. Henry Morris." Handshakes all around.

Michelle had already briefed Chris on the relevant aspects of the Deans' biographies. Stuart and Nancy Dean, both graduates of the university, were relatively new residents of the Peninsula, having recently moved from Palo Alto down to Pacific Grove. But they had been coming down for years and were quite familiar with the area. They were extremely wealthy and had already made donations to the university's new library as well as to a couple of its sports teams.

There were no surprises in the way the Deans looked; they were both dressed conservatively, with nearly matching grey suits. Chris thought he caught the slightest hint of something curious in the way they looked at him when Michelle made the introduction. But that something was fleeting, and he quickly forgot about it.

Dr. Morris, the pediatrician, was a lifetime resident of Carmel, and he dressed the part, looking like he'd stepped directly out of an outdoor catalog. While Chris had seen a different local doctor in his younger years, he was familiar with Morris and knew he had crossed paths with his mom on a number of occasions.

It was rumored that he had a golden touch with children but rubbed many adults the wrong way. Chris recalled his mom describing Morris as "a true vulgarian," meaning, he supposed, that Morris used colorful language in mixed company.

Well, it took all kinds to keep CMEx going. Far be it from Chris to let a character debate infringe on the pursuit of funds.

"It's nice to meet all of you. And to your question, Dr. Morris, I left the boat and ROV in the hands of our capable CMEx staff and students. While it's only me sitting here before you today, I want to emphasize that without our team there would be no CMEx activities for me brag about.

"I'm sure that given the longtime success of your practice in Carmel, sir, that you can appreciate the importance of a good support crew."

"Well said, Chris. Well said," came the gravelly reply. "I told your mother," then he turned to the others. "Dr. Black's mother is a well-respected psychiatrist in Carmel, and his father flew jets for United Airlines."

Turning back to Chris, Morris continued, "I was sorry to hear of your father's passing. He was a tough bastard, and we don't have enough of those around anymore."

"Thank you." It was true that Chris's dad hadn't suffered fools gladly. Ironically, one of the few fools he suffered was the doctor who worked with him when he got sick. Had Andrew recognized what an idiot the doctor was early on, he might still be around.

"Anyway, I told your mother when I saw her a couple of weeks ago that I was going to meet with you soon and that I was going to give you both barrels." He added, "She thought that you could probably handle that."

Chris laughed heartily, while the other three chuckled more tentatively. "Both barrels is precisely what I'd expect from you Dr. Morris."

With that, Chris explained to the group over the next forty-five minutes the long-range vision for CMEx and how its various academic and research programs further that purpose.

"You've done a nice job, Dr. Black, of singing the Center's praises." Mr. Dean adjusted his blood-red tie. "But we'd like to hear more about you. How have you come to be where you are today? What's *your* role been in the development of CMEx?"

Chris nodded, trying to buy time before answering. The personal line of questioning was a departure from the normal script of these get-togethers.

"Dr. Black has an exceptional record." Michelle jumped in to fill the brief silence. "He's literally worked at locations all over the world. Chris, why don't you tell them about some of your international experience?"

"Sure Michelle. Well, without returning to the Big Bang for the beginning of the story, do you remember Dr. Morris mentioning that my father was an airline pilot?"

Head nods from both of the Deans.

"One of the most exceptional perks of his position was the voucher system that we, as his family, were able to use. I was essentially able to get on any flight that I wanted, to any location that United Airlines flew, as long as there was an open seat.

"This meant that as an undergraduate at MIT back east, when I did a report on foraging behavior in coral reef fishes of the South Pacific, I flew to Fiji to dive with the fishes directly. Or when I wrote an undergraduate honors thesis on the management of the Great Barrier Reef in Australia, I flew down there to interview the managers personally and to dive on the reef."

"What a wonderful opportunity," Mrs. Dean said.

"It was. In grad school, I flew to Russia to dive in Lake Baikal for a class project. You're all probably aware that it's the deepest freshwater lake in the world. I did research in the fjords of northern Chile for one spring break and spent three weeks at Christmas one year studying white shark behavior in False Bay, South Africa."

"You must have been the envy of all your fellow students," Mr. Dean said.

"It was a unique situation. I was making little money as a teaching fellow in grad school, yet off I'd go to the exotic locales that many students only read about. It clearly changed the complexion of my education."

"We've heard that not all of your adventures were research related," Mrs. Dean offered, "that you've been in and out of trouble in some pretty rough places."

"Oh, there may have been some excitement from time to time," Chris replied, smiling.

Mr. Dean interrupted, "But Chris, we've heard stories that you've been involved in actual physical altercations in the field. Isn't that unusual for a scientist?"

Chris caught Morris giving the Deans an impatient look. "There are always challenges. But to this day I'm hugely grateful for the opportunities that my father's job afforded me. Those experiences launched me on what's been a rewarding career thus far."

"And yet," Dr. Morris said, "with all this cosmopolitan international experience, you chose to return to the Peninsula to found CMEx. What are we to make of that? An unrepentant homeboy?"

Chris chuckled. "Something like that. In fact, coming back to Carmel served several ends. In many ways, the central coast of California sits at ground zero for the interface of science and policy in the state, the country, and even the world. Our extraordinary marine environment, coupled with forward-thinking management actions undertaken by the State, makes this the perfect place to do the type of applied work that I do.

"And to be able to conduct this research in my own back yard makes it all the more compelling from my perspective. I sacrifice nothing professionally to live in a location that's dear to me."

"So why Carmel Bay specifically?" Mrs. Dean asked.

Chris explained the rationale for the current ROV cruise and specified how the Carmel Canyon project was emblematic of the goals of CMEx.

"We're not content to conduct science for the sake of science. While every one of our projects is founded on enhancing our understanding of the marine environment, each project also has a clear application to management and/or policy-making. It's this emphasis that distinguishes us from other institutions, both here in the region and throughout the state."

Desperate to get out of this conversation, he brought it back on track. "We've been successful with proposals to traditional funding agencies, but I can't emphasize enough how important donations from people such as yourselves are to CMEx, and by extension, to the marine environment."

Surveying the group, it was clear that they had additional questions. He could tell neither of the Deans was satisfied, and Dr. Morris was impossible to read through his mirrored sunglasses. The meeting had already lasted longer than any donor meeting Chris had been part of, but they talked a few more minutes as he fielded their questions.

Looking at her watch, Michelle wrapped up the meeting, thanking everyone for taking the time to come discuss all the interesting work that Chris and his team were doing. Then she walked the Deans out to their car.

Dr. Morris remained behind briefly. He eyed Chris from across the table and behind his sunglasses as though he were scrutinizing a dead flower in the middle of his rose bushes.

"Chris, I've made a great deal of money over the years. I'm grateful for it, and I have no expectation of needing it when I'm in the ground. You know that I went to the university for both undergraduate and medical school. Your program is impressive, and I'm impressed with you personally. I want to help, but I've no stomach for traditional, milk toast bullshit, if you know what I mean."

"I think I do," Chris replied. After so many donor interactions full of pleasant yet meaningless generalities, he was enjoying Morris's continued frankness, despite the fact that he wasn't quite sure what exactly the good doctor meant. But his job that night was not to question potential donors' motives. His job was to garner their interest. And that he had.

"So, I want you to think about how I might help you in ways that other people or funding sources can't. I don't want to hear anything more right now. Just think about it. Here's my card. When you've had some time to think about this, give me a call. My direct line is written on the back."

9

Chris leaned back in his chair and loosened his tie. He'd been up since dawn, and now that the primary activities of the day were completed, he let exhaustion roll over him like the incoming fog. He was contemplating the relative merits of going for a run or going to sleep when Michelle returned to the table.

"I think that went well. The Deans were complementary when I walked them back to the car. I'll follow up with them in the next couple of days to do the ask." The "ask" referred to the actual request for money. Despite his general disdain for the Development Office gatekeepers, Chris was always grateful that he wasn't responsible for the ask.

"What's their story again?" In the back of his mind, Chris was wondering about the curiously personal line of questioning the Deans had taken. "I know the basics from your briefing documents. But how did you and they connect?"

"Well, they're alums like Morris, and they both gave generously to the new library and to our sports programs. So they have a history of giving."

"Sure. But how did CMEx get on their radar screen? Did Peter organize this?"

"Actually, now that you mention it, I think they contacted us about meeting you specifically. That's why Peter was so adamant that you get off the boat to be at this meeting. You're the star."

"Huh. Well, I hope I gave them a good show."

"I'm certain of it," Michelle replied, with her characteristic enthusiasm. She would be complementary, Chris thought, even if he'd sat at the table, pooped his pants, and went to sleep in front of the donors. "Well, I've got to get back to the office." Michelle got up. "Thanks again for your help and for all the good work you do on behalf of the university."

"Oh, it's my pleasure. And thank you for pulling this together."

After Michelle had left, Chris spent another fifteen minutes watching the fog roll in. Finally motivated to move by the rapidly declining air temperature, he decided it was time to go home and began to walk back to his truck. He was parked down below the Lodge on a side street used primarily by the service staff and by employees of the golf course. A tall hedge separated the road from the grounds of the Lodge.

As he approached the opening in the hedge closest to his truck, Chris could clearly smell cigarette smoke. Must be staff on a break, he assumed, or perhaps a golfer sneaking a smoke before heading out to the back nine. But as he came through the hedge and his truck came into sight, he saw that the smoke emanated from two scruffy looking gentlemen. One was looking in the driver's side window, while the other was carelessly sitting on the hood of his Land Rover.

Yes, Chris was fit. And swimming in particular kept his upper body strong. But as he approached the two idiots sitting on his hood, Chris was once again grateful for the many beatings he used to take from his friends.

Dating back to Carmel Middle School, he, Mac, and Jase Hamilton, as well as Tony Thornburgh, had literally beaten each other to a pulp on a weekly basis while sparring full-contact Kenpo karate. Kenpo, with roots in both China and Japan, was essentially street fighting. "Street fighting with style," their instructor used to say.

Sparring was done with pads. But unlike traditional American boxing, pads in karate were intended to protect the wearer, not the recipient of the blows. So with adrenaline pumping through their then invincible bodies, the friends beat the hell out of each other in bouts that usually didn't end until someone's lip or nose was bleeding, at least a bit.

Chris was of the opinion that formal training in self-defense, with highly choreographed scenarios played out in tightly controlled environments, wasn't particularly useful unless one had direct experience with actual assailants trying to do bodily harm. There were certain reactions that simply didn't develop unless survival required them.

In the handful of instances since grad school in which Chris had been called on to defend himself or his colleagues while abroad, the instincts derived from those sparring days had served him well.

The guy sitting on the truck ground out his cigarette butt on the shiny green hood. He was wearing weather-worn, black and white checkered slip-on Vans, which Chris remembered being big in the early '80s. His buddy just stood there, one hand in the pocket of his acid wash jeans. Who are these guys? What decade am I dealing with here? he wondered.

Neither "Vans" nor "Acid" looked to be particularly worthy opponents. They were both Caucasian, which probably ruled them out as gang members from nearby Salinas. And neither appeared to emphasize fitness in his daily routine. There was a general puffiness about the two of them; skin bulging out over the necks of their jackets, paunches sagging over their belts. But, as everyone knows, it's never wise to judge a book by its cover.

Acid, the taller of the two, took a step closer and said, "We wanna know what you're doing out on that boat." He spoke with a dull, thick tongue and looked out from under heavy lids, vacant eyes suggesting to Chris that there was little going on upstairs.

"Excuse me?" Chris asked. This wasn't what he had expected. Only scientists cared about what scientists were doing offshore, but these two didn't fit the profile of budding marine ecologists.

Vans jumped into the verbal fray with, "You heard him. What the fuck are you doing out there?" He pointed in the general direction of the ocean. Vans spoke more definitively. That is to say, he formed a couple of coherent sentences and enunciated them with a gusto his buddy lacked.

A golf cart carrying four Hispanic females in white service staff uniforms rolled past. Chris hoped that one of them would sound the alarm. Neither of his antagonists seemed to care that they were being observed. Perhaps they were more stupid than they appeared.

If Chris could drag this on a bit further, perhaps the authorities would have time to respond. But then again, what exactly would the maids have had to report? Three guys talking? There was probably no help coming anytime soon. No, he was on his own.

He put the Pelican case on the ground, keeping his eye on both of the guys in the process. Then he put his hand up to his ear mimicking a phone call and said, "9-1-1? Please send an ambulance. Sorry, make that two ambulances, to the Lodge at Pebble Beach. There are two badly dressed men bleeding profusely in the parking lot; multiple broken bones."

The cogs were evidently turning for the two guys, albeit slowly, as they looked at each other, then back at Chris. Perhaps they didn't get enough sarcasm in the daily diets.

"Ah, fuck this," Vans opined, then he launched himself at Chris.

Chris maintained eye contact with Vans and pumped his arms slightly as though preparing to throw a punch. This feint conformed to Vans's expectations, so he was looking at Chris's fists rather than at his feet as Chris applied a front kick to the man's left knee.

He knew that a lot was made of shots to the groin. They were effective if landed directly but were much less so if they landed off center. Even a quick twist, or the lifting of a thigh, by a recipient can significantly reduce the impact of a groin shot, leaving an unhappy, but basically functional, antagonist. A kick to the knee, however, is usually unexpected, is tougher to defend against, and can quickly hobble an adversary.

Chris's kick landed squarely on Vans's knee. Vans's forward momentum from the charge kept him coming, but his lower-left leg remained stuck in place briefly by the kick. The net effect of these opposing forces was a loud crack as Vans's leg hyper-extended and his knee collapsed. He uttered a wrenching, guttural scream as he fell to the pavement, immediately clutching his leg.

Following through on his kick, Chris now had his back turned partially toward Acid. Puffy though he may have been, Acid moved quickly and pushed Chris from behind with enough force to send him flying face first into the hedge.

Chris had just enough time to get his left arm up to partially protect his face and absorb part of the impact. Nonetheless, he felt the branches of the hedge dig sharply into his face in a handful of locations, cutting deeply into the bridge of his nose.

Acid didn't immediately follow up on his push, but instead he stood back and pulled out a buck knife. The ease with which he flicked it out suggested at least some facility with the weapon.

Vans lay on the ground between them and, having temporarily halted the steady string of expletives, was busy working himself into a sitting position. His left leg was splayed out in an unnatural forty-five-degree angle from his body.

Watching Acid closely, Chris moved forward and stepped down forcefully on Vans's damaged knee, following immediately thereafter with a close-quarters side kick to his head. He was taking no chances having two adversaries in the game.

Acid took the opportunity to lunge directly at Chris with the knife in his right hand. Chris easily shifted to his right, grabbed Acid's arm, and let the man's own forward momentum pull him past Vans and into the hedge. At the same time Chris stepped across the prostrate Vans to keep the body between himself and Acid.

Out of the corner of his eye, Chris could see people coming down the street, but he didn't remove his eyes from Acid, who had now extracted himself from the hedge with a similar set of cuts on this face and neck. The knife was still in his hand.

"Hey! What's going on here?" said a large, red-faced man in a lime green golf shirt and blue slacks, "What are you doing?" He spoke with the air of authority that came no doubt from running a bank or perhaps a law firm. As he and his friend approached, golf cleats clinking on the asphalt, Acid bolted around the Land Rover and out of sight down the road.

"Are you okay, buddy?" the red-faced man asked Chris. Turning to his friend he said, "Scott, call the cops."

10

Two hours later, Chris was still at the scene. The Pebble Beach Company security had been the first to respond to the call. It turned out that the four maids had reported the altercation after all. The Monterey County Sheriff's Department was next on the scene. Two squad cars, as well as an ambulance, responded to the 9-1-1 call.

The paramedics checked out Vans, while the sheriff's deputies first talked to Scott Leary and Harold Buxton III, the two golfers who had interrupted the fight, about what they saw. While this was going on, a second ambulance arrived, and the second set of paramedics began ministering to Chris, who looked considerably worse than he felt. The blood from his many facial cuts, most notably the cut on the bridge of his nose, had bled profusely, then dried, giving him the look of a poorly rendered, B-movie zombie.

Chris's nose would likely require a couple of stitches, which meant a trip to the Community Hospital of the Monterey Peninsula, affectionately known as CHOMP by locals. But before Chris was allowed to leave the scene, the deputies had to ask a few questions, under the close supervision of Harold and Scott, both of whom turned out to be lawyers.

For all the jokes about lawyers he'd told over the years, and for all Chris's rants about the declining state of humanity, it was heartening to see Harold and Scott rally to Chris's side without a question. He greatly appreciated it and would have to thank them later.

Chris recounted his experience to the deputies and his impromptu legal team as the adrenaline slowly left his body. Most of the questions they had to ask, Chris couldn't answer. He'd no idea where these guys came from, or why they had singled him out. He joined the two lawyers in giving a description of Acid, who was reportedly seen running through the Lodge grounds after the altercation but had yet to be apprehended.

When Chris was finally allowed to leave, his legal team expanded their jurisdiction to include chauffeuring. Harold drove Chris in his Mercedes, while Scott followed closely in Chris's Land Rover.

CHOMP was a beautiful modern building designed by Edward Durell Stone and nestled within the pines at the top of the hill that bisected the Peninsula. Dating back to 1929, it had started as a thirty-bed clinic for "metabolic difficulties" and had subsequently evolved into a two-hundred-fifty-bed medical center by the 1960s. The building was interwoven masterfully with the landscape by sheets of glass with views of forest waterfalls. All in all, it wasn't a bad place to go, even for someone like Chris who had developed a pathological dislike for hospitals and medical offices of all types.

Harold drove through Pebble Beach, crossing into Pacific Grove at the gate marking the end of Seventeen-Mile Drive and followed Highway 68 up the hill to the hospital. He dropped Chris off at the Emergency Room entrance, walking him inside to make sure that he was helped before returning to his car to park.

Harold's ministrations were unnecessary, as Chris's appearance quickly attracted the attention of the Emergency Room staff. He was ushered into an empty room and handed a hospital gown to put on. He obeyed, sitting on the bed to protect his now exposed behind. The suturing of the cut was a quick affair relative to the interminable face washing that preceded it. While no stranger to discomfort, Chris wasn't a fan of being prodded by strangers for extended periods of time.

About the time that the stitching was complete, Harold and Scott filed into the room, followed closely by Jase Hamilton, whom Chris hadn't seen in a couple of years.

The last Chris had heard, Jase was an investigator with the Monterey County Sheriff's Department, and the brown and khaki uniform he now wore suggested that that was still the case. He was the same height as Chris. His red hair was cut shorter than the last time Chris had seen him, but otherwise he looked fit, and the perpetual crease between his eyebrows projected a serious disposition. In sum, he looked the part of a sheriff.

Like Chris and Mac, Jase, too, was a product of Carmel-by-the-Sea. On the first day of second grade at Carmel River School, Chris and Mac had run into Jase as they walked to school. After establishing each other's bona fides—mainly enthusiasm for Star Wars, Tolkien, and the beach—they'd become fast friends.

While the three had gone their separate ways for a while and hadn't been together much over the past several years, old conversations were effortlessly resumed whenever they met again.

"So, given a few years to your own devices, this is the plan you come up with to meet nurses?" Jase queried, obviously trying not to smile. "Sophisticated, Dr. Black."

Harold and Scott perked up at this. "Of course, with a face like that, I suppose that meeting people would present some challenges," Jase added.

"I was indeed angling for a nurse. But with you back on the scene, in uniform no less, and packing heat, I think my man-crush has been rekindled. Come on over and give me a big kiss."

Jase crossed the room and gave Chris a vigorous handshake.

"It's been too long, Jase," Chris said sincerely. "Life has just gotten in the way, I guess. I'm sorry."

"Not a problem. We're all going light speed. The Peninsula seems like a pretty small place most of the time, but it's obviously large enough to keep us all busy without tripping over one another."

"Excuse me, Chris," Harold interjected, stepping toward the bed. "We'll take off now and let you and Deputy Hamilton catch up. I've left my card with him so that he can follow up with me later. Let me know if there's anything else I can do."

"I can't thank you enough." Chris hopped out of bed to shake the hands of both Harold and Scott. "The two of you probably saved me from some real trouble. And your help afterward was beyond the call of duty."

"Well, I'm not sure we saved you from anything. You seemed to be doing just fine on your own."

After Harold and Scott left the room, Jase pulled up a chair and sat next to the bed. He took out a leather notepad and looked at Chris. "So, what can you tell me that you haven't already relayed to the deputies?"

"They asked what I was doing on the boat, Jase. Why would they do that? What possible interest could they have in our exploration of the canyon?" Chris stood up. Though most of the adrenaline from the fight had gone, he was still far too excited to sit still.

"All interesting questions. And we'll get to those. But before we do that, tell me about your morning prior to the encounter."

11

"We were offshore on the *MacGreggor* all night last night, and all of the previous day," Chris explained. "The first ROV dive was just after sunrise. I came ashore at Stillwater Cove a little after noon, grabbed my truck, and went home to shower and change. Then I drove over to the Lodge around two thirty." As he said this, he stopped pacing, and a series of irritating realizations started coming to him.

"So, you parked your truck down at Stillwater while you were out?" Jase asked. "Was anyone on shore aware of when you were planning to come back in? Anyone at the yacht club?"

"No. We've got a fairly casual relationship with the club. As long as we keep the number of vehicles to a maximum of three, they let us park our cars there while we're offshore. There was no reason to brief them on our plan. And I was the only member of the team to leave a vehicle there this trip. Everyone else got on board in Monterey."

"So, it's likely that the assailants picked you up when you came on shore. How they came to be there at that precise moment remains to be seen. They must have trailed you to the Lodge and decided to approach you there for some reason rather than at your house."

"The floater. They must have been on the Stillwater pier watching the recovery of the dead body from the cove. We came into the dock at the same time that the body was being removed. The pier was packed with people, so they could have easily blended in there.

"When we showed up at the dock, it would've been pretty clear that we had just come from the *MacGreggor*. I was wearing a bright yellow jacket with CMEx emblazoned on the back. Perhaps they knew I was from the boat, but they didn't know who I was."

"So, they decided to follow you to see what they could see," Jase suggested. "Exactly. We have the cell phone for the guy you took out and will be able to trace any numbers he's called. He's pretty messed up, by the way. What'd you do to him?"

"Not as much as I would've liked to do." Chris moved to the dresser to put his shirt back on. "They know where I live. Actually, now that I think about it, my neighbor mentioned two guys in a black truck had stopped by my house several times in the past week. I laughed when she suggested they were casing the joint, but now it seems pretty clear that they were."

"I sent a deputy over there just before I came into the room. He should be reporting in soon."

"Seems like the *MacGreggor* is being watched. No idea why, but depending on how crazy these guys are, there could be bigger problems."

"Yes. We should call and alert them to the situation. We need to figure out what's going on to understand the threat level. Tell me more about what you're doing out there."

Chris spent about thirty minutes describing the current project. The overall goal was to better understand how organisms were distributed along deep-water canyons, from deep water to shallow. This type of information would ultimately underlie natural resource management efforts along the coast. The team was collecting this information by using the ROV to "transect" the Carmel Canyon at numerous points.

Chris drew an improvised map of the canyon on Jase's note pad. Along the base of the canyon there were multiple Xs. "Here's the canyon. Each of these X's marks the starting point of an ROV transect. We simply fly the ROV up the canyon wall collecting continuous video and taking thousands of digital still photographs. When we're done with all these lines, we should have more than eighteen hours of video to analyze back in the lab."

Chris stood with his arms behind his head and looked out the window. He winced slightly as his cut nose reminded him it was there. "I'll tell you what. I don't think our project has anything to do with today's attack. Just doesn't make sense."

"I'm with you. No offense, but fish swimming around on rocks isn't likely to make many criminals super motivated to get involved. Unless it's a case of wrong place wrong time."

"What do you mean?"

"Well, don't you take pictures in that ROV of yours?"

Chris nodded.

"So, you may have seen something the bad guys, whoever they may be, don't want anyone to see."

"Hmmm. We haven't noticed any fishing gear, but there's been a great deal of fishing activity out there historically. And the fishing community isn't fond of scientists. The guys who attacked me didn't look like fishermen exactly, but who knows. Either way, the question is, what's down there?"

"You tell me."

"Tomorrow morning looks like a wash based on the weather forecast. Too windy," Chris said. "But the wind is supposed to lay down a bit tomorrow night, so Thursday I'm going back out to find out."

Looking at Jase, Chris smiled. "Do you get seasick?"

12

Darrell English was glued to CNN when Kevin O'Grady came in to interrupt. For the last twenty-four hours the major story on all the networks had been the capture of mobster James "Whitey" Bulger. Bulger had run a crime syndicate in South Boston that included several crooked FBI agents. When an FBI agent alerted him to a coming indictment, Bulger fled and hadn't been caught for the ensuing eighteen years, until now. He was captured without incident in a small apartment in Santa Monica.

Bulger was an "old school" mobster, the CNN talking heads said, because he participated directly in the more than twenty-one murders attributed to him. In one of those murders, the victim was literally severed in half by the rain of bullets fired at him while he was in a phone booth.

In Bulger, Darrell English saw a kindred spirit. Ruthless was a term regularly applied to Darrell during his early years, when people who knew him still felt safe enough to speak of him in anything other than glowing terms. He was the product of a broken and dysfunctional home, an all too familiar story in modern America. Xavier, an abusive, alcoholic father, had visited his rage on Darrell and other family members regularly and with impunity, sending him to the emergency room at

CHOMP on more than one occasion. His initially willful mother had lost both her will and her independence under her husband's crushing blows and couldn't protect Darrell from harm. Eventually, she joined her husband in a nightly descent into drunkenness, frequently before the dinner hour.

The beatings stopped precipitously in the following year, when Xavier English was crushed under the engine block of the Pontiac El Camino he was working on in the garage. The cursory police investigation concluded that he'd been the victim of an unfortunate accident. Darrell's mother knew better, for she'd seen the look in her son's eyes.

Now at the age of 48, grey haired but still built like a refrigerator, Darrell owned tire stores in Seaside, Marina, and Salinas, a Subway Sandwiches in Monterey, and several properties in Carmel Valley where selected activities could be conducted out of the public eye.

Darrell turned toward Kevin O'Grady as he got up off the office couch. He was wearing slacks and a crisp button-down shirt which somehow didn't get wrinkled as he spent the day watching CNN. "I guess I'm old school, too."

Kevin had no idea what to make of that comment, but he went along with it as he did with so much else that had gone on out there.

In the deep, uncharted waters of his inner-self, Kevin knew he wasn't deserving of the myth that surrounded him. Sure, he was tough, but not *crazy* tough like Darrell English. Darrell simply existed on a different playing field than everyone else; he was basically fucking crazy. He would be calm, joking about something one minute, and in the next, he'd switch on the crazy. His eyes would light up with a look that made even the toughest guys Kevin had known want to run away. Darrell was Hannibal Lecter crazy.

Over the past several years, Darrell had done some nasty shit, most of which had been attributed to Kevin. And Darrell actually encouraged that misattribution. It pleased him for some odd reason that Kevin didn't understand.

"We've got the Georges out here. You asked to be told when they arrived."

"Yes, I did. Let's go make another part of that legend of yours," Darrell said, jovially patting Kevin on the back.

They walked out of the wood-paneled outbuilding located at the rear of a large McMansion and down a short path through a eucalyptus grove. Eucalyptus, though an invasive species in this country, were commonplace along the California coastline. Kevin had heard stories that the trees were originally planted a few hundred years ago by Spaniards seeking to capture the market for ship masts. Unfortunately, the trees grew too crookedly to serve as useful mast material, and the scheme failed, both financially and ecologically.

At the edge of the grove was a vast open area that once held local, native trees and wildlife, but of late had served as a staging ground for the dumping of toxic waste. One of the disadvantages of California's growing environmental awareness was the ever-stricter regulation of waste disposal in any form. It wasn't easy anymore for an honest criminal to run a profitable business with agencies like the state Environmental Protection Agency, the Coastal Commission, and the National Marine Sanctuary dictating what could be dumped and where. Agencies never seemed to let up in the ongoing game of "Whack-a-mole" with would-be dumpers. But if they did, citizen organizations now abounded throughout the state to monitor and report even the slightest infraction.

Darrell English had first encountered this fact as the owner of several automotive repair shops around the Peninsula. Burdened by the logistics of legally disposing of used engine oil and transmission fluid, he began to look for alternatives. It was then that the man his wife called "the Sugar Daddy" offered a way out. The way out involved joining forces with a much broader group of illegal dumpers who had banded together to defeat the system and make a profit while doing it.

With no suitable spot to dump the waste on land, the group opted for dumping it offshore. Darrell had organized the use of the *Lizzie J*. Several years back the Donnadio family, longtime residents and fishermen along the Peninsula, had sold the boat to Darrell. No one knew that he purchased a fishing boat and the associated trawling permit, largely because he did so through one of his many private contacts built up over the past twenty years. The economy was bad and the price was right, so no one asked too many questions.

Darrell was also the brains behind disguising the barrels as fishing gear. This made it much easier for them to load the vessel in Monterey for the multiple dumping runs they had made in the past month.

The Georges were on their knees, neither looking defiant nor depressed, when Darrell and Kevin arrived. Though Kevin didn't have the vocabulary to express it, he would've thought that they appeared resigned to their fate.

Their fate, such as it was, was now in Darrell's hands. The couple had once been a reliable source of information for Darrell. Mr. George was a local attorney, and Mrs. George was a doctor. When their wayward son ran afoul of one of Darrell's employees, Darrell himself became involved. He spared the son in return for information from Mr. George and medicinal products from Dr. George.

The son had died last year in a drug related car crash down in Big Sur. But Darrell still felt obliged to lean on both of them, even though his primary source of leverage was now gone.

In the second curious twist of fate in the past week, Chris Black's apparent discovery of the barrels being the first, it turned out that Dr. George was in practice with Dr. Henry Morris, Chris Black's potential patron. Darrell hated these types of surprises.

He approached Mr. George first. "I thought we had this all worked out a few months ago. If you go to the cops or talk to anyone at all about my business, it won't end well for you. So, what the fuck is going on?"

"Mr. English," Mr. George replied in a calm demeanor that belied the circumstances, "I've neither the will nor the subject matter expertise to relate anything substantive about you to the authorities. To be perfectly honest, since my son died, I couldn't give a shit about what you're doing."

"Hah! I appreciate that. And I actually believe you." Darrell looked like he'd just sucked on a lemon. "But I can't say the same for your wife here. She's apparently been talking to her co-workers, and they in turn are talking with people whom they shouldn't be."

"I don't know what you're talking about," Dr. George said. "I really don't."

"Let me explain it from my perspective, Doctor," Darrell said, circling the couple. "One of your partners, Morris I believe, met on Tuesday with Dr. Chris Black, a marine scientist. I want to know what Black told Morris."

"*Margaret* Black's son? I've no idea what they would've been talking about. And if you knew anything about my practice, or my partners, you'd know that I spend little time speaking to Henry Morris."

Darrell pulled out a snub-nosed .38 caliber revolver from the back of his belt. "I expected you to say something like that. And at this point, I've no time for any further discussion." And with that, he shot her in the head twice in quick succession. Her body collapsed next to her husband as the reports from the two shots briefly echoed around the surrounding hillside.

Mr. George screamed in agony and rage. He tried to fling himself at Darrell, but from a kneeling position there was little he could do. Darrell shot him twice in the small of the back. Neither shot was lethal, but one of the two shattered Mr. George's spinal column. His torso writhed on the ground, but his lower extremities remained disturbingly motionless. English looked at Kevin with the crazy, vacuous stare that periodically gave Kevin pause. He briefly considered that he was about to be shot as well.

"I didn't expect to get any information out of either of them. They *did* talk out of turn, but I don't think it mattered. No, we need to clean up some loose ends around here in case this thing with Black gets out of control."

"Okay." Kevin was relieved that he was going to live another day. "What other loose ends are you talking about?"

Two thugs who had been standing by observing the action moved to pick up Mr. George.

"Leave him," Darrell said casually. "I'd like to spend the day thinking about him out here, wiggling around in the dirt next to his dead wife."

13

The sheriff's deputy reported nothing unusual at Chris's house. He was apparently being chatted-up by Mary the neighbor. Probably got an earful for his efforts but perhaps received some homemade cookies, as well.

Jase spent a few more minutes collecting the details of Chris's encounter with Vans, a.k.a. Jerry Smith, who had by then been identified, and his buddy who hadn't. They made a plan to meet at the dock in Monterey at 5:00 a.m. on Thursday morning, assuming no change in the weather. Then Jase went down to interview Smith in his guarded room one floor down, and Chris went home to play with Thig.

Chris drove home uncharacteristically slowly, meandering along in the slow lane at a snail's pace. As he turned off the highway into Carmel, the sunny day had given way to the fog that frequently characterized the early summer months on the Peninsula.

Having grown up with the fog, Chris was generally unaffected by its gloomy presence. Indeed, for the years he'd spent in New England, he'd actually missed the fog a great deal. It had become a nostalgic vehicle for recalling his childhood years.

Of course, all nostalgia aside, there was still the practical impact of the fog on daily life. This was why no self-respecting local was ever caught outdoors without at least a couple of clothing layers handy.

Chris hadn't forgotten that he'd have a guest over for dinner that night. He'd been working with Abigail Wilson, a new lecturer in the Marine Science program at the CMEx, for months. But recently, after a series of chance encounters around town, a relationship had begun to develop and Abigail had become Abby to him. He'd been thinking about the evening for much of the day, until Acid, whatever his name might be, and Jerry Smith decided to make that earlier appointment.

He'd been replaying the fight continually since it happened. He wasn't disappointed with his performance. He avoided serious injury and was able to stop at least one of the assailants. But his impulse following an event like this was to review and critique his own actions and frequently find those actions wanting.

Chris recalled one of the few truly memorable talks he'd had with his dad years ago. They were riding in his dad's meticulously restored Mustang back to Carmel from the Santa Cruz Beach Boardwalk. He'd just seen his father scare three potential thieves away.

Though Andrew had been a fighter pilot in Vietnam, he'd also encountered hostiles on the ground when a helicopter he'd been riding in was shot down. So when three hoods had approached Chris and his dad in the parking lot outside the Boardwalk, Andrew hadn't hesitated. He'd grabbed the guy closest to him by the neck and pinned him to the nearest car.

Stuck in Andrew's vice grip, the guy had quickly conceded defeat. The other two had fled instantly at the first sign of resistance.

"The only point of hand-to-hand combat," Andrew had said to his young son as they drove south, "is to put the other guy down as fast as possible. No posturing. No following some antiquated sense of fairness. I encourage you to never get into a fight, son. But if you do, don't fuck around."

Chris had been shocked and impressed by his father's strategic use of the "F" word, which at that young age still had a mystical quality to

Chris. "You remove the other guy from the fight however you can. You can sort out any other issues once the immediate danger has passed."

Dear old dad, Chris thought; yet another vintage tidbit. But it had been a useful tidbit that Chris had internalized all those years ago. He was no doubt alive today because of that advice.

He pulled up to Bruno's Market on Junipero Street to grab a few more vegetables and some fruit for dessert. Before going in, he first put on a fleece from the back of the truck to cover the blood stains on his shirt.

Bruno's was a classic mom-and-pop store—higher prices than supermarkets and less stock but there was something comforting about the narrow aisles, low light, and mural-painted interior walls. Perhaps, he thought, it was the timelessness of the archetype and increasing rarity.

Chris nodded to several people he recognized as he moved through the aisles, but he wasn't in the mood to chat and was thankful that no one had attempted to strike up a conversation.

"Dr. Black?" Chris was just coming up to the check-out aisle and realized his mind had been drifting. He turned to see a tall, grey-haired fellow smiling down at him. The man looked to be in his late sixties or early seventies. His clear brown eyes stared out from a face that had seen many moons pass, but the pattern of his wrinkles suggested a man of good humor. The tufts of grey hair popping out from the sides of his head gave him the look of a mad scientist.

"Yes. Sorry. I guess you caught me drifting there for a minute. How can I help you?" Chris reached out to shake the man's hand. It was a solid grip.

"My name is Abe Levine, I'm an orthopede at CHOMP," he replied, the hint of a foreign accent hanging in the air. "But I'm also on the board of the Harrison Library, and we're looking for interesting speakers to participate in our annual lecture series. I've heard that you're doing some interesting work here in Carmel Bay. Any chance I can convince you to come and speak?"

"That sounds great. I'm actually in the middle of a research cruise right now, and two more cruises follow immediately when this one's done. So, it would probably have to wait until the fall."

Levine nodded a little too frenetically, evidently not quite listening to much of what Chris had just said about his schedule. "We were actually hoping that it could be sometime in the next three weeks. The summer is just getting started, but we've already had a number of inquiries about the series. I hope that I can get you to reconsider. Perhaps during a day you're not on the boat?"

"Well, to be honest, Dr. Levine, even when I'm not in the middle of the field season, two to three weeks is generally not enough advance notice for something like this. I'll see how the next few days go and get back to you."

Levine persisted. "How about I schedule you for a week from Thursday? That should give you enough time to finish what you're doing in the Bay and come speak to our group."

Chris looked at Levine. The guy was either slow, incredibly irritating, or a combination of both. Letting irritation creep into his voice, he replied, "I'll tell you what. Give me your card and I'll call you when I can, and we'll see if it can work out."

Undeterred, Levine's mouth smiled in a way that his eyes didn't, and he made one last attempt. "I, that is to say, we, are interested in learning more about your work in the Bay. I ask that you reconsider." He even stepped in a little closer, violating Chris's personal space.

"Look," Chris offered as he moved a bit closer himself. "I've got to get going. Good luck with your lecture series."

The guy finally seemed to be getting the message. But he didn't move, and Chris could see that the man was looking at his facial wounds, so he pointed to his face and offered, "I'm having a little work done. How's it look?"

"My apologies. You've caught me being incredibly impolite. I shouldn't have been staring."

That's the least of your offenses, you obtrusive bastard, Chris thought. Aloud, he said, "It's quite alright. I would stare at myself, too. I'm hideous."

"Certainly not. But in any event, I'll let you return to your shopping. It was nice to meet you, and I look forward to your presentation."

Struggling with his desire to mash the guy's face into one of the pies in the dessert display, Chris just shook his head and turned away. He'd travelled enough to know that not everyone shared America's unique brand of interpersonal customs. This guy was probably walking away thinking Chris was the rude one.

While waiting in line to check out, Chris focused on his forthcoming dinner with Abby.

Though Chris knew it irritated her moral sensibility, the first impression Abigail Wilson made was usually a visual one, before she'd a chance to impress with her intellect. She was a tall redhead, with green eyes that effectively rendered Chris defenseless every time he looked into them. She was originally from Florida, and while the skin of most redheads seemed to tend toward pink, she somehow achieved an even tan that defied imagination.

As an undergraduate in the history and philosophy of science at Yale University, Abby had needed to make a decision between competitive swimming and academics. While she ultimately opted for academics, Abby continued to swim daily and still competed in masters swim meets.

After leaving New Haven, Abby had moved to Harvard for a Master's degree in biological statistics.

As Chris pulled out of Bruno's parking lot, he could see Levine watching him from inside the store as he spoke on a cell phone. he surveyed the traffic around him, looking for anomalous vehicles. Seeing none, but uncertain that meant they weren't there, he proceeded home.

After showering, he took Thig for a quick walk along the hidden maze of trails that wound themselves through Carmel. A trail might last for several hundred yards and run through a lush field that wasn't visible from any road, or it might be a brief, unremarkable right-of-way between two houses. Chris was sure that somewhere at City Hall there was a master list of all these trails, but he'd yet to see it.

Back from the walk, he was deep into the preparation of his chicken pesto pasta extravaganza when the doorbell rang.

This was the third time that he and Abby had dined together. Each meal had been great fun, punctuated both by interesting conversation and by many easy laughs about whether MIT and the university trumped Yale and Harvard or the reverse. Chris felt like the trajectory of the relationship was positive, but neither he nor Abby seemed in the mood to rush things. For his part, it had been some time since he'd been in a relationship, and he wasn't anxious to revisit that state again until it felt right.

Thig beat him to the door. She loved Abby. When Chris opened the door, Abby was already bent down to greet Thig first, then she rose to greet Chris. She was wearing a green dress that amplified her eyes and blue jean jacket. Her hair was pulled back in a half ponytail. The perfect juxtaposition of elegance and casualness, in Chris's mind.

"Oh, my God! Chris, what happened to you?"

"You should see the other guy," he answered. He was serious, too.

"Seriously. Did something happen on the boat? I didn't hear anything about it." She'd reached out to touch Chris's shoulder as she surveyed the damage to his face. He was momentarily incapacitated by her touch.

"Come on inside and I'll tell you the whole sordid story." As he stepped to the side to let her enter first, he added, "It's quite a tale."

He took the baguette and beer that Abby had brought and led her back to the kitchen with Thig in tow. Another promising sign, Chris thought. Wine and brie would've been fine, but an appreciation of the simpler pleasures of beer and bread boded well.

Chris began the story as he finished preparing the meal. Abby cracked beers for both of them, then stood next to him in the kitchen, one bare foot propped against the counter behind her. Abby listened closely as they dined and only interjected a couple of times for clarification. A half an hour later, the meal was gone and the story had been told.

While Chris washed the dishes, Abby sat at the bar and asked her follow-up questions. "Are you sure you've never seen either of the guys before?"

"It's possible, you know, that I'd seen them before someplace. But if so, it isn't coming to me." He'd thought about this already, but his memory for faces had failed to serve him in this instance.

"And you don't remember seeing them on the pier or in the parking lot when you came in this morning?"

"Nope, but I wasn't scrutinizing the crowd at that point. To be honest, all the activity at the pier threw me off a bit. That place is usually the picture of tranquility."

"Right. Think about that. Here we are in Carmel-by-the-Sea, where nothing major ever happens. Remember the last issue of the *Pinecone* that you showed me? The police log reported barking dogs and arguments over parking. We laughed about it, remember?"

The *Pinecone* was a curious little weekly newspaper that was well matched to its Carmel readership. Chris had a yellowed clipping from the paper from many years ago tacked up on his office wall. It chronicled an argument between neighbors in which one neighbor was convinced that his next-door neighbor had poisoned his plants because he could see it in her aura.

Abby ventured further, "Now we have a dead body mysteriously washing up in the cove and a violent attack all in the same day. What are the chances that these two incidents are not related?"

14

Chris agreed that Abby made an excellent point. But what was the connection between the two incidents? And if they were linked, how? Vans and Acid had wanted to know what he was doing out there in Carmel Bay, and an unidentified body had washed up in the Bay on the same day. Did someone think he'd witnessed a murder? Had he, without noticing? His thoughts were interrupted by a loud knock at the front door.

Chris glanced at his watch, and then at Abby. Eight fifteen. Who's coming by now? He found himself disappointed that his evening with Abby was being interrupted. Thig barked and took off for the door. As Chris followed after her, he could feel the adrenaline instantly surging through his sore muscles. Was someone following up on their failure from earlier in the day?

He opened the door to find Mac and Gretchen standing on the doorstep like disturbingly old trick-or-treaters. Mac was wearing a black pull-over sweatshirt, and Gretchen was wearing an orange fleece.

"Holy crap! You look terrible!" Mac offered with great sensitivity. "But you gotta let us in," he added while smiling and gesturing toward Gretchen. "We have something interesting to show you."

Gretchen, in turn, asked, with a twinkle in her eye, "Is Abby here? I believe I saw her car outside."

They pushed past Chris and headed back to the kitchen like they owned the place. They didn't, although Chris would've loved some help with mortgage, but they were there enough to know the lay of land well.

Chris stepped out onto the landing and looked down onto the darkened street. The lack of streetlights in Carmel left tree-lined streets like his in near perfect darkness after the sunset. His eyes searched for anything unusual in the dark. He could hear Abby welcoming Mac and Gretchen from down the hallway. Seeing nothing obvious, he returned to the house.

There was no awkwardness as the foursome came together at the dining room table. Virtually everyone at the CMEx was aware that Chris and Abby had a burgeoning relationship outside of work. The fact that Mac and Gretchen had barged right into the middle of an intimate evening was overlooked by all, given the nature of the day's events.

Besides, both Mac and Gretchen seemed beside themselves with glee at having an opportunity to observe the new relationship firsthand. Mac was Chris's oldest friend, and Gretchen was one of his closest colleagues. They were eating this up.

Gretchen sat down and opened the Pelican case she'd brought with her. She pulled out a laptop with a seventeen-inch screen and a small video editing deck. While she and Abby made sense of the rat's nest of cords and got the two devices powered up and connected, Mac brought Chris up to speed on the rest of the day's activities aboard the *MacGreggor*.

"We completed two more transects this afternoon, a three-hour run up the south side of the canyon and a two-hour run to the north," Mac explained as he pulled out the cruise plan binder and pointed to the map on the front cover where all the planned transects had been plotted before the cruise.

Every research cruise had a cruise plan that detailed each day's operations, including what scientific instruments would be deployed, by whom, and where. By the end of the cruise the map usually looked like an old pirate's treasure map, having been held so frequently throughout each day.

"That took us a bit beyond the twelve-hour day we'd planned," Mac continued, "but as I'm sure you know, the weather isn't looking great for tomorrow, so I figured you'd want us to make hay while the sun shined."

"Absolutely. That was a good call," Chris said. "The timing worked out well, by the way. I was able to point to the ship from where I was sitting at the Lodge this afternoon. The donors were impressed."

"How impressed?" Mac asked. "Am I going to be able to build the new, bigger ROV we've been talking about?"

Chris exhaled and absentmindedly pinched the bridge of his nose right where the stitches were. "Ouch. I don't know, Mac. We'll see. Just tell me what you found."

Gretchen picked up the story. "Well, after the first transect of the afternoon, we tasked Marisa, Travis and Matt with reviewing the video while we conducted the second transect."

"And they followed the standard rapid assessment protocols?" Abby asked.

"Yes. They reviewed the video at one-minute intervals and noted the type of seafloor habitat and any organisms they saw, both fish and invertebrates, at those intervals," Gretchen explained. "And of course, we also encourage them to note anything else of interest that they observe. It gives them an extra incentive to watch the video closely."

While she was talking, Gretchen had plugged a small digital tape into the editing deck and was fast-forwarding through the video. Even though digital copies were made of every ROV transect, there were still multiple tape back-ups made as well to guarantee that no information was lost. Looking up the approximate time in the logbook, Gretchen reached the spot she'd been looking for and nodded to Mac.

"Into a canyon deep," Chris said, watching the small monitor.

"Is that Shakespeare?" Abby asked.

"Not exactly. Chris offers that little cherub every time we start a dive. Pretty deep." Mac chuckled. "Anyway. So this is about forty-five minutes into the second afternoon transect. Nobody caught it during the dive, or if we did, we didn't think about what we saw. Otherwise we would've looked around a bit more."

Chris tensed. He'd known that with him off the ship, the attention to detail during data collection would suffer.

Gretchen jumped in as though she could see what Chris was thinking, "But Matt spotted it right away when reviewing the tapes on our way back to the dock." She tapped the screen, "There it is."

Mac pointed, too, and Gretchen paused the video. Both Chris and Abby leaned in to look more closely.

Eventually Chris asked, "Go forward a bit now." And then a couple of seconds later, he said, "Okay, now let's see it again, but this time start the tape a little further back so I can see the approach."

Gretchen complied, and they all watched as the muddy wall of the canyon passed by the ROV's forward camera. Suddenly an object popped into view on the camera. In the ROV's lights it showed up as bright red.

"That looks like a hagfish pot, but—" Chris said.

"It's too large," Mac interjected, "and look how deep it's sitting in the sediment. That thing is too heavy for a pot."

Hagfish, known more commonly as slime eels, were unattractive members of the taxonomic family *Myxinidae*. Usually around eighteen inches in length, they had primitive eyes and a "mouth" that featured tooth-like projections. Hagfish were scavengers and had been found on submerged whale carcasses eating the carcass from the inside out. While nothing in the natural world was gross to a scientist, hagfish came as close as anything.

Hagfish were captured using cylindrical pots, or traps, which were deployed on the seafloor in muddy environments. Though not tasty, their skin served a variety of roles. Chris had had a hagfish wallet while in college that looked and felt much like leather.

"Okay, Gretchen," Mac said, "now show them the frame grab you made."

Gretchen switched software on the laptop and brought up a close-up image of the end of the "pot." The HD camera on the ROV allowed for high resolution, particularly when making frame grabs, which were essentially still photographs "grabbed" from the video.

"Look at that," Mac said.

"That's no pot. That's the end of a barrel," Chris replied, then turned to Abby. "See that? That's the pressure release valve for a barrel."

"Now we know why it's sitting so low in the sediment. There's something in it," Mac offered. "And it's clean, too, no fouling at all. Which means it was dumped fairly recently."

Most man-made objects, anything from beer bottles to rubber tires to shipping containers, when tossed overboard, ultimately ended up covered by living organisms. These "fouling" organisms, like anemones and sponges, tended to attach to any hard surface they could find underwater.

Rewinding the tape a couple of more times, Chris suggested, "Look at the way the sediment is cleaved around the barrel. And you're right, Mac; that looks fresh. There's been little time for the disturbed sediment to settle." He looked up from the screen. "Gretchen, please clip about twenty seconds of video around the barrel and bring that, with the frame grab, to the office tomorrow."

Mac looked quizzical, so Chris added, "Jase Hamilton is the sheriff's investigator who interviewed me this afternoon at CHOMP. We discussed what would explain the attack, and the only thing that made sense was that we might find something out there these guys don't want found. I think this may be it."

"Jase. Huh. Haven't seen him in a long time. How'd he look? Keeping himself together?"

"He's meeting us at the dock at dawn on Thursday, so you'll get a chance to catch up with him then."

"What do we think is in that barrel?" Abby said, thinking out loud. "Could it be empty? Perhaps some kind of mistake that was dropped overboard?"

Everyone looked at Chris, he assumed, because he was the one with the Ph.D. Or maybe just because they assumed he'd met the goons who'd presumably dumped the barrel. "I suppose it could be empty. But why dump empty barrels offshore when I'm sure there's any number of places to dispose of them on land? And as Mac said, the barrel is sitting pretty deep in the sediment. And if it was an honest mistake, why attack me and call attention to it?"

He thought for a few more seconds. "No, there's something in it. And I'll bet there are more of them. Why go through the trouble of disguising barrels as hagfish pots if you're only dumping a few?"

He stared up at a large framed photo on the wall from a dive he'd done with his dad in Whaler's Cove on Point Lobos.

Abby followed his gaze. "If there's some kind of toxic waste in those barrels, and any of it leaks..."

"We could be looking at a bad situation," Chris finished her sentence. "We don't want any waste leaking into one of the West Coast's most biologically diverse ecosystems."

He looked at Mac.

"We need more information. We need to figure out exactly what's down there."

"Roger that." Mac leaned toward Gretchen. "On that happy note, I guess we should get outta here and let these two, er, um, friends be by themselves."

"Yeah," Gretchen winked at Mac. "I don't want to be here when things get, you know, mushy." She was joking, but Chris could see her face flush with embarrassment.

Abby smiled and Chris laughed. "I've already beaten up two people today, I don't think a couple more would be too difficult."

"Nonsense," Abby said. "I downloaded the full director's cut of *The Abyss* to my iTunes account. You guys have to stay to watch."

"Just happy to be here." Mac looked at Gretchen with undisguised mirth.

"That cherub never gets old," Chris said.

"I already mentioned cherub earlier, by the way," Mac said.

Gretchen cut a quick glance at Chris for approval. He smiled and nodded. "Okay," she said. "But someone is going to have to explain to me where the aliens come from. I just don't get it."

15

The weather the next day, as predicted, was sub-optimal. Strong winds, combined with a tricky swell, made ROV operations impossible. The *MacGreggor* sat at the dock.

Preoccupied with the threat of leaking barrels in Carmel Canyon, Chris awoke at 4:30 a.m. When none of his usual tricks were successful in returning him to sleep, he got up and ate breakfast. Thig, sleeping on the couch in an inverted position, legs sticking up in the air, cracked one eye open and looked at Chris like he'd lost his mind.

"Yeah, you're clearly the brains in this operation, Thiggo."

Moving into his small home office, Chris found a voicemail message from a neighbor indicating that he had a package addressed to Chris, another thing to remember to do later.

Unable to escape the multitude of thoughts going through his head, around seven Chris went in to work. Even if he was unable to do any concentrated work himself, at least he could supervise others.

Late in the day, Chris was home from CMEx working in his garage, tinkering with one of his bikes when Gretchen pulled into the drive-way. He nodded as she got out of the car. Having come out the other side of more than one challenging field project, words were frequently not necessary.

Gretchen pulled up a folding chair and sat next to Chris. He was trying to adjust a difficult rear brake with little success.

Looking at the grease all over Chris's hands and blood on more than one of his knuckles, Gretchen inquired, "Don't they have people who get paid to do this kind of thing? Successfully, that is?"

"Funny. Got any more where that came from?" Chris didn't even look up from his work. He'd been fighting to concentrate all day and working on his bike seemed to be helping.

"Oh, I got a lot of them. Been working with Mac too much lately."

"That why you came by? To try out some new material?"

"No, I was just in the neighborhood and thought I'd drop in. I was on the boat most of the day and missed you at the office. Here's the mail that was sitting in your box. Anything new on the barrel?"

"Thanks. A fair amount of speculation on the barrel, but no new facts. I don't think we'll know more until we get back down there."

Gretchen had worked with Chris long enough to be undeterred by his lack of elaboration when he was in a bad mood. "What about the guy who attacked you? The one who got away, that is. Anything turn up there?"

"Actually not. My friend Jase from the sheriff's office hasn't contacted me yet. But he'll join us tomorrow if we're successful in pulling away from the dock. Perhaps we'll learn more then."

"My social media announced this morning that we have a work anniversary this week."

Chris looked up. "I try to stay away from social media. But I guess you're right. Have you finally had enough?"

"You wish. No, I just—I don't know—wanted to touch base to see how things are going. We've all been so busy lately that I haven't had much time to talk with you."

Chris wanted to say how much he valued their relationship, how important it was to him beyond the bounds of work; to reiterate how

79

his relationship with her was now longer-lived than any other save his childhood friends Mac and Jase; to explain that he had awakened each morning for the past eight years excited about going to work because he worked with her, the kindest person he had ever known.

But he fucked it up. He dropped the ball and opted for a sarcastic response. "All clear on my end." He didn't even know what it meant, and he couldn't look at her as he said it.

Before he could elaborate, Gretchen's phone rang. She stepped out of the garage to field the call.

In a few minutes, she came back. "The Dianas are all bent out of shape about some data issue. I don't understand what they're talking about, but I'd better go back to the boat to check it out."

Chris nodded. He tried to salvage the conversation. "Let's resume our discussion tomorrow. If there are things that you'd like to change or improve on, I'm game to consider it."

"Roger that," Gretchen said over her shoulder as she walked to her car.

16

The wind was already blowing fifteen knots out of the northwest when the CMEx team arrived at the dock on Thursday morning at 5:00 a.m. If it got closer to twenty knots, conditions would be too rough to deploy the *Seaview* over the side of the *MacGreggor*. With the boat rocking, the ROV could either smash into the side of the ship, or worse, someone could get hurt trying to wrestle the thousand-pound behemoth swinging around the deck on its way to or from the water.

Jase Hamilton and a deputy came on board a few minutes before departure. They joined Abby, Gretchen, as well as Marisa, Travis, and Matt in the vessel's main lounge as the *MacGreggor* got underway. Gretchen had set out assorted breakfast foods along a long counter and a TV was tuned in to one of the twenty-four-hour news networks. Chris and Mac were up on the bridge with the captain.

There was something about departing a port while on the bridge of an oceanographic research vessel that never got old for Chris. Dating back to his first cruises as a graduate student, leaving land behind to go exploring seemed to stir something primal.

And the bridge always provided the best vantage point for taking in the view that passed by as a vessel left the interior of a harbor and steamed toward the entrance. Heavier work-a-day fishing boats docked in the interior of most harbors gave way to small sailboats, lonely representatives of their owners' opulence sitting at moorings waiting hopefully for the infrequent weekend visit. The structures on land followed the same pattern. Where packing houses and bustling warehouses characterized the working interior of many harbors, the structures became less utilitarian as one progressed seaward. There one found the lonely mansions associated with the lonely yachts.

But every once in a while, one came upon an outlier, a harbor that time seemed to have forgotten. Here the structures, rather than becoming more opulent, became more rustic as one steamed seaward— more authentic to the locale. Old, weather-beaten piers held memories rather than jet skis and were attached to houses held by working families for generations.

At the same time, Chris also enjoyed the bridge for its stability. All hell could be breaking loose, the weather could be raging outside, and the science labs might be bustling with activity two decks down, but the bridge and its residents enjoyed an envelope of unlikely calm: the absolute quiet of the bridge, broken only by garbled fragments of conversations broadcast over the marine radio.

These feelings were even more poignant aboard the *MacGreggor*, since Chris had been present for its maiden voyage five years prior and nearly every cruise since.

"In addition to this wind, there's a six- to eight-foot northwest swell that came up overnight. Should make for bit of a rough ride until we clear Point Pinos," Captain Bill Williams said as he steered the *MacGreggor* away from the dock. Even at the early hour the sea lions and cormorants that lived on, in, and around the end of the Monterey breakwater in large numbers were sounding off loudly as the boat motored past in the dark.

"I spoke to Peter last night and explained our plan to him," Chris said, seated to the left of the captain. "He's fully supportive, provided we don't destroy the *Seaview* or chip any of the paint on the *MacGreggor*. I told him that Mac had pledged to do neither but was prepared to resign if he does."

Looking grim on the other side of the darkened bridge, illuminated only by the green light of the ship's navigational computers, Mac grumbled, "We haven't had any time to practice with that widget you've brought on board. I wouldn't get my hopes up if I were you. I sense a Charlie Foxtrot in the making."

Normally, the ROV team would've had time to conduct test runs in a large tank back at the university before going to sea with new equipment. But the exigencies of the situation precluded that from happening this time. So they had had to mount the "widget" late the night before, and the first dive today would also serve as its maiden voyage.

The captain looked at Chris, who just chuckled as he walked across the bridge and patted Mac on the back. "If it were easy, everybody'd be doing it."

The ride around Point Pinos, the westernmost point on the Peninsula, was indeed a bit rough. The swell tended to pile up at headlands like Point Pinos, making transit through the area exciting, even in a relatively large oceanographic vessel. From their vantage point on the bridge, the highest deck on the ship, Chris and Mac had the rougher ride. But both had acquired their sea legs long before and had no difficulties.

Down below in the main salon, the graduate students fared relatively well, having each come up with a personalized medication plan before going to sea at the beginning of the summer. Some chose various over-the-counter medicines; others went for prescription patches that attached behind an ear. And others just opted to power through, eating a lot of saltines. Marisa and Travis actually worked on computers during the transit, testing their stomachs even further by trying to concentrate on a small screen while the world around them rocked back and forth.

Abby and Gretchen sat with Jase, who didn't look good, but was able to keep his breakfast. The ladies talked of anything other than the swell to keep Jase feeling okay, and he gamely fought off the frequent urge to vomit all over the place.

The deputy, however, spent most of his time outside at the ship's rail unceremoniously revisiting his last meal. He'd made it for about twenty-five minutes of the ride out of Monterey, working hard to repress the growing feeling of nausea. But when the ship reached Point Pinos, matter flipped over mind, and he succumbed to the involuntary need to empty his stomach. He grasped the painted handprints on the railing outside the galley, added by a witty engineer years before, as he stood in the chilling wind, wishing for nothing other than a break from his current predicament.

Conditions calmed a bit once the *MacGreggor* steamed south of Point Pinos and the crew began to prepare the ROV for the deployment as the ship continued steaming toward Carmel Canyon. By 6:20, the ship was onsite off Point Lobos and ready to deploy the ROV.

"I'm not sure we'll get more than one shot at this today," the captain indicated to Chris and Mac, both of whom were back on the bridge for a pre-dive conference. Any decision to deploy the ROV, or any gear for that matter, over the side of the ship was a joint decision among the key players: the chief scientist, the ship's captain, and the ROV supervisor. However, both the captain and the ROV team leader had veto power if there was anything they didn't like about the situation. "I don't like the wind or the building weather," the captain continued.

"I concur," Mac added gravely. "The wind is gusting to eighteen knots on the back deck. And the period for the swell is only about seven seconds. The waves are steep and numerous. Deploying the ROV over the side in these conditions is looking less and less likely, in my opinion. We have a narrow window of opportunity here."

Everyone, including Chris, knew that the captain and Mac, as well as the rest of the crew, would do everything possible to make any project conducted aboard the *MacGreggor* successful. That was a foregone conclusion. But these conferences presented the opportunity for all involved to express concerns freely.

"Well, we have to assume that people are being attacked, and possibly killed, over whatever is out here," Chris said. "So let's get the ROV in the water and see what we can see. If we can't get to the site today, we'll come back. And Captain, though I doubt it'll prove useful, keep an eye out while we're in the water. Someone was clearly watching us earlier in the week, so they may be at it again."

"Okay. Agreed." The captain was less than enthusiastic. "Mac, let me know when you're ready to deploy and I'll turn her into the wind."

"Will do."

Turning the *MacGreggor* into the wind made deployment of the ROV from the stern as stable as it was going to be in these weather conditions. It was critical that the ROV not swing from side to side while it was hanging from the A-frame crane. That was when it behaved like a construction wrecking ball from a Road Runner cartoon, breaking equipment and hurting anyone in the vicinity.

The deployment of an ROV, in terms of excitement for an observer watching the process, was usually a non-event. The ROV, attached to a winch wire that ran up through an A-frame crane at the stern, was lifted off the deck and lowered into the water. When it reached the water, the winch wire was detached, and the pilot was free to maneuver the ROV away from the ship. At that point, the primary concern was the tending of the ROV's electronic umbilical, for it was critical that it remained away from the ship's propellers, or screws, at all times.

Chris recalled a trip on board a large research vessel on the East Coast during grad school when an ROV's umbilical had become tangled in the huge screws that propelled the three-hundred-foot ship forward. In less than fifteen seconds the umbilical had wound around the propeller shaft and the ROV was sucked directly into the screw, where it exploded into a thousand small pieces.

On that occasion, Chris remembered, the post-dive meeting had been rather contentious. Much of the discussion focused on the fact that the incident had occurred in near perfect surface conditions, with human error being the primary explanation for the problem.

Under conditions such as those they were facing today, there was even less room for human error. Everyone had to be on their game. Communications between the deck crew working with the ROV and the bridge crew operating the ship had to be clear and unimpeded.

Fortunately, CMEx had a dedicated ROV crew that worked most of the time aboard the *MacGreggor*. That meant that they understood not only the nuances of how the ship moved, but also how the ship's crew operated. That's not to suggest, however, that the CMEx-*MacGreggor* team didn't struggle with challenges, like anyone else.

The wind blew and the waves crashed against the stern of the ship, sending a near-continuous curtain of white-blue saltwater over the back deck. Mac and the ROV team all wore their waterproof, foul-weather gear and personal floatation devices, or PFDs, as they went through the final checks for all the ROV's systems.

As part of a longstanding, but frequently humorous tension between the two groups, none of the ROV engineers wanted a scientist near the vehicle. So the science team observed the deployment from the relative protection of the upper deck. Watching the majority of the crew getting soaked by the building seas, the scientists weren't at all opposed to being excluded from this particular operation.

86

Checks concluded, Mac gave the signal to the ship's crew that they were ready to go. He then called up to the captain on the radio mounted on his PFD and asked for permission to dive.

Mac timed the distance between incoming swells and watched for any brief lull in the waves that he could use to put the ROV in the water. Seeing one, he called to the winch operator to lift the ROV off the deck. But the winch operator missed the signal at first, then lifted the ROV after the lull had passed, and a set of ten large swells approached the stern.

As the swells rocked the boat, the ROV instantly began to swing. The technicians posted on either side of the ROV struggled to hold the lines taut and to keep the vehicle from moving, but the thousand-pound beast evidently had a plan of its own.

The ROV swung to port and threatened to pin one of the technicians against the side of the ship. Mac grabbed the ROV's frame to try and stop it from crushing the technician. He screamed through his radio to have the ROV dropped back onto the deck. This time the winch operator responded instantly, not needing to hear the command through the radio, and the ROV dropped heavily to the deck without injuring anyone.

The look Mac cast up toward Chris wasn't friendly. The natural tension between the chief scientist, who sought to collect vital data, and the ROV team leader, who sought to keep the ROV intact, superseded a lifetime of friendship every once in a while. This was one of those times. However, another unexpected lull in the swells gave Mac one more chance to get the ROV in the water. The deployment went off this time without a hitch, and the group moved down to the lab to begin the dive.

The ROV's trip to the seafloor fifteen hundred feet below the ship took roughly thirty minutes. Most of this time, Mac spoke to no one. Once on the bottom, Chris punched in the coordinates from the previous dive during which the barrel had been observed, and Mac began flying the ROV in that direction.

Jase, looking pale, but remaining functional, joined them in the ROV lab, as did Gretchen and Abby. The three took up seats behind Chris and Mac, who once again occupied the lead scientist and ROV pilot seats immediately in front of the control console.

Jase looked up at the six monitors and said, "If I understand this correctly, since I last saw you, you've spent millions of dollars on a vessel and a robot, as well as untold thousands on fuel, supplies, and salaries for all these people, all to come out here and film some mud?"

"That's not entirely true," Chris said over his shoulder, "we're also out here looking for a clue. We understand that the sheriff's department doesn't have one, and we'd like to help out as kind of a public service."

From the snort to his left Chris could tell that Mac had liked that one. It also meant, now that the ROV was on the bottom and things were proceeding reasonably well, that Mac's demeanor should be improving.

"How quickly can we find one of these barrels and get the hell out of here?" Jase asked as the boat took a major roll with the swell.

"The coordinates that we picked up on Tuesday should put us fairly close to the spot where a barrel was observed. At this depth, the geographic positioning is less precise. The sonar should bring us a clear image of it."

Chris pointed to the upper left-hand screen. "Yellow indicates a target that's large enough and substantive enough to reflect the sonar's beam back at us; the brighter the yellow, the harder the target. Since, as per your keen observation a few minutes ago, it's fairly muddy down here, any hard target we see should be the barrel."

As if on cue, Mac said, "Hard target at eleven o'clock, about twenty meters out."

Everyone in the lab held their breath as the ROV approached the target, then a large boulder, not the barrel, came into view. It was greeted with several loud exhalations.

"Just like clockwork," Jase suggested.

Chris and Mac, however, were nonplussed by the incident. They had each spent more than enough time underwater to know that things rarely worked out as conveniently as they're portrayed on TV.

Mac set the ROV down on the bottom for a moment and played with a flat screen in front of him. "I'm re-calibrating the sonar. Stand by."

The ship rolled more as the swells rocked the hull. "Conditions up top appear to be falling apart," Mac said. "It'll take at least thirty minutes to surface. We need to think about ending the dive for today. We can always come back tomorrow if the weather calms down."

"Understood," Chris responded. But since he wasn't ready to give up just yet, he continued, "Let's spend fifteen more minutes looking around, then we'll call it a day."

17

Not a peep could be heard from the cheap seats, Chris thought. Jase, Gretchen, and Abby said nothing. Their attention was fixed on the sonar screen and the forward video camera.

"What's the angle of the sonar head?" Chris asked. "Can we bring the angle up a bit to look farther out from the ROV?"

"We can do that," Mac said. He directed his attention to the touch screen panel in front him. The screen depicting the sonar image instantly turned into a computer screen displaying the graphical user interface for the sonar software. The group watched as Mac moved the cursor around the screen, expertly clicking on pull-down menus and changing settings.

He finished the adjustments and re-enabled the sonar. As soon as the first sweep of the sonar beam was complete, Mac blurted out, "Holy shit! Excuse me, ladies, but look at that!"

The sonar screen now showed what appeared to be dozens of barrel-shaped targets immediately in front of the ROV, about ten meters away.

As the first target came into range of the ROV's forward camera, a large red barrel was clearly visible.

"Okay," said Chris." All cameras are recording. Sonar is recording. Gretchen, please note the barrel field at 16:43 GMT. Abby, we'll go back and count individual barrels later, but a rough count would be helpful if you can."

Keeping his eyes glued to the sonar image displayed on the monitor, he continued. "This isn't good. I don't see any obvious leaks, but I'm sure it's just a matter of time. At this depth, we probably can't say definitively where any waste would go or what the consequences would be if a leak occurred. But we're looking at a potential ecological disaster. Who would do this?"

Several minutes later, having flown over dozens of additional barrels, Chris said to the screen, "We're looking for a barrel that hasn't yet settled into the sediment. Just one cooperative barrel will do for today."

A candidate for extraction was located. The barrel was sitting at a forty-five-degree angle, propped up by another barrel which it had landed on. The weather at the surface remained rough, but it wasn't declining. Yet.

Chris leaned back and looked toward Jase. "We're now going to attempt a fairly challenging maneuver directed toward recovering one of these barrels. Using the ROV's manipulator arm, Mac is going to lasso the end of the barrel with cinching line. The line is spooled on a reel we added to the ROV late last night. After lassoing the barrel, Mac will back up the ROV and cinch the line."

"This may be a stupid question, but how is the ROV going to lift a heavy barrel that's stuck in the mud?" Jase asked, looking a bit green. "Can it handle that type of weight? Isn't there going to be some kind of suction?"

"Those are not stupid questions," Chris answered. "And no, it can't. The beauty of this plan is that it doesn't have to. Stand by one minute."

He returned his attention to the barrel visible in the forward camera. To Mac he suggested, "I haven't seen a better opportunity than this one to try out the plan. What do you think?"

Mac looked at Chris. "What do you always say?"

"If it was easy, everyone'd be doing it?"

"That's the one," Mac said.

One of the riskier moments for an ROV comes when its manipulator arm is extended. The seafloor is essentially one giant ROV trap, with numerous possible snags that could foul up an ROV. When an ROV is hung up on the bottom, since it's tethered to the surface vessel, it can essentially anchor the ship, at least until the umbilical snaps and the ROV is lost.

With a manipulator arm extending out from the ROV, the probability of entanglement increased considerably. The cinching line added to the challenge, as it could easily become entangled on the bottom and ensnare the ROV.

No one spoke as the ROV approached the barrel. Mac operated the ROV with his usual skill, but the barrel didn't cooperate initially. At one point the ship's position shifted under the building swell at the surface, and the ROV was pulled out of position, dragging the extended manipulator arm across several barrels. The cinching line that ran from the spool to the claw of the arm snagged on the rough edge of a rock and unwound three extra feet of line, exponentially increasing the chances of a snag.

Mac swore under his breath as he did what he could to keep the ROV from hanging up. He spotted a new barrel and quickly directed the ROV toward it. Using the newly created excess line to his advantage, he looped the excess around the end of the exposed barrel. He then used the claw of the manipulator arm to "tie off" the end of the line using a carabiner, creating a slip knot. Reversing the thrusters on the ROV drew the line taught around the end of the barrel.

"That's one for the record books," Mac exhaled. "I've tied up, or blown up, a number of things underwater, but never lassoed a barrel using an ROV in fifteen hundred feet of water!"

Mac then keyed his radio. "Back deck, ROV lab. We're prepared for recovery. The cinching line will be unspooling, so when we get to the surface, we need to get the vehicle on board as quickly as possible."

"You see," Chris said to Jase, "the ROV doesn't have to lift the barrel. It'll simply unspool the line as it's recovered. Then we'll wrap the line around a bollard and use the boat's winch to bring the barrel to the surface."

"We're not out of the woods yet," Mac added, "but I think the line should hold on to the barrel."

Chris stood to stretch his neck and back, which had tensed up during the operation. "Nice job, Mac. That was hairy. I'm going up to the bridge to call in a report on what we've found. I expect that a lot of people, from many agencies, are going to be unhappy about this. Jase, do you want to come up with me?"

"Yes," Jase replied. "I'll check on my deputy and meet you on the bridge.

Twenty-five minutes later the ROV was back on board and the recovery of the barrel was underway. Chris and Mac, wearing hard hats and personal floatation devices, monitored the recovery from the back deck, while Jase, Abby, and Gretchen observed from the upper deck. The deputy was still nowhere to be seen.

"What are we going to do with this thing once we get it back?" Mac asked.

"I just got off the phone with Peter," Chris replied. "He has a hazmat team standing by to meet us at the dock in Monterey. They'll take the barrel back to CMEx to open it there inside one of the new labs. It'll take a bit of time for the state and feds to pull their act together. So for now, we've the ball."

"I wonder what the hell is in those things," Mac said.

"I'm with you. This mystery could get more interesting quickly."

The barrel broke the surface five minutes later. The *MacGreggor* crew, wearing protective gear to avoid coming into contact with any of the barrel's contents should there be a leak, brought the barrel on board successfully and secured it on the back deck for the ride back to Monterey.

Chris surveyed the shoreline for any evidence of the tell-tale reflection from binoculars. "If our mere presence had irritated folks before this, the recovery of this barrel should really push their buttons. It'll be worth considering some precautions when we return to the dock."

He turned to Abby, who was standing nearby. "Perhaps we should eat dinner again together tonight, you know, as a precaution."

Abby shook her head and walked back inside. Chris had no idea what that meant.

As they steamed back toward Monterey Harbor, Chris looked down at the camouflaged barrel on the back deck. Something about it stirred a memory. There was something there, but he couldn't get it. He'd have to think about that.

18

"Wait just a minute," an angry Darrell English screamed at Kevin O'Grady across the desk. "You're telling me that this pantywaist scientist, a fucking *scientist*, beat the shit out of your two guys, then went out and recovered one of the barrels that you dumped offshore? One of those barrels that 'nobody would ever see again in this lifetime?' What the fuck is happening here, Kevin?"

Kevin hunkered down in his chair as Darrell leapt to his feet.

"Do you understand what's going to happen if our 'friends' find out about this situation?" asked Darrell as he walked around behind Kevin. "There won't be any conversations. They won't ask questions. They'll fucking waste us! Both of us. You *and* me. No discussion."

Kevin again had no response.

Jabbing his large finger into Kevin's back, Darrell said, "You need to make this problem go away."

"How?" mumbled Kevin, still hunkered down as low as the small chair would allow.

"Do I have to do all the thinking around here, for god's sake?" roared Darrell. "Find out what the psychiatrist knows. Perhaps you and your team can at least handle a single, old woman.

"Now get the fuck out of my face," said Darrell, waving his hand as he returned to his chair.

Kevin didn't think it likely that Margaret Black knew anything, or that anything she did know would be of any use. Darrell was in full-blown damage control mode now, and that had proven scary in the past.

But he wasn't paid to second-guess the craziest *mofo* he'd ever met. He would have to send one of his guys to look in on Dr. Black the elder.

19

There was no ambush waiting for the *MacGreggor* at the dock when they tied up at around noon. The ride back up to Monterey had actually been worse than the ride down because they were steaming into the swells for most of the ride. That meant that every several seconds the boat would crest a swell, hang briefly in the air, then drop into the trough on the other side. This pushed several of the borderline seasick cases over the edge. They joined the deputy, who had already re-occupied his position at the rail for the entire trip back to the dock.

Once the ship was tied up at the dock and secured from operations, the hazmat team came and went with the barrel. The guys who came in direct contact with, or who stood in close proximity to, the barrel wore full hazmat suits. The otherworldly suits, which most people associated with disease outbreaks in movies, did attract some attention from the smattering of tourists walking along the jetty. This likely meant that the press would be sniffing around in the near future.

The northwest wind was now blowing twenty-five to thirty knots and wasn't expected to relent for a couple of days. The *MacGreggor's* crew secured the vessel to the pier with sturdy lines.

Mac and Gretchen left in a CMEx truck to take the video and sonar records back to the lab. They would make copies of everything for Jase. Mac was also interested in picking up some parts for the ROV.

Chris, Abby, Jase, and the deputy—who had resurfaced looking much better now that the boat was at the dock—sat at the table in the ship's lounge snacking on the variety of fruits and breads arrayed in front of them that Gretchen had purchased before the cruise.

"Regardless of what we find in those barrels, the dumping alone constitutes a violation of multiple state and federal laws. This is going to be a bureaucratic nightmare that will fortunately be well beyond my pay grade," Jase said.

"But as to the attack on you and the body found in Stillwater Cove, we still have jurisdiction. Normally, we wouldn't confer with witnesses on details of a case, but this situation merits a different type of treatment."

"You mean you need our help?" Mac quipped between bites of grapes and cheese.

"Very funny, wise guy. I just got off the phone with the medical examiner and the district attorney. The body in the cove belonged to a guy named Joe Rothberg. It looks like he was hit over the head prior to being dropped into the water, so it appears that we're indeed dealing with a murder. Do you remember him, Chris?"

Chris looked at Abby, then back at Jase, and shook his head. "No. Am I supposed to?"

"Well, maybe you remember Brent, his older brother. Brent was in our AP U.S. history class junior year before he went away for robbery."

Chris perked up. "Oh, yeah. Of course. Joe was just a little kid back then. I think my mom might have worked with him at one point after Brent went away. What's the working theory on how he was involved in this?"

Jase looked at the deputy, who consulted his notes. "The decedent's wife indicated that he'd recently taken on a night job and was supposedly at work on the night he disappeared. She indicated that she didn't know, however, where he was working or for whom, or why he would've been on or near the ocean."

Jase resumed, "So we have, may he rest in peace, Joe, a three-time loser taking a job at night and ending up dead under mysterious circumstances. And from the District Attorney's Office I learned that your buddy with the decimated knee, Jerry Smith, has clammed up completely. The DA's read is that Jerry is no tough guy; he's scared. Also, no sign of the second assailant."

Chris processed this new information. "Jerry Smith. I liked him better as Vans. But listen, Abby suspected last night that the chances that these two events weren't related are close to nil. I'd have to say, based on what we've learned today, I'd agree."

"We'll operate based on that assumption. It sounds like your lab will have a preliminary identification of the barrel's contents by this afternoon," Jase said. "I'm going to head over there and check in with them and pick up the sonar and video records from Mac, then I'm going to talk to Rothberg's widow to see if there's anything else of relevance that she can offer." He got up to leave.

"You guys have been a great help today. But let us take it from here. All we need from you now, Chris, is a formal statement about your encounter with Jerry Smith. Maybe you can come down to the department. And I expect that someone will be contacting you eventually about recovering the remaining barrels."

"I'll pass them along to Mac. He's the man for that job," Chris said. "I'll come by the station tomorrow. With this weather, it's pretty clear we won't be going to sea for the next couple of days."

20

The eye of a hurricane is a calm respite from the violent winds of the surrounding storm, and Chris knew this firsthand. He'd been through two hurricanes, once as a graduate student volunteer aboard a NOAA plane that had intentionally flown through the hurricane to collect meteorological data, and once aboard a research vessel that had no choice on its return route from a cruise to the outer Caribbean.

The oft used metaphor of the calm before the storm was accurate in his experience if one were in the air. There the winds of the eye blew gently and all in the same direction. However, the metaphor broke down for anyone who had been at sea for a hurricane. In the ocean, the eye of the hurricane was frequently characterized by a highly confused sea state, with waves and winds converging from all directions. This made below a far more dangerous place to be than above.

It was of the latter experience that Chris was thinking as he drove over the hill on Highway 1 from Monterey on his way back to Carmel. He'd dropped Abby back at CMEx and planned to meet up with her for dinner later that evening at a French restaurant on Seventh Avenue. Rather than stay at his office, he was going home to take a swim in the ocean and go for a run with Thig.

The events of the past couple days—the attack, the death, the discovery of the barrels—all apparently related, but not yet in any cohesive way, seemed much like the confused seas at the eye of a hurricane. Though not prone to superstitions, Chris could nevertheless feel the massive walls of the metaphorical storm looming out there waiting to visit its violence upon them.

Changing his plans as he drove, he continued past the exit for Ocean Avenue and proceeded down the highway to the base of the hill. Turning left at Rio Road, the last stoplight on Highway 1 until Morro Bay some 153 miles to the south, he veered to the right and into the Crossroads Shopping Center.

Whereas the village of Carmel-by-the-Sea forbade chain stores and shopping centers, less than a mile away an unincorporated area known generally as Carmel had erected not one, but two shopping centers, the Crossroads and The Barnyard. Both were tastefully done as shopping centers go, and the former housed the office of Dr. Margaret Black, who hadn't seen her son for over a week.

The timing of Chris's impromptu visit couldn't have been better. Margaret took a planned break between noon and 2:00 p.m. every day without fail. He found her eating her lunch in the outer office while watching something on Netflix.

"Chris! I wasn't expecting...what happened to your face? Oh my gosh. Please sit down. Were you in an accident? Was anyone else hurt? Can I get you something to drink?" Chris knew from experience to hunker down for the staccato burst of questions before venturing an answer to any one of them.

His mom looked good, he thought. She was clad in her unofficial uniform, black turtleneck and black slacks. Her once-dark hair was now almost completely gray, but it was a regal gray—regal, that is, with a single bobby pin. Margaret, dating to her days at Wellesley College in

Massachusetts, had kept her hair just short of shoulder length, with the right side pulled back by a single bobby pin. She had the same hazel eyes as Chris and the same wrinkles at the corners of the eyes. Chris loved his mother but regularly admitted that she was a handful. And she was becoming more so as time went on.

Margaret was the product of an austere, and sometimes severe, childhood outside of Pittsburgh, Pennsylvania. Her mother had died of pulmonary thrombosis when Margaret was only five years old, leaving her in the dubious care of her well-intentioned, but manifestly unprepared father, William.

William Adams was an attorney, plying his trade along the Ohio River towns of Ben Avon, and the more affluent, Sewickley. The loss of Margaret's mother had hit him hard and left him unprepared for parenting and just about every other aspect of life outside of the narrow purview of the law. Even prior to Joan's death, as a parent, William was hindered by the repressed gender roles of his generation, unable to make the emotional connection that his sole daughter needed.

Cognizant of his failings, and increasingly burdened by his inability to succeed in life's many other challenges, William sought nightly refuge in the bottle. But it was a refuge for him alone, leaving the young Margaret out in the metaphorical cold. There were no beatings, none of the inappropriate touching that so frequently characterized families who'd lost their way, just the slow burn of a purgatory created by a thousand forgotten details—missed school plays, daily lunches not prepared, and parental advice not offered.

Margaret, with an intuition born of this troubled upbringing, had found her way to a career uniquely suited to someone so conversant in the vocabulary of human suffering. While she could empathize with the personal problems of almost anyone, Margaret had a truly magical touch with troubled kids. Her pursuit of an M.D. in psychiatry had provided her with a means to help the world while also salving her own long-standing emotional wounds.

For Chris, Margaret's career path in a village as small as Carmel-by-the-Sea had meant that many of his public-school peers, from primary school through high school graduation, spent more time with his mother than with him. She knew everyone and they knew her. Boundaries were the purview of other, less accessible, psychiatrists, yet Chris had thrived under Margaret's perpetually sympathetic guidance. While he nursed some powerful wounds of his own from his youth, they weren't the result of a lack parental love.

Margaret was saying, "You look tired. Not getting enough sleep. Why don't you go back and lie down in my office for a while? I don't have another appointment until 2:45."

That actually sounded good, but that wasn't why he was here. "Thanks, Mom. I'll be fine. I'm actually going to go for a swim and take Thig for a run." He gave her a general overview of the attack and some of the surrounding details.

"Well," she said with solemnity that the facts didn't deserve. "You're working with Jase Hamilton. Boy was he trouble. Of course, you and Mac were no better. The three of you together were quite a challenge."

"Mom," Chris interjected, knowing that this line of commentary could go on forever, "Joe Rothberg washed up dead in Stillwater Cove yesterday. It looks like he was murdered."

"That was Joe? I saw it on the local news last night. His poor mother must be in a state. First Brent goes away to jail and now this. Do they know what happened?"

There was something odd about the way she asked this last question. Chris thought he had detected a slight rise in tone or maybe a subtle change in her body language.

"To what extent does the doctor-patient relationship persist after death, Mom?"

"Well, if you mean privilege, there's a general consensus that it doesn't continue after the death of the patient."

"Tell me."

"I'm not sure that it could have anything to do with this. But Joe did come to see me last week."

"Last week?" Chris was incredulous. "That's twenty years after you first saw him, isn't it? That seems unusual."

"This is a small community. You know that. It's almost impossible to go out into public and not run into someone I may have worked with at one time or another. I ran into him with his wife and baby daughter at the Monterey Trader Joe's several weeks ago. He was polite. Asked me how you were doing. Said he was sorry to hear about Dad's passing. I remember having the impression that marriage had had a positive effect on him."

"But there was more," Chris said, a statement more than a question.

"Well, yes. I felt as though he was too enthusiastic to see me. The encounter could easily have involved a nod of the head and nothing more. He gave me the clear impression that he wanted to get something off his chest, but not something he wanted to share with his wife.

"So I wasn't surprised when he showed up here in my outer office a couple of weeks later unannounced. But once here, he wasn't particularly forthcoming. We talked a bit about the old days, he gave me a brief overview of his life since we last saw each other."

"Nothing related to any of his current activities?"

"Not when he was here in the office. No. It always took several sessions with Joe to penetrate the complex web of protection mechanisms he would build around himself. His parents were far more supportive of his brother when he was young, and Joe suffered as a result. But he did call me a week ago Monday," she explained, offering nothing further.

"You called me at home while I was at sea but didn't leave a message," Chris stated. He also offered no more.

"His call put me in a bit of situation. It was a protected conversation, but he brought up your name."

"My name?"

"Yes. He was apparently working with some rather tough people on a project which he was unwilling to describe. His reticence, by the way, seemed to be motivated by fear. Though I couldn't tell you why I thought that way."

She sighed deeply before she continued. "He said, and I quote, 'This guy Kevin isn't very happy with Chris. You should tell him to watch out.'"

21

Chris stayed until Margaret's next appointment arrived. He gave her an overview of what had happened the past couple of days and tried to assuage her guilt over not getting in touch with him more quickly.

She'd called, but not left a message, and had assumed that because he was going to be offshore that she had a couple of days to figure out how to work something out, to figure out how to discuss with Chris the danger that Joe had eluded to. She wasn't aware of the donor meeting at the Lodge in Pebble Beach that had brought Chris back to shore.

From the parking lot, Chris called Jase. He got no answer on the cell or at the office, so he left messages to call him. He also tried Gretchen and Mac and got no answers from either of them.

It was great, he thought, to have all this wonderful smartphone technology. But the façade of constant access was frequently just that, a façade. Twenty years ago, the failure to reach anyone would've been disappointing, but not inordinately so. But now, his inability to reach anyone today was infuriating, even though there were likely good explanations for each of them being out of contact.

Kevin.

So someone named Kevin wasn't happy with him. Was Kevin the name of Mr. Acid? Possibly, but that didn't make sense. If he'd been so unhappy, he would've likely been the driver of events that day rather than letting Jerry Smith take the lead. Was Kevin responsible for dumping the barrels? Again, possibly. Did Kevin kill Joe Rothberg? And if so, why? He became increasingly agitated as he pondered these questions. Operating, for the time being, under the assumption that the barrels contained some kind of waste, the potential for a disaster was high. Recovering a large number of barrels from the seafloor at that depth was likely not going to be an option—too expensive and time consuming. That meant that the primary response, at both the state and federal levels, would be to provide a small amount of funding for monitoring of the barrel field to track any leakage. In essence, the damage was done at the moment of the dumping. Toxic sites like these were the gifts that kept on giving, probably for decades into the future.

He thought about these things as he and Thig ran their "Carmel Loop," which consisted of a straight shot down the hill to Carmel Beach, around Carmel Point to River Beach along Scenic Drive, and back up the hill. Twice. Usually a run along Scenic with Thig was an opportunity to drink in the incredible natural beauty of Carmel, with the waves crashing against the rocky seashore and birds swooping down along the white sand beaches, all against a backdrop of Carmel Bay and Point Lobos. But on this day Chris's focus was elsewhere.

When he returned from the run at dusk, there were messages from Jase on both his cell and home phones. He returned the call immediately. "Ah, Chris. Glad you called. There's much to talk about. I'm headed your way right now. Be there in ten."

Chris was showered in five and waiting for Jase when he pulled up in front of the house. The sun had set, and it was getting dark.

"Let's go inside," a somber Jase said when he got out of his car. He looked to be all business, though he softened under Thig's friendly assault.

Before they could head inside the house, Chris's neighbor, Mary, came out to see what was going on. It wasn't every day that the authorities found their way down her private drive. Under the pretense of checking up on Thig, Mary came over to grill Jase on subjects ranging from her feelings about noisy, gas-powered leaf blowers to her theories on the two "hoodlums" who'd been staking out Chris's house.

Jase, Chris was interested to see, had evidently cultivated a way with the public. He smoothly navigated Mary through the briar patch of her many concerns and walked her safely back to her doorstep.

Smiling subtly as he walked back toward Chris, Jase thumbed toward Chris's front door. When they were inside and sitting at the dining room table, Jase began his update. "First, Jerry Smith's knee is destroyed. He won't be walking anytime soon, and his movements will be significantly inhibited for life."

Chris shrugged.

"I'm not questioning your actions, and testimony from the witnesses supports your side of the story. But I'm informing you that the Monterey County Sheriff's Office will continue its official investigation, and we may need further information from you. I'll probably not be part of that portion of the investigation, by the way."

Chris sought to comment, but Jase waved him away. "Just give me a minute to get it all out there on the table."

Then, having received a nod from Chris, Jase continued, "Second, and you may already know this, your lab opened the barrel and discovered a bizarre cocktail of used motor oil, and possibly transmission fluid, combined with some kind of heavy, sandy sludge. It's also possible that there was a human leg bone in there, what appears to be an adult-sized ulna.

"Third, the press has caught on to the story. I spoke to your Peter Lloyd today on the phone. He said the university press agent was handling the science end of things, at least until the EPA and NOAA come up to speed. We'll handle press on the investigation. But it's a small town, so you and your team should be ready for media queries.

"Finally—" Jase was interrupted by the sound of the front door opening.

"Yo!" Mac called, "where's my favorite fur ball?" He, too, was greeted with enthusiasm by the furry master of the house.

Mac came back, grabbed a banana from the basket on the counter and a glass of orange juice from the fridge, then sat at the table. For the briefest of moments, the three friends sat there enveloped by the comfort and intimacy that's only possible in the presence of old childhood friends. There was no sarcasm, no posturing, no words at all—just three friends who, now adults, shared bonds that reached back decades.

And then the moment was gone.

22

"Well, as I was saying." Jase didn't skip a beat. "Finally, we're working up all leads searching any known associates of Jerry Smith and Joe Rothberg, checking all automotive repair shops in the area. I can feel something out there, but nothing has turned up as yet."

"Speaking as a taxpayer and as a victim of an assault," Chris said, "I greatly appreciate any and all efforts by the sheriff's department in this matter. I'll help in any way that I can."

Jase nodded as though he knew more was coming.

Chris clenched his fist and looked directly into Jase's eyes. "Talking to my old friend Jase, I say fuck these guys. We need to get out in front of this. We need to take it to them. I, too, can feel something out there. We've all got friends, family, and colleagues around here, and I don't want to wait around for the next shoe to drop." He explained what he'd learned from his mom this afternoon. They both looked at Mac.

"What are you looking at me for? You know where I stand. I don't need anything else to happen. I'll waste 'em all, whoever they are, right now without a concern."

"Look, you're dealing with the sheriff's department here, not the FBI. And definitely not some black ops team." Jase replied defensively while looking at Mac. "I don't support the two of you 'getting out in front of this' in any way. You guys are scientists; do your science. Find out how bad the situation is with these barrels. Leave the policing to the police. We'll handle this."

Then his cell phone rang.

He answered on one ring.

"Hamilton here. Roger that. Where? What's her condition? Any witnesses? Okay. Shut down the scene. If they give you any problems, have them call me. We've got jurisdiction on this, and I don't want anyone stepping into the crime scene until I get there."

He clicked off. Both Chris and Mac were standing.

"Who?" they said simultaneously.

"Gretchen Clark. She was attacked at her apartment within the last half hour. She was beaten pretty severely. She's alive but in critical condition. They're taking her to CHOMP, but there's already talk about airlifting her up to the University Medical Center."

Chris and Mac looked at each other. "I can't get to both of them," Chris said.

"Okay. I'll get Abby."

"We'll meet at CHOMP and go from there," Chris replied quickly, preparing for a rapid departure.

"I'm going over to Gretchen's," Jase said. "I'll let you know what I find out. I'm sorry about this, Chris. I know that Gretchen has been with you for a long time. We'll figure out who these guys are."

Another look passed between Chris and Mac. If Jase caught it, he didn't let on.

Jase left quickly in his official vehicle. Mac jumped into his truck, which was blocking Chris's in the driveway, and backed out. As Chris was opening the door to his Land Rover, Mac's truck paused, and his passenger-side window rolled down.

Chris walked over and leaned in. "No mercy."

"Fuckin' A. They're going to pray for it before we're done with them."

23

Chris called his mom as he negotiated the narrow streets on the way to her house. No answer. He briefly fought the increasingly prevalent desire to throw his phone out the window.

Stay focused. There could be any number of reasons for her lack of response. But he couldn't think of one that was good.

Margaret lived on Carmel Point, one block back from Scenic Drive in a house she and Andrew had purchased a few years before he died. It was a moderate-sized redwood affair, with California craftsmen flourishes adding to its curb appeal. The large plate glass windows that dominated the second story had a clear view of Carmel Bay and Point Lobos when the fog wasn't in.

Narrow streets and close proximity to the beach meant no street parking on her block. As Chris approached her house, he passed a black GMC truck pulled to one side. Could be workers at one of her neighbors, or perhaps not, he thought.

He pulled up to her house and killed the engine. From under the front seat he grabbed a telescoping ASP that Mac had given him as a gift several years ago.

The ASP was essentially a retractable steel baton that, when fully extended, was an extremely effective weapon. It was illegal in California for citizens to own ASPs, but dating back to their middle school days, Mac had enjoyed giving Chris illicit gifts at Christmas. Over the years, Chris had accumulated illegal throwing stars, nunchuks, a switch blade, and more recently a tazer. He wasn't sure where Mac got this stuff, but he'd always expected it to come in handy one day.

As Chris approached the front door, he could see that it was ajar. With the ASP in his right hand, not yet deployed, he crept in the door while listening for any sign of activity. He'd cleared the first two rooms off the central hallway when he heard his mom speaking upstairs. While he couldn't make out the words, the tone sounded irritated.

Out of habit, Chris climbed the wooden steps quickly, following a line up the outer edge of stairway to minimize any sound from creaking boards that would betray his presence. Advancing on his mom's bedroom door, Chris tried to slow his breathing.

He paused at the bedroom door, which was partially ajar. He could hear Margaret saying, "This is ridiculous. You force your way into my house and expect me to pack a bag and come with you? Shame on you!"

He recognized her calm, but emphatic voice which she tended to use with people who didn't impress her.

"Either you fill the bag or I will. I don't care. But you're coming with me now." Chris instantly recognized the voice of Acid and his grip on the ASP handle tightened.

In another lifetime, Chris, Mac, and Jase had all turned eighteen during their senior year in high school. They promptly took their newly found, if tenuous, independence out for a walk and booked a three-week surf trip to Hawaii to immediately follow graduation. The fact none of the three discussed the plans with their parents became fodder for many an interesting family conversation.

Despite much harrumphing and guffawing by the three parental units, the trip came off as planned and the three weeks of unimpeded surfing were added to the mythology of the threesome's already rich history. They surfed four to five times a day at Threes, Big Rights, and the Ala Moana Bowl along the south coast of the island of Oahu, until their limbs ceased to function and they were forced to crawl back to their sketchy hotel room each evening.

But the trip wasn't without other types of excitement. The three young *haoles* proved to be magnets for the irritation of several local Hawaiian homeboys, who, unfettered by jobs or any other responsibilities, had plenty of time to harass the threesome.

The encounters increased in intensity for the first couple of weeks, starting off initially with name calling out in the surf and progressing later to trailing the boys back to their hotel. Then, four days before the boys' departure, another Californian staying at their hotel was beaten to death on the sidewalk in front of the hotel lobby.

Watching the body being unceremoniously carried away on a stretcher by the paramedics, not a word had passed between the three. None were needed. The tenor of the trip, indeed the tenor of their lives, had changed.

This was the closest the three had come to the frightening reality of violent death. No longer was the threat of great bodily harm an abstraction to be tossed about while sparring with friends. The body in the bag could have easily been any of them.

Later that evening, after eating dinner at the International Market Place in Waikiki, a woman had beckoned to Chris from one of the many merchant stalls. Dressed like a gypsy, she'd offered to give Chris a tarot card reading. When he asked about readings for his two friends as well, she'd suggested that their destinies were already set, that only his hung in the balance.

Mac and Jase had quickly taken the opportunity to abandon Chris in search of more Hawaiian shaved ice. So Chris settled into the booth to have his cards read.

The "gypsy" didn't just reek of cigarette smoke; she waged a multipronged assault on all the senses. Her weathered face and gravelly voice hit first, a one-two punch. As she drew Chris in, the smell of her yellow-grey hair and her putrid breath clocked him on the chin. Virtually incapacitated, he was then slowly pummeled by the malodorous emanations from her clothing, as well as the hundred-year-old upholstery of her booth.

By comparison, the reading itself was uneventful. But the woman did intimate that trouble seemed to follow Chris, and that he would have to become accustomed to dealing with it.

Sure, Chris thought back then. Brilliant. But as his creative young mind drifted, filling in the gaps that the uninspiring faux gypsy left in her analysis, he wondered how he would deal with trouble as it came. Would he rise to the occasion? Or would he blow it?

Now Chris conjured an image of Margaret's room in his mind. From the sound of her voice, Margaret was most likely across the room by her closet. That would probably mean Acid was also on that side of the room; close enough to grab her if he needed, but not too close yet.

Gambling that Acid had his knife, but not necessarily a gun, Chris burst into the room. In one fluid move he pushed through the door, and with a rapid tweak of the wrist he extended the ASP.

Each of the three lamps in the room was illuminated. Margaret was exactly where Chris had anticipated. She had her hands on her hips and the stern, disapproving look on her face that Chris had seen once or twice before.

Acid, an anachronism in this picture, was standing at the end of the bed, closer than Chris had expected. The walk-in closet door was open on the other side of him. He did have a gun, what appeared to be a .38 caliber revolver. He was dressed in essentially the same outfit he'd been wearing in Pebble Beach, and the gun was jammed into the front of his pants, evidently so he could use his hands to gesticulate while compelling Margaret to do as she was told. The bulge of his ample gut effectively trapped the gun where it was. That was a fortuitous turn of events for Chris.

As Acid struggled to free his gun with his right hand, he turned to Chris and instinctively held his left arm straight out, with his palm up. It took Chris only seconds to cover the distance between the door and Acid's position across the room. Margaret was clearly surprised to see Chris burst in the door, but he remained focused on Acid, watching the gun in particular.

Acid shouted, "Nooooo!" as Chris swung the ASP diagonally across his body and connected with Acid's right elbow. It was an awkward move that compromised the strength of Chris's attack. But he had to remove the gun from the picture. The force of the impact was sufficient to snap a bone in the elbow, drawing a spitty scream from Acid.

In the eternity of the moment, Chris felt an inkling of remorse for poor Acid. The guy was clearly a joke and was obviously involved in something way out of his depth.

But then again, this situation was no joke. Chris quickly recoiled from the first attack and brought the ASP down a second time on Acid's upper left arm with all the force he could muster. This was a much less awkward angle based on the direction of Chris's approach, so he was able to put a great deal more force behind the blow. He could feel the impact on the bone radiate up the shaft of the ASP.

As a spark of what looked like defiance flared in Acid's eyes, Chris followed with a front kick to Acid's chest that sent him flying backwards through the open closet door.

Chris followed Acid into the walk-in closet. He was conscious, but not moving on the floor. Chris grabbed a scarf from one of Margaret's million hangers and carefully removed the gun from Acid's waist.

Without turning around, Chris asked, "Mom? Are you okay?"

"Yes. I'm right here behind you," Margaret answered. "Chris, you, well—." She was visibly shaken. It wasn't every day that someone forced his way into her home to attempt a kidnapping.

"I know. Could you please hold on to this gun for a second while I search him for any other weapons? Keep the scarf around it. We don't want our prints on the gun." She took the gun and stepped back.

"Should I call the police?" Margaret ventured. "I think I should call the police."

"Hold on a minute. I'll call Jase in a bit. But I want to talk to this guy first," Chris replied.

He searched Acid, finding only the knife he'd drawn in their earlier encounter. Acid tried to move during the search and received a tap from the ASP to his injured left arm.

"I want to know a few things, and if you don't tell me, you aren't walking out of here." Chris could hear a gasp behind him, but to her credit, Margaret remained silent. "Do you understand me?"

Acid seemed to be calculating his odds. He nodded his assent.

Chris's cell phone rang. He switched the ASP to his left hand and, seeing that it was Mac calling, answered. "I'm here. Is Abby okay?"

"Yes," Mac said. "Abby is fine. There were two guys in a dark blue truck sitting outside her house when I pulled up. They saw me and bolted. I chose to check on Abby rather than to follow them. Who knows what their plan was?"

"I may have some idea," Chris replied, "or I will soon. Perhaps you should skip CHOMP at the moment and come directly to my mom's house. I have Acid here and we're about to have a chat."

"Got it. Be there in ten to fifteen minutes. Mac out."

Chris turned his full attention back to the man on the floor. "Now why don't we start with your name. Acid doesn't suit you."

24

Mac and Abby arrived at Margaret's house in nine minutes. They rushed in the front door together with Mac in the lead. He carried a 9 mm automatic in his right hand. Over his right shoulder was a black bag full of unspecified, but most likely lethal, contents. Abby followed him.

Chris had relieved Acid of his wallet and had determined his name was actually Tommy Campbell, thirty-five years old, from Watsonville. He'd learned that Tommy carried several credit cards, a Blockbuster rental card, what looked to be an old condom, some kind of a punch card from Hooters, and little cash.

Perhaps somewhat more usefully, he'd also established that Gretchen and Abby were the only other targets tonight besides Margaret. Campbell claimed the plan wasn't to hurt any of the women, so he couldn't account for what happened to Gretchen. Rather, they were to be kidnapped and held at a safe location.

Campbell indicated that Chris and Mac weren't targeted, based to some extent on what happened to Jerry Smith earlier in the week. The alleged plan was to use the three females as bait to draw Chris and Mac into a trap.

That made no sense to Chris. "What's the end game here? Why are you doing this?"

No answer.

"Do you understand that we're just scientists? Yet you attacked me, and now we know what's going on. The cat is out of the bag on your little dumping scheme and the authorities have been contacted."

Campbell simply returned a vacant stare.

"I think you're full of shit," Chris added. "Who are the other geniuses you're working with? Does the brain trust realize that even if you were successful in killing all of us, which you won't be, by the way, that your problems are only just beginning?"

"You can work on me all you want with that thing, but I'm not saying anything else," Campbell said. "You can't imagine what will happen to me if I talk."

Chris looked back at Mac, who said, "Five minutes. If I don't have anything by then, it won't matter if we have a week."

Campbell's eyes widened, but he didn't say anything. Evidently, he was going to continue to take the fifth.

Chris stepped back, letting Mac take over. "Okay. Mom, Abby, let's go down and call Jase. He'll tell us whether or not to alert the Carmel Police before he gets here."

Both women expressed a considerable lack of curiosity with regard to what Mac was going to do after they left the room. Chris fully expected to be explaining himself later, but he was grateful for their silence at that moment.

They quietly went downstairs to the kitchen, and Margaret made some tea. She didn't ask whether anyone wanted tea; she just made it. Chris respected people who knew the appropriate thing to do at all occasions. He respected it because it was a skill he didn't have. He didn't drink coffee or tea, so it never occurred to him to make it for anyone.

Abby pulled out some cheese and crackers. She didn't ask either, but food was always a more compelling option than tea. Plus, she was wearing a beautiful olive-green dress with a faint floral print woven into it. Her hair was pulled back in a loose ponytail, and Chris could smell the faintest touch of perfume, or perhaps scented lotion.

At dinner two nights ago, even with Mac and Gretchen there, perhaps even *because* Mac and Gretchen were there, Chris felt like he and Abby had crossed an important threshold. "We were going to dinner tonight, weren't we?" Chris recalled. "I'm sorry."

"Please." Abby looked at Chris, then at Margaret. "This situation is completely out of control. You've got stitches all over your face. Gretchen's in the hospital. Margaret was almost kidnapped tonight. We've got barrels of sludge being dumped offshore, and human remains washing up. The last thing we need to worry about is our compromised dinner plans."

With that out of her system, she added a couple of moments later, somewhat under her breath, "I was looking forward to it, though." Margaret's back was turned, but Chris could see her smile through the back of her head.

Chris didn't want to press the subject in his mom's presence and called Jase instead, who was at Gretchen's house in Pacific Grove.

Since Carmel Point wasn't part of the city of Carmel-by-the-Sea, but rather part of the unincorporated Carmel, it was county territory, and the sheriff had jurisdiction. Jase had a unit respond immediately, and he indicated that he would be over himself shortly and that none of them should leave the premises.

Mac came downstairs a few minutes later. He handed Chris the ASP, which had been collapsed back to its stand-by mode. He then casually walked over to the sink and washed his hands. His nonchalance had a sobering effect on two of the kitchen's other occupants.

No one said anything further. They ate cheese and crackers until they heard the squawk of a police radio out front.

Chris put the ASP into one of Margaret's kitchen drawers. No need to invite more trouble by having an illegal weapon lying about. He went to the front door and was greeted by two deputies coming up the walk with their weapons drawn. They ordered him to stay where he was and to put his hands up. He readily complied, grateful that he'd hidden the ASP, then identified himself as the person who contacted Jase and explained who else was in the house.

While several of Margaret's neighbors came out of their houses to catch some of the action, one of the deputies called Jase on his cell. He confirmed that everyone was who they claimed to be, and the demeanor of both deputies relaxed a bit.

"I'm sorry, sir," Deputy Ross said. "There's a lot happening, and we need to go slowly."

"I understand," Chris said. "The guy is upstairs." And then he asked, "You don't happen to know anything about my colleague Gretchen Clark?"

"No, sir. I'm sorry. We don't have any information."

After checking in with everyone in the kitchen, Chris led the deputies upstairs to where Campbell was lying unconscious on the closet floor. Moments later, the paramedics arrived and were led up the stairs by Mac.

While one deputy remained upstairs to talk with Chris, the other went back downstairs to interview Margaret.

She explained that she'd just returned home from her last appointment around 7:00 p.m. She'd stopped briefly at Safeway to grab a few vegetables and some fruit, along with some ice cream, then came directly home. As evidenced from the bag of groceries still lying in the front hall and the melted ice cream pooling around it, she'd just entered her house when Campbell had come to the door.

He'd convinced Margaret to open her front door by claiming to be an undercover detective with some news from Chris. Margaret chastised herself for not asking to see a badge. Once in the door, he'd drawn the gun and demanded that Margaret come with him. She'd evidently persuaded him to let her collect some clothing and other items upstairs before departing, an act that had ultimately saved her.

"The man seemed to be conflicted," she added, not being able to avoid a professional assessment of the situation. "He didn't appear to relish the job of pushing me around. But he also appeared to be motivated by a fear of the consequences were he not able to do his job. He kept asking me to just do what he asked so that no one else would have to be involved."

Jase arrived shortly after the ambulance left with Campbell. He was clearly not in a good mood. The bags under his eyes betrayed a lack of sleep, and his unusually agitated state suggested he was under some pressure.

"Jesus Christ, Chris!" he exclaimed after coming into the house. Clearly his demeanor had changed significantly in the couple of hours since he, Mac, and Chris had sat in Chris's kitchen.

"I haven't seen you in over two years and now, in less than four days, you've put two people in the hospital. There are people in the department, important people I might add, who want to see you behind bars so that nobody else gets hurt."

He looked around at the others in the room, including two deputies, and seemed to regret the outburst.

"Well, let me see," came Chris's curt reply, his hands firmly placed on the table in front of him. "Those two guys in the hospital were one, attacking me, completely unprovoked, and two, trying to kidnap my mom. And that isn't including the fact that three, these guys, or their colleagues, have put my longtime assistant in the hospital, and four, were staking out another colleague's house when Mac interrupted them.

"And as to anyone else getting hurt. I'd say that's entirely up to them. *We're* not attacking anyone. But I will—." Chris thought better of finishing the sentence in the presence of law enforcement. Even if Jase was a friend.

"I'm not sure what your personal or professional thresholds are for engagement these days," Chris added, "but I think I'm on pretty solid ground. Tell your superiors that I'm happy to talk to any of them."

The kitchen was quiet for a few moments.

Jase just shook his head and walked out of the kitchen, motioning to the two deputies to follow. He spoke to them briefly, then departed without speaking to anyone else.

Back in the kitchen, Mac was trying unsuccessfully to get a chunk of brie to stick to a cracker when he turned to Chris. "Kevin is a guy named Kevin O'Grady. Apparently, he's a big deal with the local shadow economy."

"Kevin O'Grady. Were you able to determine where we can find him?"

"Oh yeah. You're going to love this," Mac said. "He works the lumber desk at Home Depot."

25

One of the deputies took full statements from Chris and Margaret, then from Mac. Before leaving, he volunteered to call to check on Gretchen's status. A few minutes later he reported that her condition was evaluated at CHOMP and she was upgraded to stable. No flight to the University Medical Center was planned for now. But she was still unconscious, and it wasn't clear when she would awaken.

A few words passed among the group about Gretchen being a fighter, but no one's heart was in it. They were tired and they were concerned—about Gretchen and about whatever may be coming next.

Mac left Margaret's first and planned to stop by CHOMP to check on Gretchen before going home. The other deputy began a posting in the street outside Margaret's house under orders from Jase. Someone would be stationed there until the full measure of this situation was taken.

Chris and Abby returned to the kitchen while Margaret spent some time outside smoothing over the concerns of some neighbors and providing tantalizing details of her ordeal to others. After a while Margaret walked into the kitchen. "I guess I'm a bit shell-shocked by all of this. I can't seem to focus on what to do next or how to do it."

Chris and Abby looked at each other. "Will you feel comfortable sleeping here tonight?" Abby asked.

"Oh yes. Don't worry about me."

But Abby wasn't having any of that. "I packed a night bag when Mac picked me up just in case I ended up spending the night at CHOMP or at the University Medical Center. Since there's still a chance that they might be coming for me, too, would you mind if I stayed here? With that deputy outside, we could, for lack of a better phrase, kill two birds with one stone."

"That would be marvelous, dear," Margaret said. "We could have a ladies evening."

Chris and Abby had developed this strategy prior to Margaret's return to the kitchen. "Hold on," Chris said. "I'm on their list, too. I want to check on Gretchen, but then I think I might stop by my house to grab Thig, then come back here also. Thig and I will stay out of your way. Well, I will. Thig is probably going to want in on some ladies' night action."

Everyone chuckled. That was as much levity as the situation seemed to allow.

"Do you want to come with me to check on Gretchen?" Abby nodded in assent, so Chris continued. "Okay, mom. We'll head over to CHOMP and should be back here in a couple of hours. We'll speak to the deputy on the way out."

They met the deputy at his vehicle and explained their plan. He called it in, and the general consensus seemed to be that it was a good idea. Having three of the witnesses/potential victims under one roof would make it easier on the sheriff's department. They weren't having a good week. They were responding to violence rather than containing it.

It was also interesting to see how eager the deputy was to help. Perhaps he was just a good guy, but Chris thought he could perceive something else. It was as though having witnessed the earlier altercation between Chris and Jase, the deputy was quite supportive and enthusiastic. Perhaps he wasn't one of Jase's biggest fans.

Chris opened the passenger side door of the Land Rover for Abby then ran around to the driver's side. He was clipping in his seatbelt when Abby reached across and grabbed the front of his shirt. She pulled him across and delivered what he would forever describe as a compelling expression of affection.

This wasn't the type of kiss one has with the serially impermanent retinue of partners that often characterize early adulthood. No, this was—substantive. This kiss spoke of a permanence that most people long for but rarely attain. It was the type of event which foretells a future of deep commitment—of reading books in parallel by the fire, of grocery shopping together, and of little ones running about the house.

Uncharacteristically speechless, Chris leaned back when the kiss was complete, placed his hand on Abby's, and simply stared into her eyes.

They sat like that for a few minutes, or possibly years. The windows of the Land Rover fogged up.

He leaned across and kissed her this time. It was over quickly, but the follow-up confirmed the experience of the first.

Chris knew the poignancy of the moment, at least some of it, derived from the intensity of the crisis they were all experiencing. But he also knew that such a simplistic assessment didn't do it justice. There would hopefully be years to fully explore these issues further.

"Well, perhaps we should get moving," he said with a genuine smile.

"That sounds good. Let's go to CHOMP and see Gretchen."

As they pulled away from the house, a tow truck was removing the black GMC truck from the scene under the supervision of another deputy.

"That was a nice offer to stay with my mom tonight. I hassle her a lot, and she's a tough old bird, but I think she honestly appreciated it."

"I'm happy to help your mother in whatever way that I can. But to be honest, I've to admit that I was playing the odds that you were already planning to stay there, as well."

Then she added, "From now on, I go where you go."

26

Chris and Abby wound around Carmel Point to Rio Road then turned left onto Highway 1. As they moved up the hill toward CHOMP, Abby broke the comfortable silence. "What do you think is happening here? Sounds like you and Mac have something planned. I don't need to be conversant in the details, but can you tell me what you think the larger arc of this story is? How do we see our way through to the end?"

Chris chuckled. "The arc of the story? I honestly don't understand it either. Obviously we've somehow stumbled into something nefarious. I can feel the various threads of the past few days relating to one another, but I can't yet see precisely how they all connect.

"I do know that we can't let events continue to dictate our actions. We need to, as they say, get out ahead of this. The only way to do that is to keep moving forward on all fronts."

He paused for a moment, then continued while ticking things off on his fingers, "Courtesy of Mac, we now know the name of at least one of the people who has been motivating the attacks on us. We go after him tomorrow or maybe the next day. We find out from him what's going on, then we follow those leads."

"Would it be too obvious to mention that you guys are not police officers? That you're not vested with the authority to pursue criminals?"

"I cede that point. But we, Mac and I, don't have a history of sitting by on the sidelines while events around us unfold."

"I've heard that. There are stories about your adventures floating around CMEx. The graduate students eat them up, but I'd always assumed they were apocryphal."

"I'm sure most of them are."

"For instance, there's a story of a research trip with several undergraduates to Baja California. The story goes that a gang of banditos threatened the group for several days and that the mood among the students in the camp was approaching panic. The story continues that one night both you and Mac disappeared for several hours, and that when you returned, your hand was bloodied, and Mac was limping. No one said anything, but when the banditos mysteriously failed to materialize for the rest of the trip, a legend grew."

Chris thought for a minute. "That sounds about right."

"How am I supposed to interpret that?" asked Abby.

"I'll say this. We're on our way to visit one of the nicest people I've ever met, and she's in the hospital because of these miscreants. Had events tonight gone differently, you or my mom might be there as well. Or worse." Chris cleared his throat as the thought of harm to Abby threatened to overwhelm him.

"As I said to Jase earlier, I'll be happy to see them behind bars. But until that time, I'm going to settle up with them myself."

27

When they arrived at CHOMP, Chris and Abby, along with the growing crowd of students and staff from CMEx, weren't allowed to see Gretchen; it was family only.

Chris called Gretchen's parents back east in Scituate, Massachusetts, and told them what he knew at this point, which unfortunately wasn't much.

Mr. and Mrs. Clark booked a reservation on the first flight out of Boston's Logan Airport and would be in Monterey by noon the next day.

Without Gretchen's physical presence in the waiting room with them to ground their thoughts, the group grew increasingly restless. Everyone wanted to know what was going on, and Chris did his best to explain the situation. He stepped outside to call Peter with an update, as well.

"Look..." Peter said via his cell phone from Washington, D.C., "...tell me what you need from my end to help you, and you'll have it. I don't like having my people roughed up, and I don't want anyone else hurt. Period."

Chris took a few moments to reply. "I expect that the EPA and others are going to want to talk to us about surveys of the barrel field, and perhaps assistance with recovery and cleanup efforts. But I also expect that those requests will take some time in coming.

"With respect to the more immediate problem of our nameless antagonists, I think it'll be better if you aren't in the loop. Mac and I have the rudiments of a plan and will put it into effect soon. If anything goes awry, you won't want anything to do with us."

"I understand what you're saying," Peter replied. "But I wish I could be there to help. You know, in my day —."

This had long been fertile territory for discussion between Peter and Chris. Peter, "in his day," had been a bit of a hell raiser, at least in a scientific context. Back then, freed of the litigious quagmire that modern American society had become, he'd been able to get away with things in the field that would make modern risk management officers run away screaming. But perhaps more important, Peter had 'been there, done that' himself. Chris thought that this was, to a large extent, why Peter got along so well with him and Mac. They were aligned on quite a bit more than academics alone.

"We'll keep you as the nuclear option if we encounter real trouble," Chris said before ending the call.

In his absence, nothing much had changed except for some attrition among the well-wishers who left to grab dinner. Chris and Abby were just about to depart themselves when Jase showed up.

"I checked with the doctors working on Gretchen. They said she's doing okay. They won't know the full extent of her head trauma until she awakens, but they're hopeful."

"Thank you, Jase, for checking." Chris struggled to be relieved. "I really appreciate it. I'll relay that to her family."

Jase nodded. "We're not finding much at Gretchen's house at this point. The apartment was worked over, but apparently not by people who knew what they were doing. There's clear evidence of a struggle, but then much of the house was ransacked. Whether that happened before or after the attack on Gretchen will remain unclear until we can speak to her."

"We, Abby and I, are going to spend the night at my mom's house," Chris said.

"Yes, I think that's a good idea," Jase hesitated before he continued. "Look, I've got to run."

"Back to Gretchen's?"

"No. Do you remember Dr. Morris, the pediatrician? I was his patient as a kid. Were you, too?"

"No, but I had lunch with him on Tuesday at the Lodge just before I was attacked. He was one of the donors I was meeting with. Why?"

"Well, one of his partners and her husband have apparently disappeared. We received a frantic call from a housekeeper."

"Jase, do you think this is connected?" Chris sat up in his chair.

"I have no idea. But it is conceivable that, if someone was watching you, they saw you meet with Morris and assumed that he was involved with whatever they think you're up to."

28

The northwest wind blew all night and into the next day. The *MacGreggor* remained tied up at the dock.

The remainder of the previous evening passed without event. Chris and Abby had picked up Thig and returned to Margaret's, where all slept well after a couple more hours of additional rehashing, motivated primarily by Margaret. The day's events had evidently not dampened her natural desire to expound on a given issue from all angles, leaving no stone unturned.

The local evening news programs from the night before had reported on the activities of the hazmat crew in a characteristically vapid fashion. There were live feeds of talking heads from the dock in Monterey, coupled with stock video of the *MacGreggor* pulling away from the dock, but almost no facts.

Since the news crews had missed the actual offloading of the barrel, they had to make do with what they could. They had interviewed a family of tourists walking along the breakwater. They hadn't seen anything and didn't have much of an opinion on the subject. Chris wondered, not for the first time, how anyone actually learned anything from the news anymore if they didn't already have insider knowledge. The morning papers also held nothing of interest with respect to the barrel discovery.

Chris headed out to CMEx early, with Thig in tow, anticipating a strategy session with Mac. The Center was on the campus of the university's marine lab, about fifteen minutes north of Carmel, located at the end of Monterey's Cannery Row, just over the border in Pacific Grove. The campus was situated right on the water, immediately adjacent to the world-famous Monterey Bay Aquarium.

CMEx was housed in the newest building on the small campus. The five-story, fifty-thousand-square-foot building had created a bit of an uproar on the small, historic campus. The first floor contained a large experimental aquarium system, which drew saltwater from an intake pipe a half mile offshore. Laboratory experiments were conducted here to complement the field studies conducted in Monterey Bay and beyond.

The ground floor also housed the ROV lab and several engineering workshops for fabricating anything that scientists needed to conduct their research. A handful of lecture halls and teaching laboratories were on the floor above, and the top three stories served as offices for faculty, staff, and students associated with CMEx.

The building's façade was constructed entirely of glass, which, when the fog didn't get in the way, reflected sunsets to an extent that Chris had never encountered before. The entire building seemed to act like an amplifier designed solely for the purpose of projecting the beauty of a Monterey Bay sunset over the whole campus.

The planned meeting with Mac didn't materialize; he was a no-show. Moreover, Mac's voicemail message didn't offer much in the way of details as to where he was or what he was doing, just that he was looking into something and would be back in touch shortly. He'd gone off the reservation before, and Chris knew better than to question what Mac was up to.

Chris took the time to manage the Charlie Foxtrot in his office that always developed before, during, and after a research cruise. It was better than letting his worry for Gretchen overwhelm him.

His office was on the fifth story of CMEx, with a large window looking over Lover's Point. Usually spectacular under any conditions, today the view was one of unending grey, with the ocean and the sky seamlessly blended in a soup that locals called the June Gloom. Bookshelves lined two of the remaining walls. The desk was normally occupied by two large flat-screen monitors, a keyboard, and a couple of other laptop computers.

In the ramp-up to a research cruise, particularly in the final days before departure, everything not related to the cruise was put to the side. This included everything from draft masters theses that required the care and feeding of an advisor to inter-campus mail folders containing all manner of bureaucratic paperwork to anything else that might come in.

This all collected on every flat surface that his office had to offer, creating an increasingly claustrophobic fire hazard.

The building was pretty quiet. The semester was over, so many of the faculty would either be out conducting their own research or would be off recreating. A few dozen or so graduate students were mulling about looking for anything to divert them from the tedium of data processing.

Thig sat over in the corner in his large basket chewing on something.

Chris propped open his office door and sat down to dig into the messages. Two phone messages from Peter. The first related to the Tuesday donor meeting. The second was about the purchase of SCUBA equipment for the diving program. Chris needed to get with the Diving Safety Officer and order the equipment ASAP before the end of the state's fiscal year on June 30. Peter always left messages on these sorts of issues so that he wouldn't have to think about them anymore. There would probably be at least a dozen similarly themed emails waiting for him.

The fifth message was from Michelle Tierney at the Development Office. She was calling to follow up on Tuesday's meeting. The Deans had evidently been impressed and were looking forward to conferring with Michelle when they returned from their trip to Hawaii. She hadn't talked to Dr. Morris yet, but she had the impression that he was also excited about supporting CMEx. That sounded good to her ears.

There was the non-message from Margaret that had accompanied the non-message that she hadn't left at his house. And then there was a message from a new voice he didn't recognize.

"This is a call for Chris Black," a meek voice said. "This is Sarah Rothberg. My husband Joe drowned last week. He was talking about you the day before he died and I, well, I don't know. Maybe I shouldn't have called. What?" she said to someone in the background. "Sorry, I just—." The message ended. He played the rest of the messages, but there was no return call from Sarah.

He broke out his notebook and jotted down a few names:

Joe Rothberg
Sarah Rothberg
Kevin O'Grady
Jerry Smith
Tommy Campbell

Chris looked at the list for a few moments and then added two more names:

Dr. Marilyn George and Mr. (?) George

Looking out at the grey, Chris pondered the list for a few minutes. Then he grabbed the notebook and nodded for Thig to come with him as he trotted down the deserted hallway and took the stairs to the fourth floor. Abby's door, about halfway down the hall, was open, and Thig beat him to it.

"Hi, guys!" Abby scratched Thig's backside vigorously, then stood to meet Chris. "I was hoping you guys would stop by."

Surveying the clean and orderly condition of Abby's office, Chris quickly concluded that she didn't suffer the same cruise-related organizational maladies that vexed him. Abby's office beckoned to visitors, with a nice Persian rug, several healthy indoor plants, and many surfaces unburdened by clutter.

Chris pushed the door closed with his left foot and stepped over to Abby. They kissed and all was right with the world. It was impossible to worry about anything while holding Abby.

"What are you working on right now?" Chris asked, experiencing great difficulty focusing on anything other than Abby.

"Well, to be honest I've been sitting down here for an hour daydreaming and not getting much done." She looked at Chris. "I don't know what's come over me."

"That's seriously unproductive," Chris joked. "On my end I've already moved around several stacks of mail and listened to twenty voicemail messages."

"There's a reason you have that Ph.D.," Abby returned, rising to the appropriate level of sarcasm for the company she was keeping.

Chris passed the list he'd made across the desk. "One of the messages on my voicemail was from Sarah Rothberg, the drowned guy's wife. Her voice was shaky, hesitant, and she didn't leave a number. But she mentioned that Joe had been talking about me the day before he died."

"Hmm."

"Yes. Hmm," Chris replied. "It got me to thinking that perhaps we could leverage our considerable in-house research capabilities to flesh out the picture a bit." He paused. "What do you think?"

"I think Jase and his team should be working up all angles." She looked out her window. "But then again, I don't see the sheriff's department spending a lot of time on web searches. Give me a while to look around, and I'll see what I can find."

Though Abby had formally trained in biological statistics, her real talent lay in web-based research. While Google had effectively made researchers out of anyone with an Internet connection, a select few still distinguished themselves as true masters.

Chris smiled as he recalled an incident in which a mysterious donor had surfaced with an alleged interest in donating to CMEx. Faced with going into the donor meeting blind, Peter had authorized Abby to find anything she could. She'd swept in and, within a couple of hours, provided what amounted to a comprehensive review of the donor's activities and interests over the past forty years, including high school photos, various corporate documents, and a record of a DUI from thirty years ago.

Technology was amazing. But it was old-fashioned analysis that made the difference.

"Thanks. Mac's gone AWOL, so I'm going to head downstairs and hassle the grad students for a while. I'll be in the lab if you need me."

"You can leave the furball here if you'd like. She and I'll get along fine."

Thig was wagging her tail as though she grasped the nature of the conversation and clearly wanted to stay.

"I'd rather stay here, too," Chris said looking at Thig. "But where would that get us? I'll see you two ladies later."

A kiss for the road and he was out the door.

29

The solid foundation on which Darrell English had built his criminal empire was crumbling around him. He'd learned last night from a contact in the sheriff's department that Campbell had been caught while trying to grab the psychiatrist. And if his source was correct, Campbell was caught and beaten by Chris Black. Unbelievable. Who was this fuckin' guy?

Darrell had worked hard to develop his various businesses. And he could credibly claim to be self-made. But even self-made men needed help from time to time, and Darrell had had his benefactors along the way, people interested in exploiting some new off-the-book opportunity; people who understood what a little crazy could do for any situation.

He was now sitting across the desk from the longest running of those benefactors. And the man was pissed—seriously pissed.

"You've fucked up this relatively simple operation, English."

It was always shocking to hear this guy swear. To look at him one wouldn't expect him to lower himself to such language. His casual tone belied the gravity of his words. "I needed you to do a simple job, and you fucked that up. I ask you to clean up that mess, and you fuck that up, too. Now we've got sheriff's deputies all over us, and the EPA will be coming soon."

The man thrust out his right hand and ticked off Darrell's shortcomings with his ample fingers. "I told you not to let the scientists in on your surveillance, and you fuck that up. I told you not to go near Margaret Black, and your guy gets his arms broken while trying to kidnap her. Now the Georges are gone. I'm sure you're behind that, and that will inevitably come back to you as well."

He shifted in his chair and stared out the window. "You've had a good run these past few years, Darrell, but maybe this is all beyond you. Perhaps I should think about some other options."

Looking down at his shoes, Darrell responded, "Sir, I understand."

"Don't give me this 'sir' bullshit!" he hissed as he stood up and walked to a liquor cabinet behind Darrell and began pouring a drink.

"Okay, Sir—." Darrell caught himself and held up his hand. "I understand why you're unhappy. This has been a shit sandwich from the beginning."

Over the sound of jingling ice cubes, the man asked, "What are you going to do about it? Dare I ask what your 'plan' is?"

"I think we have to clean house a bit," Darrell said. "Beginning with the scientists, at least Black and Johnson. They've proven to be serious problems. I thought we could do this without a bloodbath on our hands, but now I don't think we can avoid it."

The man returned to his seat, swirling a glass of whiskey in his hand. Darrell waited to be yelled at. When it didn't come, he continued, "The psychiatrist will probably have to be dealt with, as well."

The benefactor leaned back and stared at the ceiling for a few seconds. The only sound in the room came from the ticking of the tall clock standing over against the far wall. Somewhere out in the distance a leaf blower could be heard.

When the man leaned forward again and returned his gaze to Darrell, his face was grave. "You take care of the scientists, I'll take care of

Margaret Black." He paused. "And before this is over, I want you to get rid of O'Grady as well. He's a liability."

"I understand."

"Now get the fuck out of my face and do something productive."

30

In the mid-afternoon Chris met Gretchen's parents at the Monterey Airport. The airport was small, but convenient, and situated on a plateau just out of town facing north/northwest along Highway 68. The terminal served a handful of the major carriers and their subsidiaries, though the number of daily commercial flights was low. But it was only five to ten minutes from anywhere on the Peninsula, the parking was cheap and easy, and the security line was virtually non-existent if one planned it right.

Chris had met Gretchen's parents several years ago. He'd brought Gretchen along on a mission to the *Poseidon* Undersea Laboratory in the U.S. Virgin Islands. The lab was actually an undersea space station where scientists got completely acclimated to the pressure underwater and spent up to fourteen days SCUBA diving for nine hours a day without returning to the surface. Diving all day gave unparalleled access to the coral reef around *Poseidon* and served as an incredible platform for education and outreach.

The Clarks' initial trepidation about having their only daughter living underwater for fourteen days with five strange men turned to unprecedented enthusiasm once the mission was underway. Gretchen's parents followed the CMEx team's daily efforts, watched everything they could on the live web cams streamed from inside and outside of Poseidon. They read and commented on every blog the team produced, wrote in questions to each of the four broadcasts the team had made during the mission, and it was rare to have a new entry on the CMEx Facebook page that wasn't immediately "liked" by at least one of them.

As the passengers slowly meandered through the glass doors separating the secure from unsecured areas of the terminal, Chris spotted the Clarks and waved. They were clearly tired, and the stress of their situation was visible on their faces.

Mr. Clark was a tall, thin man in his late fifties. He had the body of a distance runner, which wasn't a surprise since that's what he did with much of his time. His grey hair was cut short. He carried himself with stateliness, but his eyes betrayed the turmoil within. While the Mr. Clark that Chris knew was usually the picture of animation, moving fast and happily in all directions simultaneously, the man who stood before him now was a slow, grey replica of that other person.

Mrs. Clark was the opposite of her husband. She wasn't tall, and not thin. Her dark hair was grey in streaks. The smile that usually emanated from her face would illuminate any room she entered. It made her beautiful. But today was different, and it saddened Chris to think that she looked, well, she looked *less*.

Once the brief pleasantries were exchanged, Chris led them out of the main doors to the short-term parking immediately adjacent to the terminal. Chris tried to buoy them with the hope he'd been provided by Jase. It was, he was certain, a small comfort, but he couldn't think of an alternative.

Arriving at CHOMP, Chris led them directly to Gretchen's room. The thin veneer of control was shattered as they were confronted by their only daughter lying unconscious in a hospital bed, head wrapped in bandages and multiple tubes extending from her arms, nose, and mouth.

Mrs. Clark cried quietly as she dug three small charms out of her bag and lined them up along a shelf next to the bed. A zebra, a giraffe, and possibly a beaver, they looked to be cherished tokens from Gretchen's youth. The touching poignancy of the act was too much for Chris to bear. He offered himself for any help he could provide during their stay then quietly left.

As he was walking back down the hall toward the entrance, wiping his eyes as he went, Chris ran into Dr. Morris. Morris was wearing a white lab coat and carried a stack of paperwork under one arm. He was standing in front of a "No cell phones" sign talking loudly on his cell phone.

"Ah, Chris. What brings you here today?" Morris pocketed his phone and shook Chris's hand in an iron grip.

"Hello, Dr. Morris." Nodding his head back down the hall, Chris continued, "A close friend of mine is here. She was attacked at her house earlier tonight and she's in pretty bad shape."

"Attacked? That's terrible. Who's treating her?"

"I'm not sure."

"What's your friend's name?"

"Gretchen Clark."

"I'll find out who's treating her and report back. How can I reach you?" Chris gave Morris his cell phone number. "Thank you, Dr. Morris."

"Not at all. My pleasure. Please say hello to your mother for me."

"I will."

Morris patted Chris on his upper arm and was off down the hall in a flurry of activity, barking orders and commanding the nurses.

As Chris watched him walk away, he suddenly remembered that Jase had mentioned that Dr. Morris's partner was missing. Chris berated himself for not asking about it and expressing his concern. He'd have to check-in with the good doctor as soon as Gretchen recovered.

———

The scene in Gretchen's hospital room had been too much. Chris was depressed. CHOMP was within striking distance of Carmel, so before returning to campus, Chris headed home to grab a quick run to hopefully clear his head.

He stopped first by the post office, a necessity for getting mail in a town that did not have street addresses. No home mail delivery meant that the post office served as an informal gathering place for locals. Chris wasn't surprised when he rounded the corner in search of his P.O. Box and ran straight into the Deans.

"Mr. and Mrs. Dean, how nice to see you," he said.

"Chris, yes, nice to see you again as well. We, ah, we're here to pick up our mail," Mr. Dean stammered.

"Convenient place to do it," Chris replied, thinking that there was no reason for Mr. Dean to sound awkward.

"Well, nice to see you," Mrs. Dean said, and they moved off before he'd a chance to respond.

After retrieving his own useless pile of junk mail, Chris walked out the front door. As he did so, he noticed the Deans pulling away from the curb in a silver Mercedes. He realized only then that they were supposed to have left for Hawaii by now.

As he stepped off the curb Chris turned around and looked back through the glass door of the post office. There he saw Dr. Levine, the man he'd encountered at the market days before, watching him. The look on Levine's face wasn't a pleasant one.

31

After an hour-long run through the fog, Chris felt better, if only because of the resulting endorphin rush. He'd run hard and for the most part had been successful in blocking out the vortex of emotions associated with recent events. He took a long, warm shower and was standing in front of the bathroom mirror contemplating removing the stitches out of the bridge of his nose when Abby called. She'd had some luck with her web research and suggested that she and Thig meet Chris at Margaret's to go over the results.

Chris got off the phone feeling like a teenager prepping for a first date. He liked the feeling. It had been a long time since he'd spent any time with a serious prospect. After suffering twice in succession at the hands of women who didn't know what they wanted, from him or from life, Chris had effectively sworn off women. Then Abby appeared. Well, they did say that one will never find happiness if one looks for it.

With Gretchen being seriously hurt and attacks coming from left and right, he couldn't characterize this as happiness exactly. But his feelings in Abby's presence did transcend all the other issues. The feelings tempered the lows somewhat. Powerful juju, Mac would say.

The removal of the stitches came off without a glitch. He still looked like hell, but it was a move in the right direction.

He killed a few minutes checking email, then tried Mac, who finally picked up after more than nine hours off the grid.

"Yo! Where have you been? Doing something constructive, I hope?"

"If by constructive you mean getting prepared to pull your ass from the fire once again, then yes, I've been doing something constructive," Mac answered.

"I did have some lower GI discomfort this morning after all those peppers last night. That felt like fire down there. Is that what you're talking about?" Chris knew that Mac had something useful to report, but that he didn't want to talk about it over the phone.

"Why do I still talk to you?" Mac sounded as though he was in a car.

"Because I saved your life that time off Mauritius when you ran out of air twenty meters down?" Chris was referring to an incident in the Indian Ocean a few years back. The first stage of Mac's SCUBA regulator had malfunctioned during a dive along a coral reef at eighty feet down, meaning that neither his primary nor his secondary regulators would work. As Mac's dive buddy that day, Chris had been close by and volunteered his back-up regulator, or "octopus," to Mac. The visibility had been extraordinary that day, and the patch of reef they had been surveying was covered with fish. So they had actually continued the dive for fifteen more minutes before surfacing.

Thanks to their training and to the fact that both Chris and Mac were as comfortable underwater as above it, the incident was actually a non-event. But that certainly didn't stop Chris from using it frequently to his advantage.

"All right, as my grandmother says, 'this conversation is going nowhere,'" Mac said. "Where are you going to be in an hour?"

"I'm meeting Abby at my mom's in about forty minutes."

"Abby. At your mom's. Is there anything I should know? Should I pull out my tux when I get home? You know, to make sure it still fits?"

"Very funny. And no, leave that thing wherever it is. When I take the plunge, there won't be any electric blue tuxes in the mix."

32

"You gave me five names, none of which has a significant web presence." Chris, Abby, and Mac sat at Margaret's dining room table going over the results of Abby's efforts while Margaret prepared an exquisite vegetarian meal for the group. Outside, the cold northwest wind continued to howl as the sun shrank toward the horizon. "I looked at Joe Rothberg first. Not much there. He had a Facebook page, but it looked like he'd set it up, then lost interest."

"Poor Joe," Margaret interjected without turning away from her dinner preparations.

"The only two other references to Joe that I could find came from yesterday's *Herald* which reported on his drowning once they I.D.'d his body. No use there. And there was also a wedding announcement for his marriage to Sarah Haskins." She passed those two sheets around.

"Now Sarah Haskins has more going on. I had to open an account on Classmates.com, and 'friend' her on Facebook, which she accepted, almost immediately I might add. But first through Classmates.com, then through Facebook, I confirmed that Sarah had once dated Kevin O'Grady."

"Was there a good picture of him?" Chris asked.

"He doesn't have his own Facebook account as far as I can tell, but he was 'tagged' in a number of old photos on other people's pages."

Abby passed a color copy of a photo over to Chris and Mac. "He looks strong."

The picture showed Kevin sitting on a couch drinking a beer next to someone identified as Dave. He wasn't looking at the camera, so the picture didn't offer much, but it was true that he dwarfed Dave even in a sitting position.

"I've never seen this guy before." Mac was unimpressed. After his days as a SEAL, nobody scared Mac.

"I'm not so sure," Chris said.

"I found the 1982 Monterey High School yearbook on another site. Kevin is there as well." Abby pointed to two other photos.

The first photo showed several graduating seniors standing around the sign for Monterey High School. Kevin was leaning casually on his right arm, which, because of his height, was resting on top of the sign.

"Here's a picture of him in white gi." Abby passed it over. The picture was one of several in which students posed for the camera with the uniforms or equipment of their favorite sports. There were football, basketball, and baseball players, of course, but there were also surfers, golfers and Kevin in his karate outfit in a fighting stance.

"Check out the brown belt," Mac said. "You never know anymore."

"Know what?" Abby asked.

"Whether he earned that belt with his skills or his cash," Mac replied. "In some dojos it can take years to earn your belts, while in others you can get a black belt in less than a year."

"Zero to hero," said Chris.

"Well, the real pay dirt comes from the *Monterey Herald* archives. Here we see Kevin in the police log on three separate occasions, twice for disorderly conduct and once for burglary."

Looking at Mac, she added, "You said he works at Home Depot. I wonder if they know his history."

"I'd be surprised if they had a clue about any of their employees," Mac replied. "It's easier not to know."

"Mom, I hope that our presence here isn't cramping your style too much. Please let us know if we should, you know, go for a walk."

Margaret looked at Chris as though she were evaluating what to make of this latest comment. "Of course not. You're more than welcome to stay here."

"We don't want our presence to deter your new friend." Chris smiled. Mac pretended to duck under the table while Abby just shook her head.

"My new friend? I don't know what you're talking about," Margaret replied casually.

"Ah, you're right, 'friend' isn't the correct term, since word on the street is that you and he have been spotted out and around at several of Carmel's finer eateries. Perhaps we should call him your special friend."

"Word on the street, honestly. Abby, do you see what I've had to put up with?"

"I think I'm getting a sense of it, Margaret. I don't know how you do it," Abby said.

Chris and Mac looked at each other and shrugged. "Well, please pass along to Mr. Mysterio that he has a standing invitation to dine *chez Black* anytime," Chris offered. "We'd love to have him."

"I'm not sure what the chances are that we'd get him to come over to your house," Margaret said, changing tactics. "He's afraid of you."

"Of little old me?" Chris said. "There's absolutely nothing to be concerned about. But make sure he understands that I won't be calling him 'Dad' until he takes me to Disneyland."

Mac almost fell out of his chair laughing. Abby looked aghast. And Margaret just shook her head as she stood.

"You tough guys wouldn't know how to deal with the details of my relationships if for some reason I decided to share them. It's better for you if you remain in the dark." With that, Margaret nodded to Abby, and they got up from the table, leaving Chris and Mac staring after them.

33

Abby and Margaret retired to their rooms upstairs; Margaret doing so only after bringing hot tea and pastries out to the current deputy on duty in front of the house.

Chris and Mac took Thig out for a short walk. The fog was in, but the temperature was mild, and the wind had begun to abate. "Okay. Tell me," Chris said as they walked around the corner.

"I don't like the way all this is heading, so I flew down south to talk to a few of my former team members." Chris knew Mac was referring to his old SEAL buddies.

"A call wouldn't do it?" Chris asked.

"This kind of business requires face to face contact. You've met Hendrix. He doesn't like the phone."

Recalling just one mental image of Hendrix from the only time he met him, Chris understood. Hendrix was shorter than Chris, but gained a few inches based on toughness alone. His head was shaved, and his neck was permanently scarred from what appeared to be a failed hanging.

Hendrix usually wore sunglasses with reflective lenses, so one rarely got a direct look at his eyes. But during the few moments that Chris had seen Hendrix without his glasses, he'd looked right into the eyes of a warrior. Sure there was kindness and mirth visible from time to time, but when Hendrix wasn't directly engaging him, Chris could see Hendrix constantly taking the measure of everyone and everything within his cone of vision.

"So, Hendrix and a few others have a security consulting firm. It's called Omnipresent Security Services, or OSS."

"OSS. Cute," Chris said, recognizing the acronym from the Office of Strategic Services, the CIA precursor formed during World War II.

"Yes. Cute," Mac continued, "though I wouldn't say that in front of Hendrix. Anyway, they've tried to get me work with them a handful of times in the past couple of years. Much better money. More women. A little danger."

"All things that CMEx provides in abundance."

"Right. So I obviously turn him down whenever it comes up. But something tells me that we might need some help this time around."

"Do they have the bandwidth to come up here if needed?"

"I think so."

They reached the end of Margaret's street and turned onto Scenic Drive where it ran along the cliff above Carmel River Beach. The surf was pounding along the beach's steep profile, the sound made more ominous by the fact that the waves were completely invisible through the fog.

Chris didn't ask about money. He knew that this type of job wasn't undertaken for remuneration. The SEALs never abandoned a team member when he was down. They never left anyone behind.

"Yesterday, I was ready to go after Kevin O'Grady directly. But today, I don't know."

"Yeah, we probably should have done it yesterday." Mac obviously felt the same way. "A couple of academics kicking ass when confronted by evil dudes sounds compelling, newsworthy even."

"Yeah. But a couple of academics going on a rampage, actively pur-suing trouble outside the law," Chris finished, "that seems kind of unseemly."

The conversation was interrupted by Chris's ringing phone. He didn't recognize the phone number, but with so much going on he answered anyway.

"Chris?"

"Yes. Who's this?"

"It's Mitchell. I've been trying to track you down for a couple of days." Mitchell Tartt was a friend from graduate school. He was a computer modeler Chris still worked with on projects from time to time. Mac yawned and looked at his watch.

Chris noted the time as well and said, "Sorry, Mitchell. We've got a lot going on out here. What's up? It's after midnight back there." Mitchell lived outside Washington, D.C.

"Yeah, well, wait until you have a baby," replied Mitchell. "You'll find hours to work you never knew existed. I just wanted to confirm that you received the stack of material that I sent you via *FedEx* three days ago."

Chris was helping Mitchell on a chapter of his new textbook. "Where'd you send it? Office or home?"

"Home."

"Nothing yet. They have a tough time finding houses here with no street addresses. It's probably sitting on my neighbor's front porch. I'll check around. If you send me anything else, make sure it goes to the office."

34

At 10:00 a.m. the following morning, six miles out into Carmel Valley and a good four miles beyond the fog line that currently occupied Carmel-by-the-Sea and surrounding environs, three vehicles slowly wound their way up a long, tree-lined private drive to a guarded gate. A black Mercedes sedan led the way, followed by a green Range Rover and a silver Lexus SUV. The guard at the gate emerged from a small, unremarkable kiosk, spoke briefly to the driver in the Mercedes, then waved all three vehicles through.

At the top of the road, the vehicles pulled into the circular drive and parked in front of a large Mediterranean-style villa. The "villa" was a three-story monstrosity built three years prior during the height of the real estate boom in California. It was a contractor's vision of Tuscan life, rendered by a contractor with neither the native skills nor direct experience with Tuscany.

Five people emerged from the three cars. All appeared to be solid citizens at the older end of the age spectrum. Each moved up the steps and into the gaping maw of the monstrosity with the confidence that comes from having too much money to be bothered by much of anything.

"Thank you for coming," their host said as they settled into the comfortable leather seats arrayed in a cavernous great room. His mouth smiled but his eyes, as always, told a different story. "We have a situation developing. Quite quickly, I might add.

"Some of you are aware of the discovery on Tuesday of the waste in Carmel Canyon. A barrel was recovered by researchers from the Center for Marine Exploration."

"Led by Chris Black as I understand it," interrupted one of the five.

"Yes, that's correct," the host replied gracefully, though with some difficulty. He would've preferred to rip the head off the imbecile, but the time for that hadn't yet come. "Our sources indicate that Chris Black led the effort to locate and recover a barrel."

"How did anyone find evidence of the barrels? We thought the plan was to dump the stuff so deep that no one would ever see it again," the wife of the imbecile interjected. "Of all the different scenarios we discussed for getting rid of the waste, dumping offshore involved the most logistics and the greatest risk. And now we find that it didn't pay off at all."

The host took a deep breath. He stared at the woman. He had to admit that she was more impressive than her mealy-mouthed husband. Her long hair was pulled back into a tight ponytail that gave her face a severe look. She maintained her body in top condition for her age, and the host appreciated that. He'd even considered having an affair with her once or twice. But she was even more trying to deal with than her weaker half.

Unimpeded by anyone else, the woman continued her diatribe, "You also told us, once this problem arose, that you had the Blacks under control. Now look where we are."

"Don't doubt that I understand exactly where we are and how we got here," the host continued, raising his voice a couple of notches.

"Now as I was saying, the discovery of the barrels is quite a setback, insofar as the authorities have been alerted to the location of the dump site. The state and federal involvement goes beyond our collective ability to control the situation. So I've authorized the next most effective approach."

"And what's that?" asked a large man to the left. His suit coat strained under the size of the man's biceps.

"We insulate ourselves from the authorities by removing any connection between us and the waste disposal," the host replied.

"You mean we burn the network," the large man said.

"Precisely." The host nodded.

"More killing? Is that what we're talking about here?" the woman asked.

"How do you think we've made it as far as we have?" the large man replied, raising his voice to the woman. "You've been privy to almost every decision we've made as a group over the past decade. What the fuck do you think our options are?"

The woman looked to her husband, assumedly for support. Finding none, she ignored the yelling and looked directly at the host. "You're talking about more widespread killing than we've condoned to-date."

"That's true," the host replied. "The full extent of this plan will be wider than we've considered up to this point. And it'll involve removing some of Carmel's upstanding citizens."

The large man sounded off again to the woman and her husband, "Face it, you're not part of some kind of a shadow government trying to right the wrongs of a failed administrative structure or unjust laws. You're part of a group that has been making money, quite a bit of money, for more than two decades by thwarting the law. Now isn't the time to develop higher ideals about the group's activities. We can't afford those ideals, and I'll personally kill both you and your husband if you try to compromise our objectives in any way."

"Thank you for that crude, but effective, reaffirmation of the group's orientation," the host replied, then turned to the woman. "I'm not happy with this, but we must take action before we're exposed. If we're ever exposed, all of our collective wealth, and the well-being of our families, will be destroyed, our careers ruined. And, depending on the extent of the authorities' inquiries, we may even be looking at prison time."

The woman collapsed back into her chair. The rest of the group remained quiet. And so the host laid out a plan for handling the problem. There were no further outbursts as the group listened.

35

Chris was up and out early as usual. After finding no evidence of his package with any of his neighbors, he drove toward dock in Monterey.

The weather had finally calmed down to the point that resuming sampling efforts in Carmel Canyon was worth trying. However, a problem had developed with the *MacGreggor's* starboard diesel engine. The engineering crew was working on it, but departure wasn't imminent. Hurry up and wait, as they say.

Mac took the opportunity to conduct some necessary maintenance on the ROV, replacing one of the aft thrusters and swapping out the tracking beacon. Chris made sure that Travis, Matt and Marisa were making headway on the analysis of the imagery they'd collected so far.

The students were quite content with staying on board the *MacGreggor*, whether it was at sea or in port, for the three square meals a day and an endless supply of snacks that Gretchen had purchased before the cruise.

Chris grabbed a few snacks himself and left for CMEx to deal with some other business.

Back in his office, Chris was two hours into the third, and hopefully final, revision of a scientific manuscript that he and Peter were planning to submit for publication by the end of the month, when he decided to take a short break.

Chris left the main building with a couple of files in hand and walked out to the road and past the Aquarium to Cannery Row.

Entering the café halfway down the Row, Chris ordered a bran muffin and an orange-strawberry smoothie and settled down at the bar to read a ragged copy of the local weekly newspaper on the counter.

The smoothie and muffin arrived in a few minutes. He'd had enough time to try the smoothie and take a large bite out of the muffin when he could sense someone approaching from his left.

"Excuse me, are you Chris Black?"

Chris turned to see a woman standing next to him holding a baby. The woman was a little heavy—in all the wrong places—and was decidedly unattractive. The unattractiveness was enhanced by the lack of spark in her grey-blue eyes and by what appeared to be a perpetual frown based on her wrinkle patterns. The baby was in what looked to be a well-used sling device attached to the woman's torso and was asleep at the moment.

He nodded while still chewing the large bite of bran muffin. She added, "I'm Sarah Rothberg." No follow up, just her name. Evidently, she figured that was enough. She was right.

Chris gulped down the muffin and gestured toward a nearby table. "Hi, Sarah. Let's sit down over here."

After sitting, he continued, "I'm sorry about Joe. I knew his brother, Brent, when I was a kid and met Joe a couple of times a long time ago."

She picked at some fuzz coming off the sling and looked lazily over Chris's right shoulder as she spoke. "He worked with your mother."

"Right. I remember that," Chris said.

She waited a few beats, then, still addressing someone over his shoulder, Sarah said, "I left you a message."

Again, another dramatic pause. This was like pulling teeth. She'd sought *him* out, so he sat back and let her come out with it. Since she wasn't making eye contact, it was difficult to get a good read on her state of mind.

The seconds dragged on. Chris felt pity for her under the circumstances. But too much was going on to cater to her problems with communication.

After a few more seconds that felt like hours, he stood. "It's nice to meet you, Sarah." She looked down and away.

Chris pushed his chair in and began to walk away.

"He mentioned you a couple of times. Joe did."

"Yes. You mentioned that in your message."

"He thought that Kevin O'Grady was asking about you too much, that he was planning to do something to you." She paused, then added, staring in the general direction of his face this time, "From the look of your face, maybe he did."

Chris took a couple of steps back toward the table and put his hands on the back of the chair he'd just left. "What can I do for you, Sarah?"

"Joe was working with Kevin. I think he was going out on a boat, but he never told me exactly what he was doing."

"We know about Kevin now. Why do you think he was going out on a boat? What gave you that impression?"

"He was going out at eight or nine at night. A couple of times he even did it on Tuesdays, which was one of the nights he liked to watch TV. He always brought lots of jackets. When I asked why, he said, 'They say you gotta wear layers. The wind can come up fast out there.' And one time I found seasickness medicine in one of his pockets."

This was nothing that they didn't already know, but it was confirmation of the events. "Did he tell you anything else?"

"Not directly. But we were at the Monterey Round Table Pizza a couple of weeks ago, and Joe saw someone he recognized. He said something about a guy named Darrell English."

"Darrell English. Did Joe say anything else?"

"He said that if you guys kept snooping around, he thought Darrell would have Kevin kill you."

"You didn't say anything about Kevin or Darrell to the sheriff. Why not?"

"I'm worried about my baby."

"That's completely understandable. My friend Jase is the lead investigator for the sheriff on this case. They can protect you."

"Not from these people."

"I hear that Kevin is a tough guy, but police protection is a different thing altogether. I don't see him penetrating law enforcement."

Quietly, looking around to check out the other people in the café, Sarah responded, "I'm not talking about Kevin and Darrell. There are much worse people out there. People who don't care about the cops. They don't have to."

36

Sarah, despite her obvious limitations, seemed to have strung together a narrative from things Joe had mentioned combined with comments she'd heard from Kevin back when she and he were dating. The upshot was that she seemed to think there were some prominent people who supported Darrell English's activities. Darrel himself was wealthy and anyone who'd support this would be wealthy as well. No news there. Darrell did their dirty work for them, and they kept money and opportunities coming his way and made sure the cops didn't mess with the operations.

She didn't know any names and didn't know how many there were. She thought one might be a doctor, but that was just an impression from comments Joe had made at one point about a doctor "who liked to give shots back in the day." But she clung tightly to the fact of their existence, and Chris had to admit that, though she wasn't a convincing person, there was no reason to doubt her story.

Chris strongly encouraged Sarah to call Jase and reiterate her story to him. Then he left her and the baby in the café.

He walked back to his office to grab his stuff then worked his way back to the truck, stopping to field a few questions from students. He didn't want to intrude on the Clarks, but he felt like sitting next to

Gretchen for a while. A few minutes later he was up the hill in Pacific Grove headed toward Highway 1.

Something about Sarah's story raised the hairs on the back of Chris's neck—a conspiracy of rich and powerful citizens doing bad things via proxy. It was the stuff of fiction. But Sarah's frank delivery didn't feel fictional. Given the other details Chris had learned, it felt very real. As he drove, he once again felt the walls of the hurricane looming.

Just shy of Highway 68 his cell phone rang.

"Chris!" It was Abby, and she was whispering urgently. "It's Kevin O'Grady. He's come after me."

"Where are you?" Chris said, automatically checking traffic around him.

"On the boat. He followed me up the dock, and I think he's on board. I'm hiding in Stateroom One. He can't get me in here, at least I don't think he can. But I'm worried about what will happen if he runs into anyone else."

37

Chris floored the car as he tried to call the captain of the *MacGreggor* on his cell and on the ship's satellite phone, but got no answers on either. When the boat was at the dock it wasn't always easy to reach the busy crew.

Chris reversed course and drove back down the hill. He frantically wove through the slow-moving tourist traffic on Lighthouse Avenue, but the lights were largely with him as he sped through New Monterey.

Arriving in the breakwater parking lot, he could see flashing lights of police cars out by the *MacGreggor*, about two-thirds of the way down the pier, so he continued out onto the breakwater road. A crowd of onlookers had already formed on the road, blocking the approach to the boat. He nudged the Land Rover through the crowd and pulled right up between Abby's hybrid and the police cars.

As Chris hopped out, he bumped into some big Coast Guard guy watching the action. He apologized to the man and jogged down the pier to the gangway. A Monterey Police officer was holding station at the base of the gangway. Chris showed the officer his CMEx ID, and he was allowed to board.

He stepped into the galley first to find two police officers talking to his student, Marisa.

"Are you okay, Marisa?" Chris asked quickly.

"Yeah, I'm fine." Marisa tried for blasé. "I didn't see anyone." Thankfully she seemed more interested by the excitement of having the police on board talking to her than by the actual threat that had brought the police here.

Looking at the two officers, Chris asked, "Where's Abby? Is she okay?"

"I'm right here, Chris," Abby said, coming into the galley, followed by another officer. She looked irritated. "There was no sign of anyone when these officers arrived. I think they probably believe I imagined it."

"No, ma'am," the officer closest to her said. "We're just glad nobody was hurt. It's always better to call us and find out it's nothing than to not call and run into trouble."

"You didn't see anyone out here on the breakwater when you arrived, officers?" Chris asked.

"There were several citizens fishing and sightseeing along the wall when we arrived, but none matched the description that Ms. Wilson has given us."

"And the entire ship has been cleared?" Chris asked.

"Yes, sir," the officer who had been talking to Marisa said. "We'll look around again on our way out."

"Officers, this incident isn't isolated," Chris said. "One of my employees is in the hospital, and I was attacked, too, just a few days ago." He added this last part while gesturing toward his face. "We think it's all related to a toxic waste dumpsite in Carmel Bay we discovered last week."

38

The officers departed after another sweep of the *MacGreggor* with a plan to "keep an eye" on the ship for the next few days. Chris called Peter and asked him to investigate whether they could get some campus guards to come down and monitor the boat.

Though access to the breakwater was limited to daylight hours by the Coast Guard, and though the dock adjacent to the *MacGreggor* was fenced off, it was still fairly easy for someone pretending to know what he or she was doing to walk right onto the boat. Peter said he would work on it right away.

Next, he called Margaret at her office. "Hi, Mom. Anything happening there?"

Margaret evidently picked up on the edge in Chris's voice. "What do you mean? Has something else happened? Is anyone else hurt?"

"No, everyone is okay. But it looks like someone, possibly Kevin O'Grady, followed Abby onto the ship this afternoon. He was probably trying to intimidate her."

"How is the poor girl?"

Chris looked over at Abby. She was clearly pissed off about the entire situation. "Are you going home soon?" he asked.

"No, well, not exactly," Margaret answered.

"Not exactly? Come on, Mom, help me out here. I just want to make sure everyone is safe."

She paused for a minute. "I'm going to have dinner with an old friend this evening." Chris could hear her cringe through the phone.

"No bullshit from me today, Mom. I promise. Is this really an old friend?"

"Yes, I've known him for years, and I'm certain I'll be fine. We're eating at that small Italian restaurant, Giuseppe's, way out in the Valley. You remember that place, right?"

"Okay. Have a good dinner. We'll be at your house when you get back. Be careful."

Chris signed off and watched Abby talking to Diana. In the back of his mind something about Margaret's dinner concerned him, but his head was still spinning over Kevin's apparent intrusion on the ship, and whatever it was drifted away.

He motioned toward one of the galley tables. "Let's sit down and you can tell us everything you remember."

Abby explained that she'd left Margaret's about an hour ago to run a few errands and to check on the status of her house plants in Monterey. She lived in a small, one-bedroom mission-style house on the hill in "Old" Monterey. Spaghetti Hill, as it was known among the locals for its history of settlement by Italian fishing families in the early 1900s, rose steeply up from Pacific and Alvarado Streets facing northeast into southern Monterey Bay.

Her house had a deep, sunflower-yellow façade surrounded by lush foliage. A small garage was accessible at the back of the property from a driveway set to the immediate right of the house. While no place on the Peninsula was completely immune from the occurrence of daily fog, at two-thirds up the hill, Abby enjoyed regular sun on her front patio, and the healthy plants attested to that fact.

After watering her house plants, Abby had come over to New Monterey to visit a dive shop on Lighthouse Avenue. She was looking for a new dive knife after the kelp had claimed her favorite knife on a dive at Monastery with Gretchen before the research cruise. Divers were particular about where they carried their knives. Abby was in the two-knife camp; one knife mounted low, usually on the inside of her calf, and one smaller knife mounted high, usually attached to one of the straps of her buoyancy compensator vest. This provided a diver access to a cutting tool regardless of where he or she was entangled. But this double configuration provided twice the opportunities for entanglement. Abby's knife handle had been only one centimeter away from her leg, but that single centimeter had allowed a giant kelp frond ample opportunity to reach in and grab it. The central coast of California nurtured some of the largest giant kelp forests in the world, and the seafloor along Monterey's coast was littered with gear for this very reason.

After acquiring a replacement knife, Abby had decided to stop by the *MacGreggor* to download some of the ROV's navigation files depicting the exact routes the ROV had travelled on each of its dives. Since the ROV's position was updated electronically every three seconds during a dive, the route data were fairly accurate and could provide scientists with a useful correlation of the ROV's position to important features on the seafloor like rock pinnacles or sunken treasure.

Generally, the team reserved this type of activity for the end of a research cruise. But when weather interrupted a cruise, it was critical to take every opportunity to keep ahead of the avalanche of information that characterized field operations.

Because there was some Coast Guard activity earlier on the narrow road out onto the breakwater, Abby parked in the outer parking lot and walked out to the *MacGreggor*. About halfway out to the ship, she happened to turn back to see a man in a dark blue jacket and baseball cap walking about two hundred feet behind her. At the time, the man's outfit had been similar enough to the standard Coast Guard uniform that she hadn't thought twice about him.

However, when she reached the top of the ship's gangway, she noticed that he'd continued to follow her and that he'd closed half of the distance between them. It was then that she realized first that the man wasn't a Coastie, and second that he looked much like the pictures she'd downloaded of Kevin O'Grady.

She turned to face him to see if he would change his plan if under direct scrutiny, but he simply looked at her and proceeded up the gangway. With no other convenient way to get off the ship besides jumping, Abby had quickly moved through the nearest hatch, then up a single flight of stairs to the stateroom from which she'd called Chris, then the police.

She hadn't seen or heard any more from her pursuer.

Marisa, for her part, explained that she had been taking a break from data analysis by sitting in the galley and watching CNN. She hadn't seen Abby or anyone else come on board until the police arrived.

"I suppose I could have been wrong," Abby said without any conviction. "Maybe it *was* a Coastie who had come on board for some other reason."

"But you don't think so."

"No. I don't think so. It was Kevin, whether the police believe me or not."

The three of them briefly perused the main passageways of the ship one more time for any evidence of an intrusion. Finding nothing, they closed up and left the ship together.

Coming down the gangway from the ship, Chris saw something strange sitting on the front windshield of the Land Rover. Down on the dock, he moved past Abby and Marisa and walked quickly to his truck.

Under the windshield wiper on the driver's side was a stuffed *Winnie-the-Pooh*. Gretchen had bought it during a trip to Disneyland the year before when the CMEx team was working off southern California. He knew it was Gretchen's because it was wearing a small SCUBA mask that Gretchen had added after bringing it home. The bear had participated in several research cruises since and was well known to all participants.

Someone had taken it from its position of honor on Gretchen's bed the night she was attacked.

Chris removed the bear from under the windshield wiper. It was clearly Gretchen's bear, and just as clear was the fact that it had been sliced open from the crotch to the neck.

39

Abby gave Marisa a ride back to campus with Chris following closely. Thinking of Gretchen as he looked at *Winnie-the-Pooh* sitting on his passenger seat, Chris tried the Clarks on both of their phones. He ultimately got Mr. Clark on the phone, but the connection was so bad that he terminated after a few seconds.

Abby dropped Marisa off at her car and made sure that her car would start. As she drove away, Abby climbed out of her car and into Chris's.

"Tell me the truth. Are the stories accurate? Have you done any of those things that the students like to talk about?"

Chris sighed. He felt deeply fatigued. "Yeah, I'd say most of them are true. And to be perfectly honest, they usually don't know the half of it." Although he didn't relish the thought, he felt it was necessary to offer more detail about the Baja incident.

"At first the thugs looked harmless enough, walking up to camp chatting casually in broken English, feigning enthusiasm for our SCUBA diving activities. They were asking the students all kinds of questions, but Mac and I could tell they were eyeing everyone, looking for opportunities to exploit.

"One night they showed up after dark, and they had this woman with them. She looked beaten up and submissive. She was wearing a battered

skirt and an old t-shirt, and bruises were evident both on her upper arms
and lower thighs. The three thugs kept pointing at her, then pointing at
the female students and smiling. It wasn't entirely clear what the idiots
were suggesting, but we couldn't envision an explanation that wasn't
bad news. So we asked them to leave, and they weren't happy about that.
For the first time their body language became overtly threatening.

"We had no interactions with any law enforcement and weren't
hopeful that any help would be forthcoming. I didn't want to be responsible
for a student getting hurt or worse. And given the obvious escalation in
their behavior, I decided to go after them myself. Fortunately, Mac was
there to join me."

"Couldn't you have simply left?" Abby interjected. "Isn't that what
most people would do in those circumstances?"

"Perhaps, perhaps. But it would have taken us at least a day to break
down the camp, and we expected them to return."

"So you went and looked for trouble?"

"No, we simply confronted it. That night while the students were
playing board games, Mac and I snuck out of camp and waited. The
generator was running in the camp to power the lights. It was an old
Honda that had seen better days, and it was loud. So the students couldn't
hear much of what was going on beyond the camp.

"We staked out the main road, just over the hill from our camp.
When the thugs approached in their truck, it was a beat-up old Nissan,
Mac stepped out into the road and held up his hands.

"The truck skidded to a stop and sat there for a full minute. We could
hear quiet, but urgent talking going on inside over the idling engine of
the old truck. Then they started whooping, getting up their courage.

"When the driver jumped out of the side door holding a machete, I
stepped out of the darkness and beat him over the head with a lead pipe.
No thinking involved. Just action. I hit him so hard he just dropped. The

next guy out of the truck got the same. Mac had run around to the other door and dragged a third guy out of the car and throttled him."

"Wow," Abby said.

"That was when one of the side windows erupted with gunfire. Mac dropped below the field of view, and I jumped into the driver's side door. It looked as though they didn't have any more bullets, because they didn't fire again.

"One of the guys in the back seat kicked out at me and knocked my hand into the rusty gear shift. I grabbed his leg, pulled him toward me, and punched him straight in the face. At the same time, Mac reached in the blown out window and grabbed the guy with the gun.

"The last guy spoke a little English and begged to be left alone. He was apologizing and yelling. We pulled him out of the truck while we jammed the rest of the guys back into it. Then I pointed down the road and encouraged him to leave."

"How did you do that, exactly?" Abby asked. "What did you say?"

"Nothing I'm particularly proud of," Chris replied, shaking his head slowly. He looked up at Abby and could tell that his answer wouldn't suffice.

"I told him that if he didn't get out of there I was going to rip his fucking head off. I told him that if he or any of his friends came after us again that we would kill every one of them. He looked like he believed me."

"Wow."

"You said that already," Chris replied, pretty sure that he was turning Abby off as he spoke. But what was he going to do? This stuff happened and would probably happen again.

"I'm not sure how other people would've responded in that situation. Some probably would've rolled over for the banditos and would likely never have been seen again. Others might have found some peaceful way out of the situation. Our reaction was forceful when the time came, but was, I don't know, proportional? Appropriate to the seriousness of the situation?

"I've been shot at by pirates. Not Johnny Depp-type pirates, but real nasty guys with nothing to lose. Been beat up by corrupt police officers, too. Perhaps I attract trouble somehow, and I don't know any other way to respond to it. All the violence, the wrongdoing, it touches something primal in me.

"The thing is, all this stuff happened in other countries, frequently out in the boonies. It felt like the frontier, and we did what we had to do to protect the team." He paused.

"But now we're here at home. Not only in the U.S. but literally at home in Carmel and Monterey. Here we're supposed to be protected from this madness. We cede control over this type of lawlessness to the authorities as part of the social contract."

"And yet, we aren't protected," Abby said quietly.

40

Chris got voicemail again for Mac, so he left a message and drove straight to CHOMP to find out how Gretchen was doing. The sun had moved through its zenith and was headed into afternoon.

He parked in the visitor's lot and walked up the hill to the main hospital entrance. As he walked, he scratched at the scar on the back of his left hand. He hoped that Abby wasn't put off by his reactions to the violence around him.

CHOMP's circular drive, which was once accessible to cars, had been closed off for some time to normal traffic, perhaps a legacy of 9/11. But today there were three sheriff's vehicles parked there. Something was up.

Chris walked into the main entryway into the sunlit atrium. There he saw Jase conferring with a couple of uniformed deputies. As he approached the trio, Jase noticed Chris and immediately moved toward him. The deputies stared at Chris.

"Chris, man, I'm so sorry."

The brain works in mysterious ways. The portion of the brain that controlled muscles clearly understood what was coming and Chris's entire body tightened up. But the conscious portion of the brain seemed to be slow on the uptake.

"What are you talking about?"

"Oh, man. I thought that's why you were here. Fuck." He paused and looked briefly toward the ceiling. His gaze then returned to Chris. "Gretchen passed away early this morning. There was hemorrhaging in her brain that worsened quickly, and there was nothing anyone could do. She never woke up."

Chris just stood there.

"Chris, I'm so sorry."

Chris managed a weak nod. "Where are her parents?"

"They were here all night. A deputy took them back to their hotel downtown a couple of hours ago."

Chris walked over to the edge of the koi pond and sat on the rim. The koi, apparently thinking he might have bread for them, meandered over to him.

His brain, watching the fish swim, cycled through a variety of random thoughts, a slideshow in his head of the immediately accessible memories of Gretchen—struggling with long hair after a SCUBA dive and laughing about it; with short hair after she'd become fed up with it and sold it to a wig maker; running with his father through the hills while his dad trained for a marathon; coming out to the *MacGreggor* earlier in the week and bringing chocolate.

Jase was still standing there, staring at his shoes and looking for an opportunity to provide solace for his friend. "You worked with Gretchen for a long time, didn't you?"

"Yeah. Years ago," Chris chuckled at the memory, "I put an ad out on a bunch of different listservs for a research assistant position. Within a week, I had more than a hundred applications, including people with Ph.D.s. But she..." He took a couple of deep breaths before continuing.

"Gretchen was the first person to follow up on her application with a phone call. I was impressed with her immediately. She gave me two references to call, graduate students on whose research projects she'd participated. It turned out later that both of the graduate students were her roommates, but it didn't matter.

"We gave her an on-the-job interview. She had to come out with us in the field for a week-long research cruise. And we didn't pull any punches. The work was hard and the hours were long.

"We did three of those interviews, and nobody came even close to impressing us the way she did." He took another couple of deep breaths. "She was amazing. One of the hardest workers I'd ever seen, but also one of the nicest people. She had the perfect disposition for this work. The rest of us would swear and get all worked up from time to time, but not Gretchen. She appeared serene under even the tensest of circumstances."

Chris shook his head a couple of times and stood. "How much closer are we to ending this cluster fuck, Jase?" He'd spoken too loudly and Chris could see heads turning throughout the lobby.

"We're not making much headway. Both of your buddies Smith and Campbell have lawyered up and are not talking."

"What about Kevin O'Grady and some guy named Darrell English?" Chris asked. "We know that they're involved."

Jase looked momentarily taken aback. "Not sure where you got that information," he said. "We've talked to both of them and the investigation is ongoing. But there's no evidence to suggest that either of them was involved at this time."

"I just came from the *MacGreggor*, where a man fitting Kevin's description followed Abby onto the boat. When I arrived, the police were already there. Kevin must have been still around because he left a stuffed animal on my windshield that he'd taken from Gretchen's house. He'd gutted it, the fucker.

"If that isn't enough, talk to Sarah Rothberg," Chris continued, somewhat exasperated. "She's got all kinds of theories about what happened. She thinks there's a group of local power brokers funding English and O'Grady."

Jase was getting visibly irritated listening to these apparently new revelations. "Monterey PD didn't alert me to the incident at the ship. And Sarah Rothberg told us nothing of any of this. Some information from her might give me some purchase on English. Then I can bring him in and sweat him a bit." He kicked the side of the Koi pond.

"I just saw her this morning near campus. She sought me out. She's afraid. I told her to call you."

"I've got to go follow this up. I'll get in touch with you later. Again, I'm sorry." He put his hand on Chris's shoulder then went back to the deputies.

Chris watched the deputies leave with Jase. He looked around for a few minutes for anyone he knew. Seeing no one, he walked back out to his car in a haze much deeper than the late-afternoon fog weaving its way between the trees surrounding the hospital.

Without a conscious effort, he navigated his way back to Margaret's house. Cars full of smiling people doing interesting, fun things flashed by in his peripheral vision, happy tourists visiting the lovely Carmel-by-the-Sea. He knew they had their own challenges to deal with, many with burdens far in excess of his own, but at this moment he couldn't see beyond the crushing sadness of Gretchen's death.

New SCUBA divers, he thought, frequently experience what's referred to as a perceptual narrowing in which an irritant such as a leaky face mask causes the diver to focus entirely on the irritant at the expense of all else. They stop monitoring their depth in the water, they disregard their pressure gauges that report how much air they have remaining, and they lose track of their dive buddies. The danger can be significant.

Gretchen's death was far more significant an irritant than a leaky mask, and he could feel the perceptual narrowing accelerating as he drove.

41

Word of Gretchen's death spread quickly once it got beyond the hospital. Chris fielded calls from Peter and several of the graduate students on his cell phone. He had to borrow Abby's charger on the fly when his phone gave out during one of the calls.

When speaking to one of the graduate students who was calling from the lab at CMEx, Chris could hear Mac talking in the background, but he'd yet to call himself. Chris thought he understood. Other than Chris, Mac was the closest to Gretchen. This was going to hit him hard, as well.

Twenty-five years ago on a summer day much like today, when Chris and Mac were in their early teens, Mac had lost his younger sister. Chris had been over at Mac's house, which at the time was in the Mission Fields neighborhood below the Carmel Mission. They were playing a game of Dungeons and Dragons. Jase was the DM, or Dungeon Master, while Chris and Mac were each playing several different characters. The game was spread out on the dining room table, and it was a tense one. Nobody wanted to deal with any distractions.

This was before the days of organized play dates and intricately planned summer activities for kids. So Chris and his friends were left largely to their own devices during the summer as their parents went off to work each day. In Mac's case this frequently meant that he was nominally responsible for making sure his sister, Melissa, who was two years younger than he was, didn't get into any major trouble.

The day's activities had panned out this way for years and could easily have done so forever without incident. But on this particular day, when Melissa announced that she was going out to ride her bike, fate had something different in mind. She'd taken off out the back door with little recognition from the foursome battling for supremacy of Middle Earth.

An hour later, when a sheriff's deputy had arrived at the front door with terrible news, the boys hadn't even realized that Melissa was gone.

She'd been riding her bike on the street in front of their house and had evidently got bored with endless circles of the same cul-de-sac, so she'd ridden out of the neighborhood onto Rio Road, a heavily trafficked street that linked Carmel-by-the-Sea and the Carmel Mission to Highway 1. Drivers coming off the highway, accustomed to the faster speeds of the open road, would regularly speed along Rio Road despite the fact that it was in a residential neighborhood.

One such driver, an old guy in a van towing a collapsible camper behind him, had simply not paid enough attention when rounding one of the curves on Rio Road. He hadn't even known he'd hit Melissa until the vehement honking of a car behind him drew his attention.

When Gretchen moved west with Chris to work at CMEx, Mac had come on board shortly thereafter. He'd initially wanted nothing to do with her. She didn't fit into any useful role for Mac; she wasn't an engineer, had no training in electronics, and didn't have a lot of experience working on mechanical devices, period. However, Mac's general good humor and the fact that Gretchen was clearly intelligent and strongly motivated to learn should have made them instant friends.

But that hadn't come to pass initially, and it had been difficult for Chris to reconcile.

It was only after Chris sent Mac and Gretchen on a road trip to San Diego to pick up a new umbilical for the ROV that the bonding between the two of them finally occurred.

While most of the story behind their adventures during that road trip remained a secret between the two of them to this day, the trip had clearly changed Mac's attitude. And in the ensuing six years, Mac and Gretchen had become the siblings they each desired. Chris had greatly enjoyed watching the friendship develop.

Yes, Mac was going to have a tough time with this.

In the late afternoon, Abby and Margaret found Chris sitting downstairs in the living room. Abby had been doing more web searching and had something to report. "Check out this anonymous blog by salinasmother72, this is interesting," Abby said. "In 2004 this woman's son was murdered in Salinas. She blames Kevin for his death and claims that Kevin works for Darrell English."

She continued, "Her son apparently got involved with Kevin through some friends. He started 'working' for Kevin and Darrell, though it's not clear what he was doing, then one night he just disappeared.

"The woman claims that her son isn't the first kid to disappear after working with these guys. I couldn't find anything to substantiate that, but she refers to at least ten people who had disappeared. And this was in 2004. She wasn't happy with the sheriff's department at all. We should talk to Jase about that."

"That's a lot of missing people," Chris said. "But then again, anybody remember how many gang deaths there were in Salinas last year? 'Cause I sure don't."

"Next I started looking for anything on Darrell English," Abby continued. "Google returned 4,730,000 hits in 0.24 seconds. The only reference I could find to anyone by that name in the vicinity of Monterey was the meeting minutes from the January 2007 meeting of the Marina City Council. He apparently testified before the Council on some land development issue. Unfortunately, the Council's website didn't archive video of the proceedings."

Margaret chimed in here, "I spoke to Abby earlier in the day." She paused to look at Chris, probably thinking that he would need an explanation, "To make sure that she could get into the house whenever she came home. And she mentioned the names you had on your list. Well, I thought I recognized the name Darrell English, so I went back into the archives at my office. And I found him."

Chris, who had been staring out the front window, re-focused at that and waited for Margaret to continue.

"Way back when I first took over the practice in Carmel from Dr. Fitzhugh. Remember him, Chris? He was such an interesting man."

Chris nodded. "Dad didn't care for him much, if I recall correctly."

Margaret sighed. "Few people passed muster with your father. That was one of the things I always loved about him.

"Where was I? Right, on his way out the door to retirement Dr. Fitzhugh transferred to me several cases that he'd been working on for the county's Office of Child Protective Services. They were all tough cases, children who had experienced a variety of horrors at the hands of adults. Chris and Mac have heard me talk about the cases from time to time.

"Anyway, while I never met with Darrell English, Dr. Fitzhugh did. His notes indicate that Darrell is believed to have killed his alcoholic father, though charges were never pressed. Apparently, the father put Darrell in the hospital on more than one occasion."

Margaret waited for comments, but receiving none, she continued, "I don't see how any of this helps us with the current situation. But it set me to thinking about the role of parents or authority figures in the formation of our adult selves. Let's assume, for the moment, that Darrell English is indeed behind all this trouble. Think about the pathologies that would motivate such antisocial behavior. It's not hard to imagine that the origins of those pathologies began, as they do with so many of my clients, with monstrous abuse by a parent."

Chris sensed that the train had switched tracks and was moving off in a different direction. "Bring it home for us, Mom."

"My point is this—Darrell English committed his first murder more than thirty years ago, during his formative years. And he may have committed many more in the three intervening decades for all we know. Even though most of this is just supposition, we have to consider that Darrell is capable of extreme violence, and we shouldn't underestimate him."

With the conversation about Darrell English having run its course, Chris drove over the hill to Monterey to talk with the Clarks. Their hotel was at the base of Munras Avenue, a street known for the proliferation of hotels and motels along its length. They were staying in a newly renovated stucco behemoth that had been completed the previous year. He met them in their room.

Chris found them to be more poised than anyone had a right to expect. The room was clean and organized, when the opposite would've been entirely forgivable under the circumstances. The curtains were open; CNN was playing on the TV in the background.

Mr. Clark was sitting at a table by the window making notes on a laptop computer, while Mrs. Clark answered the door with a smile. It was the wan smile of someone in great pain. She was clearly trying. Both were dressed casually, and again, were looking better than they needed to, given the passing of their only daughter.

Chris's eyes were drawn to the three small plastic figurines that he'd first seen in Gretchen's hospital room, which were now lined up along the table in between two queen beds. Looking at them once again put Chris on uneven ground.

His mind raced and his heart sank as he imagined a young Gretchen packing a small bag full of her "friends" to take along on a family road trip, thinking carefully about which of the multitude of small figurines in her room she should bring with her and which to leave behind. He could see those same "friends" surviving the purges of early adolescence to remain prominent on the bedroom shelf, emblems of a cherished childhood. When the time came to move on to a dorm room in her freshman year at college, the "friends" had somehow, against great odds, survived a transition yet again and remained poignant reminders when other tokens had been tossed away unceremoniously.

And now these "friends" had outlived their owner.

The Clarks both asked questions about the investigation to bring the situation in the room onto less emotional ground. They tried to put *him* at ease, which of course made Chris feel much worse.

But a halting conversation was initiated, and they ultimately spoke for an hour, first discussing the logistics of a memorial service and funeral, then moving on to much more comfortable ground, reminiscing about Gretchen's exploits.

After a few uncomfortable minutes, the conversation found a rhythm that allowed the three of them to switch between laughter and sadness. The Clarks told stories of Gretchen in her youth that Chris had never heard. Indeed, as he listened, he realized how little he knew of Gretchen's life before she started to work for him. She'd played her cards close to her vest in all ways.

Evening approached as Chris took his leave of the Clarks for the day, and his anger at the unjustness of this loss began to rise to the surface, yet he realized as he drove through the tunnel into New Monterey on his way to the *MacGreggor* that his new relationship with Abby had somehow tempered his need for vengeance. His soul, his very essence, seemed to be in conflict with itself. What to seek? Righteous fucking vengeance or the eternal grace of the high road? He parked by the boat and made his way onto the ship. The flag on the *MacGreggor's* conning tower was at half-mast. On the back deck, the hatch covers were off at two locations, and several bags of tools were placed around holes within an arm's reach. The engineers were still working on the starboard engine.

The ROV looked to be in one piece on the back deck, with none of Mac's team visible. The ship's dry lab was congested with graduate students. Most were talking quietly in small groups, while a brave few were trying to watch some ROV video.

"Anyone seen Mac?" Chris asked the group.

"He left suddenly about half an hour ago," one of the Dianas said. "We thought he might be going up to the hospital."

A few hesitant glances were passed among the students. "We all really liked Gretchen. Do the police know who did it?"

"They're working on it," Chris said with no conviction. "None of you have to be here today, by the way. Take some time off, and I'll call everyone when there's something to know, either about the case or about when we're heading back out to sea."

"Is there going to be a memorial for Gretchen?" another student asked.

"Yes. I spoke with her parents this afternoon. The timing isn't yet clear, but there will be something. I—." He almost said he'd pass along word through Gretchen, which until last week was his standard protocol for years. "Thank you, everyone, for your hard work. I know this sucks. We'll get through it."

Chris went to his stateroom, closed the door, and collapsed onto his bunk. He kicked off his shoes, lay back on the pillows, and within minutes was asleep.

An eternity passed in fifteen minutes, and he awoke to call Mac, who picked up on the first ring. "Mac, where are you?" "Sitting out front of Kevin O'Grady's place." Mac had a dangerous tone in his voice. "It's off Highway 68, across from the airport. Remember that industrial park where we used to rollerblade back in the day?" "How could I forget," Chris said. Back in the early '90s, when inline skates were still cool, Chris, Mac, and several others had combed the area looking for the best place to practice their moves. The industrial park that Mac was referring to was situated around a cul-de-sac. Both the approaching road and the cul-de-sac had recently been repaved. That, coupled with its isolated location and consequent lack of traffic, made it an optimal location for group of miscreants armed with Rollerblades and rubber-tipped ski poles. Chris hadn't been out there for years.

"Is he there?" he asked.

"Yep. Along with a couple of others. I picked him up when he was leaving work at Home Depot and followed him out here. Shortly after his arrival two other vehicles pulled up; a windowless van that immediately drove around back and was carrying an unknown number of humans, and a black truck that two people got out of. I could use some backup."

42

Weaving through traffic on Del Monte, Chris tried to call Jase. No answer on the cell. He called the office. No answer. He called Margaret at home and asked her to take the phone to the deputy out front.

"This is Anderson," the deputy said.

"Deputy, this is Chris Black. I've been trying to reach Jase Hamilton and can't raise him on any of his numbers. Do you know his location?"

"No sir. I'll try to identify his twenty and get back to you. Please stand by." A few seconds passed. Chris could hear a conversation in the background, but it was too garbled to understand. He did recall that identifying your *twenty* meant your location, in law enforcement speak.

The deputy returned. "Sir, Inspector Hamilton doesn't respond to his radio. This is concerning. We'll find him and have him call you. Thank you."

This is concerning. No shit.

Chris turned right up Camino Aguajito, which ran along the east side of El Estero Lake, then San Carlos Cemetery. There he was slowed momentarily when a family of ducks decided to stroll across the road. Even pressed for time he was happy to wait; he'd seen people swerve intentionally to hit ducks in the past, and it wasn't pretty. He then turned

INTO A CANYON DEEP

left onto the Highway 1 on-ramp. Staying to the right, he took the Highway 68 off-ramp at over seventy miles an hour.

Mac was parked a few hundred feet up the hill from a former auto repair shop, which must have been Kevin's house. There was a black Chevy Tahoe parked along the side and several trucks parked out front. Next to Kevin's was a silk-screening operation. On the other side of it was a pool cleaning business. And, based on the stickers on the windows, the remaining building on the cul-de-sac was what looked like a surfboard shaper. None of the three businesses appeared to be open.

Why anyone would choose to live in one of these buildings was unclear to Chris. Perhaps he'd find out.

Chris got out of the Land Rover, left the driver's side door open, and jumped into Mac's truck on the passenger side. "Jase is out of communication. That's not good. What do we have here?"

"A few minutes after I got here, a van pulled around back. O'Grady followed in that Tahoe and parked where you see it. The other two trucks came along shortly after that. So we have at least four bad guys and possibly more." Mac looked to be in his all-business mode; the mode one didn't want to mess with.

They improvised a plan. Not a great plan, but it was a plan.

Mac grabbed his small black bag of tricks from under the driver's seat and hopped out of the truck. In seconds, he was across the street and out of sight around the back of the building.

Still no movement visible from the front.

Chris took the new ASP that Mac provided and hefted it in his right hand. Three minutes later Mac was back. He'd been moving fast but talked as though he was lounging by the pool.

"Okay. The situation has changed," he said as he looked at Chris. "I think they have someone back there, and it sounds like they're roughing him up." He paused, then added, "We need to go in now. And we need backup."

"Righteous fucking vengeance it is," Chris finished the conversation with himself from earlier.

"What?"

"Nothing. Go. I'll call the cavalry then join you from the front as planned."

Chris called 9-1-1 and gave them the location, asking that a message be passed along to Jase if anyone could determine his whereabouts. The operator asked him to stay on the line, but as Mac disappeared for a second time around the back, Chris couldn't wait around. He grabbed a clipboard from the back seat and walked up to the front door. He slowed his breathing then knocked emphatically.

Someone other than O'Grady answered the door, looking pissed. The guy was average height, which in the U.S. made him about five foot nine. He was drug-addict thin and had visible tattoos down both of his forearms and poking out of the neckline of his dirty Pabst Blue Ribbon T-shirt. He held a can of Budweiser in his right hand—serious brand confusion.

He looked up at Chris through pharmaceutically enlarged pupils and asked, "Fuck do you want?" in a tone that begged for an abrasive response.

Not knowing whether anyone else was there with this joker, Chris took a different tack. Using his best manic smile he enthused, "Hi! I'm from EnviroCal! Are you aware that the island of debris in the Pacific Ocean, now known as the Great Pacific Garbage Patch is twice the size of the State of Texas?" The clipboard was in his left hand. The collapsed ASP was in his right.

The guy reached to slam the door, saying "Fuck y—." But he was prevented from completing what would certainly have been an insightful soliloquy by the ASP wrapped in Chris's right fist. The punch landed squarely on the man's nose. Chris could feel the nose crunch as the man's enlarged pupils rolled back to white as he fell. He hit the concrete floor with a thud that left little doubt that he was out cold.

Chris ducked into the room and shut the door as quietly as he could. He lucked out. No one else was in the room. He grabbed two of the large plastic tie wraps that Mac had given him from his back pocket and quickly bound the man's wrists and ankles. It probably wasn't necessary, but one couldn't be too careful. He didn't have a nice little bag of tricks like Mac.

He looked around. He was in what was once the office of the repair shop. The interior walls of the room were frosted glass from the halfway point to the ceiling. He could see bright yellow light beyond the wall directly in front of him as well as blue flickering light coming from the left. There were several shadowy figures moving around in the vicinity of the yellow light.

Chris assumed that with no light in the room to backlight him, he was fairly safe to move around without being seen. He dragged Mr. Pabst over to a corner and dumped him out of the way. The guy must only weigh a hundred and twenty pounds, Chris thought. He searched for a wallet but found none. Who doesn't carry a wallet?

A quick survey of the room revealed nothing of interest. It looked as though it wasn't used too frequently. The dust on the floor had accumulated to an extent incompatible with lived-in space.

Chris checked his watch—time to move. He crept to the door, waited for a three-count, and slowly cracked it open.

The room on the other side of the door was large, at least twenty feet by forty feet. It must have been the main work area for the repair shop. Now it had been converted to the quintessential bachelor pad. Maximum cheese. There was a large flat screen TV on the wall with what looked like ESPN tuned in. Only porn would've been more appropriate.

There was what looked to be a well-used free weights station set up in front of a mirror; a bench press and a few barbells resting on a black pad. The "cardio center" was immediately to the right, with a not-inexpensive LeMond Revmaster stationary bike and a LiveStrong treadmill. They both looked used but reasonably well maintained. Even idiots, it seemed, made good choices once in a while.

The bachelor's heaven was made complete by the accoutrement that occupied the primary living area. Toward the center of the room was a horseshoe formed by three plush vinyl couches. In the middle of the couches was a pool table illuminated by a large stained-glass lamp hanging four feet above it.

There were three men standing around the table, two were holding pool cues. The third, Kevin O'Grady, was looking down at a body lying on the table.

The body was Jase Hamilton.

43

The pool lamp directly above Jase cast a halo of light around the table and the three men. The surrounding darkness provided Chris with sufficient cover to slip into the room unnoticed.

O'Grady kidney punched Jase from behind, using what looked like brass knuckles. At least he was still alive, Chris thought. Even these idiots probably wouldn't work on a dead body. The other two just watched, awed, or perhaps scared, by the violence that Kevin was visiting upon a sheriff's department investigator.

Chris slowly adjusted his position. He now noticed that sitting on the couch beyond the pool table was Sarah Rothberg, with her baby sitting in her lap. She still looked oddly detached, but not particularly scared, which was interesting. What was she doing here? A reunion with her old flame?

He couldn't see any guns in plain sight, but it was certain that they were near. No self-respecting group of shit-kickers such as these guys would be without guns around somewhere.

As he tightened his grip on the ASP handle and prepared to move, there was a large crash on his right. From the shadows at the other side of the large room Chris saw the blue light of Mac's taser arc across the space and strike Kevin in the chest.

"Yo! Fuckos!" Mac yelled, still from the cover of darkness on the right side of the room.

Before the other two had a chance to react to Kevin's incapacitation, there was a loud report from the same direction as the voice and the man closest to Kevin was struck in the face with a bean bag. It was a non-lethal weapon for crowd suppression, and it suppressed the guy instantly.

The third man was quick enough to dodge the second projectile and jump toward Sarah and her baby, landing behind the couch. Reaching over from behind the couch, the guy pulled out a knife and held it within range of the baby, who was now crying loudly.

The room remained largely dark, with the exception of the illumination provided by the pool table light and the flickering images of ESPN from the big screen TV. It was also quiet. Mac was hidden somewhere unseen, while the knife-wielding man had yet to notice that Chris was in the room.

Chris took a deep breath, put the ASP in his back pocket, and stood with his hands out in front of him. "Okay. Take it easy, tough guy. I'm unarmed."

"You! Stay right where you are, or I'll cut her and the kid!"

"No problem. I'm not going anywhere," Chris replied, walking slowly to his left as he spoke, but moving no closer to the couch. He needed to check on Jase but kept his eyes on the man with the knife.

"I said stop moving!" the man yelled as he pressed the dull side of the knife into Sarah's neck. She whimpered and the baby continued to scream. "And shut that kid up!" he added, looking down toward Sarah.

"Listen, man. Calm down. I'm just going to move over to the table to check on the cop. Nothing to worry about." Jase was breathing, but it was labored, wheezy. Up close he looked bad. Both eyes were swollen shut, and his nose was broken. Blood from the nose and other injuries caked up the side of his face. Chris was sure that those brass knuckles had done some damage internally, as well. They needed to get him to a hospital.

"You've got no way out of here. The cops will be here shortly, if they aren't already outside. Why don't you put the knife away and talk to us," Chris soothed, hands still out in front of him.

"What do you mean by us?" asked the tough guy, scanning the room in front of him.

As he spoke, the two metal prongs of a taser press into the man's right temple as Mac appeared behind him. "Get it now?" Mac said. "Why don't you drop the knife?"

The man hesitated, looking first at Chris, then at his two incapacitated colleagues. "Okay, okay. Shit!" He finally put the knife down on the couch.

Chris moved quickly over to grab the knife. Sarah also moved quickly to get away from everyone. She got up, carrying the crying baby, and ran through the door from which Chris had entered without saying a word. He briefly considered running after her to find out exactly how she had been involved in Jase's capture, but opted to stay and interrogate the remaining henchman.

While Mac kept the taser pressed against the guy's head, Chris started asking questions. "Where can we find Darrell English?"

"Ah man, they'll kill me if I tell you that."

"Who's gonna know? We'll tie you up just like the rest before we get out of here. Time is running out. Once the cops get here, we lose control of the situation. *Tell me*."

"Look. You're Black, right? You're already too late."

"Too late for what?" demanded Mac.

"I'm not saying anything else," said the man.

Mac jammed the taser into the man's thigh and activated it.

The henchman screamed and fell to one knee. Spittle flew from his mouth as he cursed Mac. Mac redirected the taser to the man's chest and again hit him with a jolt. The man fell onto his side barely conscious.

Chris knelt next to him. "The next jolt's going to be even worse."

"No. Stop. I'll talk."

"What's English's next move?"

"He's going after your mom and the redhead right now," sputtered the man.

"To kill them?" Mac dangled the taser in front of the man's face.

"No. I...I don't think so. At least not your mom. She's not supposed to be hurt."

Chris's brow furrowed. "What? Well, where's he going to take them?"

"Darrell hangs out a lot at a ranch in the valley."

"Which valley? Salinas? Carmel?"

"Carmel. It's—" The guy was interrupted mid-sentence by a gunshot coming from the door. A bullet struck the man directly in the chest. He ceased talking to cast a surprised look down at the bright red blood bubbling out of the hole just to the right of his sternum.

44

Chris dropped behind the pool table as several more shots struck the guy and the couch around him. The man on the couch was dead. Chris couldn't see where Mac had gone when the firing started, but he assumed Mac was behind the couch. Whoever it was kept firing, but at what?

Then Chris risked a quick look around the table. From his vantage point he could see two bullets hit the already prostrate Kevin. Both were shots to the torso and were likely fatal. And two more hit the guy Mac had downed with a bean bag. One of the shots took out the man's right eye. The remaining eye, now lifeless, was looking at Chris crouched behind the pool table. Kevin wasn't moving either.

The shooting stopped for a second. In that instant Chris heard Mac's shotgun blast away from behind the couch. The shooter went down by the office door from which he'd emerged.

Mac leapt up from behind the couch. "Chris, it's the cops. We've got to get Jase and get out of here!"

"The cops?" Chris motioned to the downed men. "What do you mean? Why would they take out all three of these guys, even the ones you had already incapacitated?" He thought about it. "What the fuck is going on?"

"Grab Jase," Mac said. "Dirty cops. They're cleaning house. Let's hope there are only a couple of them. In which case, they won't be able to cover all of the exits. If there's anyone else, I bet they're coming in the back and I only hit these guys with bean bags, so they're going to wake up. I'll cover you. Let's move!"

Chris hefted Jase up onto his shoulder. The groaning he heard was a good sign. At least Jase was still alive. He moved toward the door, stepping over the downed police officer as he went.

At that moment, three more shots rang out from the back of the building as Mac had anticipated. The shots were off their mark, but were close, shattering the glass to the right of the office door. The shots were followed immediately by return fire from Mac's shotgun.

Seconds later, Mac joined Chris. "Got him. And this, too." He flashed Chris one of the fallen cops' badges as he knelt over the second cop and grabbed his badge as well. Taking the badges would serve two objectives; it would provide them with solid intel on who they were dealing with, while at the same time putting both cops in a difficult situation. It would be hard for them to maintain their innocence with people out there in the world holding their identification.

"I'll pick up Jase, but we should check to see if any of those three guys are still alive." Chris assumed they were all dead, but he wanted the check just the same.

Chris could hear and feel Jase struggling.

"O'Grady. Note. Notebook. B- black." Jase was trying to speak. "Get notebook." He tried to nudge his head back toward the room they'd just left.

"Jase says there's a notebook back there that we need to get. It's O'Grady's," Chris said.

"I'll go," Mac volunteered. "Get Jase out to my truck and I'll meet you there."

Chris hefted Jase higher onto his shoulders, and they emerged into the darkness of the deserted industrial park. As hoped, there were no flashing lights from additional squad cars. The only illumination came from three street lamps.

Chris made a dash for Mac's truck. His thighs were screaming by the time he reached the truck. It was unlocked, and he gently placed Jase in the back seat, leaning him against the side and buckling his safety belt.

"We're out of there, Jase. Just hang tough. This is Mac's truck. Mac is going to take you to CHOMP in a second." Jase didn't respond.

Chris tried again. "Jase, is there anyone in your department you trust? We need a safe contact." Still no response.

Mac followed a couple of minutes later. He came out the door, quickly checked out the area, and ran up the hill.

"Got the book, I think. It's a black notebook that was on O'Grady's desk. Looks to have a lot of notes and phone numbers in it. Hard to know what O'Grady would've written down that was any use to us, but maybe he confesses to everything." He climbed into the driver's seat. "Also got a couple of cell phones. Perhaps they'll give us some good intel."

"I'm going after my mom and Abby just in case that guy was telling the truth. Can you get Jase to the hospital?"

"Roger that. Once I make sure he's covered, I'll come to you. Let me know what you find out. And be careful."

"Anderson," Jase said from the back seat. Then again, "Anderson."

"What?" Mac looked at Chris.

"I asked about anyone in his department he can trust. Who knows how far the corruption goes?" Chris answered. "Anderson is the guy I spoke to earlier. I'll call him on my way to Carmel and tell him you're en route to the hospital."

45

For the second time in a week Chris was speeding toward Margaret's house. His mind was racing. Whoever was running this show had cops on the payroll. That first cop had acted quickly, shooting at Chris and Mac as well the other guys without hesitation. Did Darrell English have that kind of reach? He may be crazy and dangerous, but he still sounded more like a two-bit tough guy, not someone who manipulates dirty cops. Perhaps there *was* something to Sarah Rothberg's conjecture about the prominent supporters pulling Darrell's strings. And whoever they were, how many departments had they compromised? With Jase out of the picture, who was it safe to talk to?

Calls to Abby's cell phone went unanswered. Same with his mom's. He risked a call to 9-1-1 and asked the operator to alert Deputy Anderson of the threat at Margaret's. He stayed on the phone while she attempted to do so.

He was moving down the hill on Highway 1 at about ninety miles an hour dodging the light traffic. There were a couple of cars behind and in front of him. He saw a black truck pull up to the stop sign at Hatton Fields, one of the two roads below Ocean Avenue that turned directly onto Highway 1. He didn't think much of it until he drew abreast of it and the truck leapt out and center-punched the Land Rover.

Chris rolled twice on his way across the other lane and down the embankment on the other side of the road. The roof collapsed and the windshield crumpled. His responses were quick, but there was little for him to do but go along for the ride.

"Black truck!" he yelled. But he'd no idea where his cell phone was or whether the 9-1-1 operator on the phone could hear him. Later he remembered thinking that he was glad that Thig wasn't in the car. Then nothing.

46

Way back in fifth grade at Carmel River School, Chris had broken his hand in a fight during morning recess. He was playing Four Square, which was serious business back then, on the lower playground when one of his largest classmates, ironically named Eugene Small, started hassling a younger and smaller kid also playing in the game.

By that age Chris had already been indoctrinated by Margaret with regard to two things: first, you never made fun of other people, particularly those less fortunate than you, and second, when you observe that type of treatment, you do what you can to intervene on behalf of the recipient.

Chris had defended the younger kid with as much righteous indignation as he could muster at that age and had broken the fifth metatarsal in his right hand when he punched the larger opponent in his fat stomach. His hand just seemed to disappear into the folds of Eugene's cellulite deposits.

That was hardly the first punch he'd thrown, but he wasn't a particularly large person at that age. The bone had broken in two places, and by the time he'd gone to the hospital, the bone fragment had migrated into the middle of his hand. The surgery to repair the break and insert a metal pin to hold the bone in place was the first and only time Chris had been under a general anesthetic.

He remembered waking up in the recovery room after the surgery with Margaret standing next to him. The nurse had asked if he knew where he was. He'd responded, "I'b in da recabery rooooom."

Some twenty-seven years later, Chris spoke those words again, now to no one in particular, as he awoke lying on a cot. He blinked several times and tried to lift his right hand to rub his eyes. It was then that he noticed an IV tube attached to that hand. He rubbed the crust from around both eyes and wiped at the drool that had evidently ran down right side of his cheek.

The room he was in felt dry and hot. He could see sunlight streaming in through a narrow window about five feet above the small door. Both the walls and the floor were made of unfinished wood. So, he thought, not in a hospital.

Chris felt dizzy. Even without moving his head, the world spun madly. He closed his eyes and tried to calm his stomach.

Before sitting up, he took stock of the situation. What had he been doing? No answers were forthcoming.

Keeping his eyes closed for the moment, Chris wiggled his feet. They were both still attached and functional. He slowly began tensing the muscles in his legs. There was soreness, but nothing appeared to be broken. His left arm, however, was in a cast and didn't feel great. He could wiggle his fingers, though.

His head also hurt like hell. With his right hand he gently felt around his head and found it to be wrapped in bandages. His hand brushed his cheek during that tedious effort, and he could feel at least a couple of days' worth of stubble growing there.

Chris put his arm back down, exhausted from the effort. He could feel his heart pounding in his chest. What the hell had happened to him?

There was something. What was it? He lay there for quite a while struggling to focus. Every time his mind seemed to lock onto an image or a concept, it would just as quickly spin away to be replaced by something completely unrelated. He thought of Thig, then of dense sponges growing along the underside of sunken ship. He could see the house he grew up in quite clearly before it dissolved into an image of the Bat Signal shining in the sky above Gotham City.

This must be madness, he reflected at one point, then that notion also passed into oblivion.

Several hours, or minutes, later, Chris finally found his mental state stabilizing. His ability to focus returned. He opened his eyes again to find the room remaining stationary. Sunlight still shone through the single window in the room, but not as strongly or directly as before.

A car crash? Yes, that was it. He'd been driving down the hill on Highway 1, and he'd been in an accident. That black truck had jumped out and ran right into him—intentionally.

Even with half his wits, it didn't take much of an imagination to figure out who had been behind the accident—Darrell English and crew, though he could effectively rule out Kevin and the two other guys with him.

So where was he now? He'd survived the accident only be taken to what? A barn? Why wasn't he at CHOMP? And, perhaps more curious, since he was not a CHOMP, why was he being cared for at all? How would his continued existence serve Darrell and his group of thugs?

The synergistic effect of the head trauma and the multitude of unanswered questions exacerbated Chris's headache. Clearly, they, who ever "they" were, weren't administering any type of pain medication through the IV.

Motivated by his total uncertainty about his current situation, Chris forced himself to sit up. It was a tricky maneuver given a cast on one arm and an IV tube sticking out of the other. But he persevered and negotiated his way to a sitting position. His head immediately swooned, but he remained sitting.

Looking down at the rest of his body for what felt like the first time in a while, he could see that he was wearing a traditional hospital gown, as well as a pair of shorts made from the same material. There were pale blue socks on his feet. He sat for several minutes, contemplating the eight feet between himself and the door.

He'd had some experience with this type of situation before. In college, he'd broken all the bones in his right foot while surfing in large winter waves. He was a "goofy foot," which meant he stood on the surfboard with his right foot forward. As he dropped down the fifteen-foot face of what would be his last wave for several months, a small bit of chop popped his foot up off the board for a split second. But in that split second the entirety of his weight, moving quickly down the face of the wave, landed on the foot and bent it in half.

The break was bad, almost a compound fracture, and he'd spent the first few days on the couch elevating his leg so that the swelling would come down sufficiently to allow the doctors to cast it.

Of course, nature called and he'd tried to make his way to the bathroom. Halfway to his destination, right in the geographic center of the room, with no source of support, he toppled, landing right on the broken foot. The pain had been excruciating, and he'd not tried to move again for the next twenty-four hours after he'd returned to the couch. But, as he learned when the doctor next looked at his foot, the fall had actually set the five bones.

So Chris's one data point from this type of situation suggested that there might be a long-term benefit to attempting a run for the door. If he'd learned anything as a scientist, it was "trust the data." Logic suggested that in all likelihood the door would be locked. But he needed to get his body used to moving around, so if it was locked, so be it.

Delaying no further, Chris stood and took his first steps toward the door, using the IV stand to stabilize himself. Those steps were followed by two more in the opposite direction, and he found himself dropping back onto the cot exhausted and in pain. Within seconds he passed out.

47

Chris awoke twice more over the next twelve hours. In each case the darkness of his room was complete and his exhaustion remained. But it was also notable, he thought, that while some pain persisted, the swirling disequilibrium he'd experienced earlier was definitely abating.

When Chris awoke the next time, the sun was once again shining through the window. He sat up quickly with little discomfort. He could feel the wooden floor vibrate under the approach of someone coming down a hall outside his room.

Choosing not to feign unconsciousness, Chris waited as the footsteps stopped immediately outside the door. The door opened to reveal a stern-looking pear-shaped woman carrying a tray of food with what looked to be two very strong arms. She looked like an artist's conception of an evil nurse, too authentic to be believed.

"Ah, you're awake. Good." Her gravelly voice suggested to Chris a lifetime of smoking.

She set the tray down on the bed beside Chris and grabbed his right arm to take a blood pressure reading. Next, she held Chris's chin in a vice-grip and flashed a pen light across both pupils. Looking into her eyes, Chris saw nothing, neither evil nor kindness. She was an automaton conducting her responsibilities with little relish and no extra effort. She examined the fingers extending from his cast and re-wrapped his head in new gauze.

Evidently content that he wasn't in imminent danger of dying, the woman returned to the door, offering over her shoulder as she pulled the door closed, "Eat. I'll be back in an hour to pick up the tray."

Chris didn't need to be encouraged to eat. He would've eaten the bed sheets soon if food hadn't arrived. The plate of apple sauce, mashed potatoes, steamed broccoli, and a wheat roll couldn't even qualify for a coach class airline meal. But Chris wouldn't have complained had anyone been listening.

Without his watch, Chris disconnected from time. He recalled reading once that the ability to accurately measure the passing of time without a timepiece was a mark of high intelligence. His inability to do so in his current predicament irritated him.

Maybe he was brain damaged, he thought, with his possibly damaged brain.

He slept again for what felt like hours. The nurse returned within some period of time, pushing a wheelchair.

"I'm happy to walk if you tell me where I am and where I'm walking to." Chris tried to stand. He feigned dizziness and dropped back onto the cot. The truth of the matter was that he actually was beginning to feel better. "Or not," he offered. There could be benefits to perpetuating the notion that he was in weakened state.

The impassive gaze he received in reply to his request suggested he wouldn't be learning much from Nurse Ratched, the only nasty nurse from popular culture that he could remember. She'd terrified the young Jack Nicholson in *One Flew Over the Cuckoo's Nest*.

"Is this CHOMP's new western wing? They've really taken 'western' to heart, haven't they?" offered Chris, warming up.

Nurse Ratched didn't appear to be amused, so he followed with, "I'm certain you're laughing on the inside." When in doubt, antagonize, antagonize, antagonize.

The nurse lifted him into the chair with surprising strength. He decided to dial back the antagonism.

48

Nurse Ratched wheeled Chris out of the room and into a long hallway. They appeared to be in the worker's quarters on a ranch somewhere. Chris noted five numbered doors on either side of the hallway, all closed. The building was eerily quiet, the only sound coming from the slow hum of the wheelchair as it rolled across the creaky floor boards.

They exited the hallway and came out into the warm mid-day sun. Chris was temporarily blinded as his eyes struggled to adjust to the infusion of bright light. Looking down, he could see he was on a path made of decomposed granite.

As his eyes adjusted, he took in more of his surroundings. The path was lined by low-relief shrubs and what appeared to be dry grasses. Small, solar-powered light fixtures were planted at three to four-meter increments, and he could see rabbit droppings under some of the low bushes.

He was in a valley. The golden, grassy hills around him were dotted with oak and eucalyptus groves, a stray cow visible here and there among the trees. It certainly felt like California, but precisely where was less certain. He could be two miles, or two hundred miles, from Carmel in a landscape like this.

The nurse wheeled him across the garden to a large marble patio. Uncomfortable, ironwork patio furniture sat unused on the patio. Someone's idea of what a patio should look like, but not a patio that was regularly enjoyed.

The patio abutted the rear of a large house. Chris had never been to Tuscany, but that was the first association that came to mind as he looked up at the looming structure. Massive stucco walls were painted a deep ochre. Regularly spaced windows were accented with ironwork planters, and many of the second and third stories had small iron balconies large enough for two people to stand abreast.

Darrell English "hung out a lot at a ranch in the valley." That had been what the guy at O'Grady's had said right before the police shot him. This could be that ranch. But if that were the case, what was he doing here? Again, he asked himself why anyone would first try to kill him, then go to the trouble of convalescing him? And what were the chances that Mac and Hendrix were going to find him?

With no answers forthcoming, their walk across the patio ended at two open French doors. It was interesting to Chris that he'd yet to see or hear evidence of another human being—no car engines, no distant weed whackers, no radio or television.

Nurse Ratched wheeled Chris across the threshold and into a cavernous room two stories high. Elaborate, dark wood bookshelves lined the walls. Tapestries and large paintings filled any wall space not occupied with books. Three crystal chandeliers evenly spaced across the room provided illumination, though the natural sunlight coming in through the French doors and the surrounding windows needed no support.

Of greater interest than the room's decor, however, were the people sitting in the room. Several brown leather chairs and couches had been arranged into a U-shape at the center of the room. Nurse Ratched wheeled Chris into the opening of the U and set the brake on the chair.

To Chris's immediate left sat Mr. and Mrs. Dean. Around the rest of the half circle sat six other people—all appeared to be in their sixties or older and all were looking at him with a mixture of interest, curiosity, and open hostility in at least one case. The gender ratio was slightly tilted toward the males. The body language of everyone in this room said very clearly that Chris was the only one held against his will.

Seizing the initiative, Chris reached out with the cast on his left arm and wacked Mr. Dean across the forehead, sending him reeling back into his chair. The move was extremely painful for Chris, but worth it nevertheless. While he didn't yet understand what was going on here, it probably was not good, and he intended to go down swinging.

"Went a little overboard on the sunscreen, didn't you, Mr. and Mrs. Dean, or whatever your names are. Or was the trip to Hawaii as big a load of crap as everything else you've said?" Chris let a little irritation creep into his voice but betrayed no overt concern over his situation. He wasn't yet feeling panicked, and he definitely didn't want to convey it either way.

A couple of tough guys materialized out of nowhere to approach Chris. They were both large, and they didn't look as stupid as Vans and Acid, but before they had a chance to visit their toughness upon Chris, they were waved away by the stern-looking man sitting immediately to his right.

"Now Chris, there's no reason to be rude. We're hoping that we can have a reasonable discussion with you."

The man was wearing a bowtie. How reasonable could Chris be expected to be with a man who looked like Orville Redenbacher?

"On the contrary, my dear Orville," Chris replied, the essence of reasonableness, "I would counter that if you and your friends are expecting a reasonable conversation, you're all fucking crazy."

While speaking to the man to his right, Chris could see that Mr. Dean had regained his position at the front of the chair. So he reached out again, nailing Dean on the nose and bloodying it.

"Son of a bitch!" came the muffled scream from Dean as his hands went to his nose to stem the bleeding. Mrs. Dean leaned over with a handkerchief to help her husband.

This time the heavies came over and grabbed Chris forcefully by the upper arms. He didn't try to resist, but he also refused to cower before them.

"We've made every effort to treat your wounds following your unfortunate accident," countered bowtie with some obvious frustration. "I should think some gratitude is warranted."

Speaking as though he were having a cocktail with friends, Chris replied, "You appear to have made every effort to cause my unfortunate accident and to keep me from a real hospital. My gratitude knows some limits, I'm afraid."

The woman to the right of bowtie spoke up. She was pleasant enough looking, the model of an aging business woman. "Please understand that *we* didn't cause your accident. And we've done everything we can to return you to health."

"I stand by my earlier assessment," Chris said. "I think we can debate that point. But nevertheless, perhaps we can discuss why I'm sitting in a wheelchair, with a cast on my arm, bandages around my head, in a house I understand to be owned by Darrell English." He was going to have to get these people riled-up to see what he was really dealing with.

"This house isn't owned by Darrell English," Mrs. Dean said.

"Fine, rented, stolen, whatever. I don't know English personally, but I see his sense of style, or lack thereof, is about what I'd expect. Aren't we a little far from Tuscany?"

The man on his right spoke up again, this time more gravely. "Mr. English is no longer with us."

"With us? You killed your own guy?" Chris said, astonishment in his voice. "I wish you'd done that a little sooner."

"He outlived his usefulness, I'm afraid, and his unorthodox methods ran counter to our interests. So, he was dealt with in the most severe terms."

"Unorthodox methods!" Chris yelled. "Listen, motherfucker, one of my closest colleagues is dead. She was the nicest person I've ever known, and she's dead because of you and this band of throwbacks." He tried to get out of his chair but was constrained by the heavies.

Having calculated his odds of survival as grim, Chris decided to press onward.

"Two of your goon squad attacked me. And I caught one of those guys later trying to kidnap my mother. I don't know what you're expecting of me here, but I have to tell you that each one of you is fucked once I'm back up and running. I'll not stop until you're all history."

"Please, Dr. Black, vulgarity isn't necessary," the woman said. "You are quite isolated here. No one is coming to rescue you. You've got no choice but to listen to what we have to say."

"Right. Less swearing," said Chris. "Fuck you."

"Dr. Black," said the man to his right, now clearly irritated, "I'll remind you that you're a guest here."

"A guest?" Chris laughed. "That's rich, man."

Undeterred, the man continued, "And you're at our collective mercy in your current condition. I believe it would be best for you to hear us out."

"I'm all ears," Chris replied.

"The six of us here in the room represent a business consortium of sorts, along with a few others. This consortium has persisted for decades through the judicious allocation of power and influence."

"A business consortium?" Chris said. "You've got to be kidding me. I feel some more vulgarity coming up."

Bowtie's eyes flashed. "Oh, we've worked on behalf of society. Since the early 1960s the greater Monterey Peninsula has benefitted from many of our initiatives, all of which have occurred beyond the public eye."

"I'm riveted, please continue."

"For instance, in 1982 CHOMP was going to be shut down, and the Peninsula would've been without a major medical center. We intervened in the real estate deal at the eleventh hour and made sure that the deal was altered to make a renovation of the hospital more profitable than removing it. Now we have the stunning structure that you and the rest of your generation have come to know and likely fail to appreciate.

"In 1972, still before your time, water politics on the Peninsula threatened to make golf—one of the most redeeming qualities of the area and also one of the most profitable—no longer feasible. After several of the people before you intervened, the focus on the water got diverted away from our cherished golf courses.

"I see that you're unimpressed. Perhaps an example that's closer to home will help." And the man nodded to Mrs. Dean.

Mrs. Dean explained, "In the late 1990s, the placement of a new building on the grounds of the university's marine laboratory was anything but assured. However, this group imposed its will upon key state and local officials, and the building was approved. So you see, without our efforts there would be no Center for Marine Exploration."

"Perhaps I might interject," Chris jumped in, ignoring the propaganda. "Can you clarify for me how dumping barrels of automotive waste and human remains offshore is in the interest of society? I'd be interested to hear that rationale."

Bowtie returned to the discussion. "As I mentioned, there have been times when the unorthodox methods of our personnel depart from our long-term goals. The waste disposal was a regrettable turn of events. We're certain that the authorities, along with your capable assistance, will be able to rectify the situation."

"Bullshit. It would be charitable to suggest that these 'personnel' are capable of independent thought. You guided them. And how about murder and kidnapping? How does that benefit society?

"You tried to have my mother, a child psychiatrist and longtime member of the community, kidnapped. All because her son happened to have located the sludge your stooges dumped in Carmel Canyon. I would venture to say that you and your group are full of crap. You've been drinking your own Kool Aid too long. Drop the altruistic bullshit and stick with the business motives. At least it's authentic."

The man sat back. "We had hoped that you were someone with whom we could reason. Someone worthy of inclusion in our consortium."

"If by inclusion you mean beating the shit out of all of you, then yes, I'm with you. I very much look forward to attending the next meeting."

The man looked around the room at each of his colleagues. In his defense, Chris thought, he did look genuinely dismayed.

Bowtie waded in for one last attempt to bring Chris around. "If you joined us, Dr. Black, we could multiply your contributions to the field ten-fold. Our donors could support your research beyond your wildest dreams."

Chris looked at the Deans. Right. Bowtie continued.

"You would leave a legacy that surpassed all other marine scientists in the region. The CMEx would become a focal point for cutting-edge research that exceeded even the Scripps Institute of Oceanography down south or the Woods Hole Oceanographic Institution back east. You can't tell me that such an offer doesn't interest you.

"And, I should say, nothing more would happen to your family and friends. Once you're in the fold, as it were, we'll be able to contain this latest outbreak of unpleasantness and cease the hemorrhaging of vital information."

"Even if I were of a criminal mind, why would I associate with a group that's so clearly inept? You dumped waste within sight of shore. The authorities will be able to trace that waste whether I'm around or not. Your tough guys failed to get the better of a few scientists. You guys seem to be a textbook case of how *not* to commit crime."

Bowtie nodded, then motioned to one of the goons standing behind Chris. "We no longer require Dr. Black's presence. Please see to it that he's dispatched with all due haste."

"Well, let's hang on a second." A newcomer walked in the door from the interior of the house. He was carrying an automatic weapon in his hands and didn't look happy. "Why don't you put that gun down." He motioned with his own weapon to the man behind Chris.

Two other men, also carrying guns, followed the newcomer in and spread out to the left and right. One took up position on the far side of the couches, while the other stopped somewhere behind Chris.

"Darrell, what a surprise," Bowtie said with little enthusiasm.

49

Chris turned to look at Darrell English more closely. Now this was interesting. Risen from the dead, it seemed—all the better.

Darrell looked at Chris. "That's right, Black. I'm your man. I've been keeping this group of old fucks going for years. They wouldn't know which end was up if it weren't for me." Chris had never seen English before, but he looked somewhat worse for wear. His face was dominated by dark circles under red-rimmed eyes.

He turned to Bowtie, showing open scorn. "Harvey, you never send one of my own boys to kill me. Never. Poor Skerry, he had no idea what he was doing. The idiot came sneaking up the side of the repair shop right in view of an external camera. I was waiting for him when he burst through the door. End of story."

Darrell then pointed his gun at Bowtie, whose name apparently was Harvey. Harvey looked at Darrell with a defiant look that suggested no one of Darrell's poor breeding could possibly harm someone like him. He sat up straight and neatened his bowtie. He looked like he was prepared to resolve this petty crisis with his characteristic aplomb. He'd no doubt weathered many a crisis over the years.

Then Darrell smiled and shot him in the stomach.

There was a collective gasp from the group. Mrs. Dean screamed.

The loud report from the weapon left a ringing in Chris's ears.

Harvey looked down at his hands, now covered with blood. He coughed twice and more blood erupted from his mouth. He still looked more shocked than anything else. The bullet had gone straight through the abdomen, piercing the stomach. As Harvey sat there his stomach juices flowed out into his body cavity and mixed with the massive amounts of blood collecting there. Even if he weren't going to die in a matter of minutes, the toxic cocktail of stomach acid and blood being mixed in his abdomen would've killed him anyway.

"Help him for God's sake!" The woman to his right moved to the edge of her seat. "Somebody do something." Her vehemence tapered off as she finished her sentence and looked around at the rest of the group.

Darrell, weapon still in front of him, looked around the group, challenging each member of the consortium to attempt something. "I don't think so," he said evenly. "Let's let Harvey enjoy the experience. Hurts, doesn't it, Harve?"

Harvey was now fading fast. He'd coughed up more blood, and his eyes were glazing over.

"Now, we're not all here," Darrell observed. "Where's the good doctor? Too uncomfortable with the dirtier side of the business?"

Doctor? Which doctor? Chris wondered.

"Doesn't matter. I'll deal with him later." Darrell looked at Chris. "Now, Black. You've been a real pain in my ass. A real pain. The whole operation was moving along swimmingly until you came along and fucked it all up."

"Darrell English," Chris said. "I've been looking forward to meeting you." Out of the corner of his eye, Chris saw a small red light flash three times high on the wall behind English. He recognized it immediately as a laser sight. The three flashes were a signal. Mac and Hendrix had found him.

English's eyes flared a bit. "Really? I'm sorry we didn't get a chance to meet earlier before you had your little accident. I would've liked to kick your ass when you didn't have a cast on your arm as an excuse."

"Yeah, that's a real shame," Chris said. "The rest of your team is dead, and your own team tried to kill you. You're not doing too well."

In the next couple of seconds, several things happened in quick succession. Before English had a chance to respond, English's guy behind Chris grabbed for the wheelchair. Too focused on grabbing the chair, the guy missed the red laser dot hovering on his chest. Before he was able to put his hand to the chair, the guy was shot from somewhere out on the patio. The shot was silenced, but the thwap of the bullet hitting a body, combined with the tinkle of glass resulting from the bullet's trip through the window, gave it away as the man dropped to the floor.

English dove for the ground as more tinkling glass fell.

English's other guy was hit, but he remained standing long enough to open up with his semi-automatic. He sprayed bullets in the general direction of the patio. Glass from the French doors and all the rear facing windows rained down upon the travertine patio outside.

The two other henchmen, now willing to unite with Darrell's group, also turned and manically fired outside with their pistols. Sweating and wild-eyed, their shots went wide, high, and low, in perfect counterpoint to the strategically placed, laser-focused shots coming from outside.

Harvey, now dead, sat morbidly erect in the chair where Darrell had shot him, his face a grotesque mask of the surprise and pain that consumed him in his last seconds of life. The five remaining members of the "consortium" cowered on the floor between the couches, too afraid to move. One of the Deans had been hit by a stray bullet and was bleeding onto the floor, but they were cowering so close together that it wasn't possible to determine which of the two had been hit.

Like the others in the room, Chris sought the cover of the chairs so as not to be hit by the random shots fired by Darrell's goons. Working his way around the chair on his elbows, to avoid putting direct pressure on his injured left arm, Chris found Darrell sitting behind one of the couches, checking the clip on his automatic weapon.

Several more bad guys flooded into the room from the interior door and took up firing positions behind the couches. As their number and rate of fire increased, so did the strength of the assault from the patio. The roving red dots of laser sights danced about the couches and walls.

A flurry of bullets struck the couch immediately next to Chris, hitting the bad guy next to him in the neck and face. The man died instantly and dropped where he stood.

After a few seconds, Chris looked up to find Darrell English nowhere in sight. He grabbed the gun from the fallen bad guy, including a couple of extra clips visibly protruding from the man's jacket pocket.

About half of the newly arrived bad guys were already down, either dead or critically injured, and the attention of those still alive was directed out the French doors onto the patio. Not knowing where English had gone but guessing that he'd left through the door immediately behind his previous position, Chris crouched and moved as quickly and quietly as he could through the door, his no-slip socks proving useful for the occasion.

Through the door, he found himself in a wide hallway leading away to the right and the left. Paintings and large tapestries lined the walls in both directions. Chris did a quick double take when he spotted a suit of armor standing along the wall to the right. Was that a common design move in faux Tuscan villas? Medieval armor?

Where did Darrell go? Pausing for a moment, Chris could hear a muffled crash coming from somewhere to his left. He checked the weapon again and ran down the hall. If Darrell chose to come back this way with his automatic weapon, Chris thought, there would be little cover available in this hall. But fortune favors the foolish.

The hallway ended at a grand entryway dominated by a chandelier with elaborate marble staircases on either side. Chris had covered the open area in seconds, but English was still nowhere to be seen.

Seeing the front door ajar, Chris moved over to investigate. He tentatively poked his head around the door frame and was greeted with a hail of bullets that sent wood and stucco fragments flying in all directions. He dropped to his left and hoped that the front wall was constructed of something other than cardboard. He tried to roll to avoid putting any weight on his left arm, but the move was incredibly painful nonetheless.

The wall held, and he was briefly protected from the hail of bullets. Chris collected himself and took stock again of the situation. His cast was still solid, but the arm inside it was screaming. His right hand hurt and was bleeding from where he'd torn the IV out when he ran from the wheelchair. His head also hurt like hell, but his mind was clear. He also lacked shoes. But among his many problems at the moment, at least he'd yet to slip and fall, thanks to the blue booties.

Chris briefly assessed the weapon he'd grabbed from the dead thug. Mac had taught him a thing or two over the years, for which he was grateful at the moment. The gun looked like a 9 mm pistol. He ejected the clip and found it to be nearly full, probably ten or eleven rounds remaining. He found the safety and turned it to what he hoped was the off position, then checked to confirm that there was a round in the chamber.

The hail of bullets stopped abruptly. Chris's ears continued to ring loudly through the new silence. The gun battle at the back of the mansion, if still going on, was out of earshot. The sound of a car engine being gunned penetrated the ringing and broke Chris out of his trance.

English represented a clear threat to Margaret and Abby. Plus, Chris owed him for Gretchen's death. He couldn't be allowed to get away.

As Chris peered around the shattered door jamb, a black Land Rover was fishtailing at the far side of the gravel drive as English made his escape. Stepping through the door and on to the outer landing, Chris pointed the pistol at the rear of the Land Rover and pulled the trigger.

The first pull on the trigger took some effort, but the action became significantly easier as he continued to pull. The rapid pace of his shots precluded an accurate count, but he thought he must have fired at least a dozen shots at the Land Rover in the first couple of seconds. The rear window shattered, and the tailgate took several hits, but there was no other obvious damage to the vehicle.

Chris stopped to slap in a new clip, but in the next moment the vehicle swerved awkwardly and shot off the road. There was no overcorrection this time, and the truck launched over the side and out of sight down an embankment.

50

"Chris!" It was Mac coming from behind him. Chris couldn't give words to the solace that washed over him.

"Mac! English just went down in that ravine over there. He may be injured, but he's definitely armed. I'm going in."

Mac looked Chris over briefly and tossed him another weapon. "Just happy to be here. You, however, look like shit. I heard you firing, your clip's shot. Take this one. Safety's off. Let's go." And then he added, "Watch your feet." The blue hospital socks weren't optimal off the marble floors.

"Abby, my mom, are they alright? Did anyone get to them?"

Mack answered quickly, looking right at Chris, "They're both fine."

Perhaps, Chris processed quickly, the group's attempt to kill Darrell had inadvertently saved Abby and his mom.

Chris and Mac ran together across the drive. Now that he was outside again, Chris could hear scattered fire behind them on the other side of the mansion. He and Mac slowed as they approached the ravine. It would be a pity to have survived this far only to be shot for not being patient enough. At the edge of the ravine they saw the Land Rover leaning against an oak tree about thirty feet down a gentle embankment.

They approached the vehicle slowly, Mac on the driver's side and Chris on the other. The airbag had deployed, its saggy remnant hung from the steering wheel, draped onto an empty driver's side seat. There was no sign of English, but blood was dripping down the front of the seat and covered the door handle.

Instinctively, Chris and Mac both paused and listened for any sign of English's retreat through the brush. The wind blew through the oaks. The crows squawked at each other from perches high above the ravine. The shoot out behind the house had quieted. Hearing and seeing no sign of English, they slowly began to work their way farther down the ravine in search of his trail, Chris doing so as quickly as his socks would allow.

Oak trees were scattered at varying intervals along the edge of the ravine, their curved, gnarled trunks evoking haunted thickets. Mac signaled that he was going to move off to the left and up the opposite edge of the ravine. Chris gave Mac the okay sign and continued along his current path.

He'd barely traveled fifteen feet when English suddenly appeared from a tree immediately in front of Chris and fired a burst in Mac's direction. Chris saw Mac go down with unspecified injuries. Mac was wearing a bullet-proof vest, and Chris hoped it was enough.

English looked toward Mac and then began turning the weapon toward Chris.

Chris stepped forward to close the distance between himself and the barrel of English's automatic weapon. He thrust upward with his cast and disarming English as he fired. Pain radiated back up Chris's arm and stars burst in both eyes. He struggled to retain consciousness while trying to also anticipate English's next move.

That move came quickly. Darrell jabbed at Chris with his left fist and hit him squarely in the sternum. As Darrell was a big guy, the punch carried significant momentum behind it, but he stood slightly below

Chris on the hill and off-balance, standing on the uneven ground of the ravine. The blow wasn't what it could have been.

Chris knew that if he fell to the ground, Darrell would gain the advantage. His foot connected with Darrell's wrist, stopping the incoming punch.

Darrell screamed out in an unintelligible combination of anger and frustration. As he did so, he dove toward Chris and hit him in the midsection, knocking the wind out of him and forcing him to drop the gun Mac had given him.

Now both on the ground, Chris on his back and Darrell on his stomach, Darrell began to claw up toward Chris. Chris in turn kicked out again with his right foot, hit English on his bloodied left shoulder and sent him sprawling backward down the hill.

This put Darrell within reach of the gun Chris had dropped. As he reached it, Chris sat up and grabbed along the ground for anything to throw. His hand closed around a fist-sized piece of granite. In the instant before Darrell raised the weapon to fire at Chris, Chris threw the rock with accuracy he would've been hard pressed to repeat.

The rock hit English squarely in the throat. He dropped the gun, reached up to his throat with both hands, and fell backward onto his back. He landed hard on the rocky bottom of the ravine.

Running now on pure adrenaline, Chris got up pretty quickly under the circumstances and moved down the hill toward English. He bent and picked up the gun, then looked down at Darrell. The man's lips had turned blue, and his eyes, now devoid of life, were frozen.

Chris walked gingerly up the other side of the ravine to where Mac was rising to a sitting position.

"Got me in the shoulder," Mac said. "Just over from the vest. Do you think we're on the CMEx clock out here? I could use the workman's comp."

"Team-building exercises. Or maybe, extreme management training," Chris replied, slowly lying down next to Mac in the tall grass. "I'm your man. What's his status over there?" Mac gestured toward English.

"Code blue," Chris said, looking up at the sky through the canopy of oak trees above them. "He's gone."

51

Chris could hear sirens approaching from far off. He felt like he'd been dropped from a very high place, but it was okay as long as he didn't move. Mac appeared to be doing okay, as well. The experience of being shot wasn't a new one for him, though Chris had never been present to see it.

Hendrix and his team were the first down into the ravine after the action stopped in the house.

"Look at this yard sale." Hendrix peered down into the ravine to survey the situation. "Impressive, Black. You've totaled a $75,000 vehicle, taken out a bad guy, and got Johnson shot again. All while wearing your hospital nightie and those lovely blue socks. What are you going to do with the rest of the day?"

"I thought I'd go home and look at my abs in the mirror for a while," Chris replied, wincing at the pain in his ribs as he did so. "Maybe do a few other SEAL poses, then go out for a run in some tight shorts and reflective sunglasses."

Hendrix scowled, but a couple of the other guys laughed. "Make sure you don't drop Black on his head on the way out of there, guys. We wouldn't want to cause any more damage."

"On the other hand," Chris pushed his luck, "a little more brain damage and I'll be ready to work for you, Hendrix."

Now Mac was laughing from the stretcher he was being helped into. "You've got to admit, Hendrix, that for a nerdy scientist he did pretty well."

"There's always room for somebody who's willing to tackle dangerous situations wearing only a nightie. I can think of several jobs coming up where we could use that particular skill!"

"I'll have my people talk to your people," Chris offered, then he rested his pulsating head back down.

Eventually two of the team members helped Chris to his feet and, with his arms over their shoulders, carried him up the edge of the ravine. Two other guys carried Mac out on the stretcher behind Chris.

Back up in the main courtyard, the vehicles were beginning to pile up. Two unmarked vehicles with U.S. government plates were parked in front of a sheriff's deputy. Chris assumed that the rest of the vehicles belonged to the members of the consortium.

There was also some excitement as a variety of uniformed people tried to turn off the water on a fountain spraying water in all directions. It sat in the middle of the circular drive, and English ran over it during his flight in the Range Rover. The rainbows that formed in the mist created a bizarre counterpoint to the violence of the hour before.

Ambulances arrived to assist Chris and Mac and to tend to the wounded in the main house. Harvey's body was brought out in a body bag. Chris saw no one else come out, dead or alive.

That was explained quickly. A couple of additional cars arrived on the scene, which turned out to belong to lawyers who had been called by the surviving members of the consortium. The lawyers took in the circus outside then proceeded inside to consult with their clients. They used very nice handkerchiefs, Chris noticed, to wipe the drool from their mouths. He figured they'd quickly calculated the billable hours this fiasco was going to generate.

Chris and Mac shared a twenty-minute ride to CHOMP in the same ambulance, where Chris's considerable physical discomfort was amplified by his frustration at being unable to talk with Mac about what had been going on while he was in captivity. That would have to wait until they had some distance from prying ears.

52

Chris survived the ride to CHOMP, though his grasp of reality was faltering when he arrived. The same doctor who had stitched up his nose the previous week reviewed the work that was done on him while in captivity. An X-ray confirmed that the break in Chris's arm was well set. He'd broken both the radius and the ulna about halfway up his forearm, as well as at least two ribs. Chris requested a new cast anyway to distance himself from the experience. That, and he wanted a nice new blue one.

His head also seemed to be healing well. There were a number of new cuts all over his body from his pursuit and fight with English. His feet were particularly dinged up. But those would resolve on their own in time.

It must have been a slow day at CHOMP, middle of the day, mid-week, because Chris was eventually rolled into his own room; no annoying chattering or snoring roommates to put up with. There wasn't even another bed.

Chris had just gotten comfortable, pillows in exactly the right place under his arm, no throbbing, and was sitting back to watch a rerun of *Californication* when in came Margaret.

Tears were welling in her eyes as she came over to give Chris a hug. "My God. We thought we'd lost you. Are you okay?"

"I'm okay, mom." Chris gave her a one-armed hug with his right arm. It was good to see her.

"And how are you? Any more trouble?"

"No, no. No more trouble on our end. We've just spent the past forty-eight hours worried about you." She looked back toward the doorway.

Chris could see an older man in a doctor's white coat standing at the door looking down at some charts. He seemed more interested in the charts than he should be.

"Steven, please come in," Margaret said. "Chris, this is my friend Dr. Steven Larsen. Steven, this is Chris."

The man walked over and quickly surveyed Chris before approaching and clasping Chris's hand. He was of average height and weight and had close-cropped hair that was thinning at the top. But his presence was somehow commanding. He moved with the confidence of a surgeon who regularly holds peoples' lives in his hands.

He reached out with one of those hands and grasped Chris's. "Nice to meet you, Chris. I'm sorry it's under these circumstances. Your mother has told me a bit about your ordeal. It's all incredible."

"The truth is stranger than fiction. But it's nice to meet you as well, Steven," Chris said genuinely. This guy seemed solid. "I'm afraid I owe you an apology."

Steven and Margaret looked at each other quizzically, then back at Chris. "I'm afraid I was referring to you as Mr. Mysterio rather than the more appropriate Dr. Mysterio. No offense was intended."

Margaret sighed and Steven smiled. "Dr. Mysterio. I like the sound of that actually. Much more compelling than Dr. Larsen. I may have to use that."

"Be my guest!" Chris laughed, causing his ribcage to remind him that it had had enough for the day.

"I think we'll let you rest for a while, Chris. We won't be far. And there's someone in the hallway who wants to see you. I'll check on Mr. Johnson and come right back." Before Chris could suggest that she stay, Margaret swept out of the room.

"It was a pleasure meeting you, Steven. I look forward to getting together under more favorable circumstances."

"I'm in complete agreement. Rest up for now, young man." He too swept out the door.

Chris watched them go. As Abby's head appeared in the doorway, he smiled and waved her in.

Abby's approach was tentative, the expression on her face difficult to read. Was she happy to see him, but tentative because of his injuries? Or was there something else going on? Chris felt like his heart was in his throat as he awaited the answer.

She sat on the edge of his bed, resting her hands on his. "How are you, Chris?" she asked, her eyes not meeting his.

"I've had better weeks, but I'm glad to see you."

They sat quietly. Then Abby sat up as if to compose herself. "I don't have any experience with this, you know. Losing people through all this violence. Sitting up all night wondering what had happened to you, what was happening to you. It's just not normal."

Chris wasn't sure how to read her.

"It's absolutely horrible to miss someone so profoundly that you can't breathe," she interrupted. Chris couldn't breathe himself just listening to her explain this to him. "Right in the middle of all this stuff going on, you just simply disappeared." She took a deep breath. "So I've made a decision."

His heart had withstood a beating in the past couple of weeks, but he wasn't sure he was going to survive this encounter. Any remaining defenses he'd had were rendered useless at this point. He felt like he was dangling over the side of Bixby Bridge wondering how it would feel to hit the rocks below. Then Abby continued, "I don't ever want to lose you."

He turned his hand over slowly to clasp hers. "I'm not going anywhere," he whispered. "I, well—." He loved her. Right now, that felt more important than breathing.

"I have no experience with this type of life," Abby said. "I grew up in a stable, supportive environment in which no one was threatened, attacked, or killed. I've only lost one person in my life, and that was my eighty-nine-year-old grandfather. He'd had a good life, and his passing wasn't a surprise."

She drew a deep breath and continued, "I'm not proud of this, but I don't believe I have the constitution to live this type of life. As much as I may want to support you and the rest of the CMEx team, and as much as I may want to spend all my time with you, doing so in the context of this potential and realized violence just isn't going to work for me."

"But, Abby, these past two weeks are not normal for me either. I didn't like what was happening any more than you did. We could go the rest of our lives without another incident like this. In fact, I hope there will never be an incident like this again."

For the first time, Abby looked directly into Chris's eyes. "I don't know if you're drawn to trouble or trouble is drawn to you. But the net effect is the same. You live a dangerous life. Sure, so far you've been fairly lucky. But Gretchen is *dead*. She's not coming back."

She continued, her cadence increasing, "I'm not blaming that on you. Not at all. But think about the number of times you and Mac have been in these situations. You yourself admitted that the stories the students tell are only half of it."

Tears welled in Abby's eyes as she struggled to complete her point. "You guys don't look away when trouble comes, and that's so respectable. I'm in awe of what you guys have been able to do. But it's also extremely dangerous for yourselves and those around you."

Chris felt like he'd been decoupled from his body, as though he were observing the conversation from a position on high. He had once again put himself out there. He'd welcomed Abby into his life and lowered the defenses that had so effectively served him over many years. The payoff had been extraordinary. The affection he felt for Abby was clearly the most mature, the most complete, of his adult life.

Chris had allowed himself the luxury of envisioning a future with her, which he'd never done before. He'd ventured into otherwise unknown territory in which he considered a family and all the trappings of a "normal" life.

And yet, that life looked as though it would continue to prove elusive. However, as much as he wanted a life with Abby, he knew from her words that she was resolute. And he wasn't going to counter that resolution. Even from on high, a penetrating sadness overwhelmed and weakened Chris in a way that the fight with Darrell never even threatened. But almost as quickly as the sadness came, he felt the familiar numbness returning, as well. He rejoined his body, welcoming the numbness that would insulate him from the crushing sadness, the numbness that filed love and romance away in a virtual closet somewhere, possibly to be revisited at some point in the distant future.

53

"Yo, did somebody order a pizza?" Mac said as Margaret wheeled him into Chris's room in his wheelchair. His shoulder was wrapped and his color was off a bit, but he was otherwise unscathed. And he was indeed carrying a pizza.

"Wait just a second," Jase said as he wheeled himself in behind them in his own chair, followed by Dr. Mysterio. "How'd he get a solo room? I've got two phlegmy old men in my room. Makes me want to upchuck just thinking about it." The swelling had gone down considerably around his eyes since Chris last saw him, but his entire face was a deep purple.

Still numb from the conversation with Abby, Chris was happy to see his friends. "I think your plastic surgeon might need to be brought up on charges," he joked. "Or was eggplant the look you were going for?"

"Charges?" Mac added. "I don't think so. Given what the poor man had to work with, I think he should be congratulated. If it were me, I would've pulled the plug!"

"Honestly. The three of you are insufferable." Margaret looked at Steven. "They've been doing this since middle school. It's relentless. I don't know where it comes from. Certainly not from me. And both of their parents are completely normal," she added, gesturing toward Mac and Jase.

Once they were done with their friendly sarcasm, they began to review the past three days.

Jase had been here at the hospital recovering from the severe beating he'd received at the hands of Kevin and his goons. Fortunately, the internal injuries were minimal, so Jase had been able to direct all his attention to continually revisiting how he should have responded when the goons attacked him at Sarah Rothberg's house.

Mac, on the other hand, had been busy. Following their hasty departure from Kevin O'Grady's warehouse, he'd taken Jase directly to CHOMP. He'd driven him up the emergency room, left the truck sitting outside, and stayed with Jase while he was rushed back to be checked out.

Then Mac's first call was to Margaret. He spoke to her and everything seemed to be okay there. Abby and Thig were with her and the deputy was outside. He'd explained that Chris was on his way there and that there may be a new threat to her and Abby. Chris was to call him as soon as he arrived.

Expecting that Chris had called Deputy Anderson, Mac's second call had been to a former SEAL he knew with the FBI back in Washington, D.C. Mac had apparently saved the guy once upon a time in an operation that he wasn't at liberty to describe to the group without killing them after. But he suggested that the value of his assistance back then was sufficient to warrant support in the present. The call panned out exactly as he'd hoped. His friend had contacted agents at the Bureau's local Residence Agency in Watsonville, and Mac had decided to stay with Jase to wait for two FBI agents to arrive.

The nature and extent of Jase's injuries had attracted a great deal of attention among the emergency room personnel, so much that the doctor working on him had felt compelled to alert the police. There had been some tense moments following that alert.

Mac tried to explain the situation to the doctor, but the doctor was young and wasn't convinced of Mac's story. He went ahead with the call. However, when two officers from Monterey PD arrived, the doctor had hedged his bets and asked them to stay outside the room. They weren't thrilled to be told that they couldn't see Jase, but their attention had been drawn away when they spotted Mac. They noted that he had blood over much of his shirt, jacket, and pants and began to question him.

Having just been engaged in a fight with two dirty Monterey PD officers, Mac hadn't been particularly cooperative. "I was pissed and not in a mood to talk to them. I had no idea whether they were bad or not. In fact, I assumed they were probably fine, because how far could this little conspiracy really lead? But I still didn't want to talk."

Fortunately, the two FBI agents, Agent Smith and Agent Jones, had arrived in the middle of the growing altercation. Apart from wielding the power of the federal government, Agents Smith and Jones were both massive. Smith was a large black man with a shaved head and shoulders too large for any suit coat. Jones was a comparably large Caucasian with a flat nose that looked as though it had seen a fight or two.

They were quickly able to impose their federal control over the situation and keep Mac out of handcuffs, at least for the time being. The patrol officers, though not happy about it, clearly understood this was above their pay grade and decided to back off willingly to avoid being removed by Smith and Jones.

"What happened to the two cops who killed everyone at O'Grady's?" Chris asked.

"They've both disappeared," Mac said. "According to Smith and Jones, no one has seen them in the last seventy-two hours. Whether they're dead or not is unclear."

"Taking their badges was a sly, move Mac," Chris said. "Any evidence that other cops are involved in Monterey or elsewhere?"

"The Feds are working on it. I don't know where that stands."

Mac continued his recounting of the events. An hour had passed without word from Chris. Mac called Margaret's again to find out that Chris hadn't arrived. Unclear as to whom he could trust within the authorities, he decided to look for Chris himself. As he came down the hill on Highway 1, he encountered the scene of the accident. He found Chris's Land Rover demolished and lying in a ditch on the eastern side of the highway—no evidence of the other vehicle and no evidence of Chris.

There was some confusion as passersby tried to explain what they had seen. The accounts differed, but Mac found one tale particularly compelling. An American Eagle pilot was on his way to the airport from his house in Carmel Highlands when he saw the second vehicle in the collision pull away and move down the hill quickly with its lights off. When he reached the accident site and pulled over to stop, he could see several people removing Chris from the truck on the other side of the trees that lined the road. By the time he'd worked his way down the embankment and through the trees, the men had left.

"I always try to fly American Eagle when I can," Chris commented. "What are the Feds up to now?"

Mac replied, "I think they're going slowly until they can flesh out precisely who among local law enforcement was on the payroll. As you know, we didn't get a chance to question either Kevin or Darrell on that subject."

"It's probably a wash," Jase said. "Because O'Grady probably knew nothing about it. It's possible English didn't know either, but that's less likely."

"The consortium," Chris said. "The group out in the valley; that's how they described themselves."

Jase nodded. "I don't know everything that's going on out there today, but it seems likely that that's the explanation. They've evidently been at it for a long time."

Phone records on the recovered cell phones pointed to several properties in Carmel Valley that English and O'Grady had used for various nefarious purposes. Mac had called Hendrix and his team, and they'd arrived by 6:00 a.m. the next morning.

Mac and the team had spent the next twelve hours checking out the three locations that seemed most likely to be where Chris was being held, as well as looking for English.

English hadn't been located. After watching the three houses, they'd decided to move on the Tuscan villa once a trace of Chris's cellphone had placed it close to the building.

The team moved into place right before Chris was wheeled into the main house. They were outside watching and listening to the conversation through a directional microphone and moved only when they thought it was absolutely necessary.

"Cut it kind of close, didn't you? I mean, I was probably only seconds from pushing up soil." Chris was only half joking.

"Nah. On our way in we found what appeared to be a kill zone out behind the stables. It looked like they liked to take people out there to ice them. So we knew we had at least a few minutes. Besides, you looked like you were having so much fun. I enjoyed when you slugged the guy next to you with your cast. That showed real panâche."

"I'll show you some panâche," Chris said.

"Also, farther out, beyond the kill zone, we found a dump site that appears to be where they were filling the barrels with waste and other fun things before dumping them," Mac said.

Chris nodded. "I've been thinking about that. Since we found that barrel, I knew I'd seen barrels like that before, just couldn't remember where. Remember when we were talking to the local fishermen in Monterey about conducting a trawling study?"

"Vaguely."

"Well, at one point we went down to the fishing pier in Monterey to talk to a couple of captains, and I saw a bunch of barrels on the deck of one of those boats. I think it was called the *Lizzie J*."

"That makes some sense. Abby thinks that English might have owned a fishing boat. Anyway, the appearance of English and his goons was a bit unanticipated. He must have arrived before we did and stowed away in the house for a while."

Chris looked at Jase again. "So do we know who the members of this consortium are? I'd met the Deans, or whoever they are, before. But the rest of the crew was unknown to me."

"Dean is their real name. Harvey Williamson was the guy English shot. The other three were Patricia Mace, William Knight, and Susan Armstrong. All three are Carmel Valley residents and as far as we can tell have no records. They give every appearance of being solid citizens."

"Apart from the obvious, of course. But who put my cast on and worked on my head injuries? Nurse Ratched must have had help."

"Nurse Ratched?" Mac asked.

"*One Flew over the Cuckoo's Nest*," Chris answered.

"Ahh."

"We don't know," Jase said.

"English, when he first came into the room, said something about the doctor not being there," Chris said. "I remember thinking at the time that the group in the room seemed like real milk toast. The guy whom English shot was wearing a bowtie.

"It's tough to imagine them spearheading a major criminal enterprise and impossible to imagine them working with English and O'Grady directly on a regular basis. There has to be someone else, someone running the whole show."

"And that person is the doctor who worked on you?" Margaret asked. She looked at Dr. Larsen standing next to her, then back to the group. "Someone whose profession is dedicated to healing is orchestrating all these criminal activities—dumping, kidnapping, murder?"

"It wouldn't be the first time in human history that a doctor has done something like this," Chris said. "The question is, which doctor is it? Apologies to Dr. Mysterio here, but prior to meeting you, it had occurred to me that someone was trying to get close to my mother, possibly to learn more about what was going on."

"When was that?" asked Margaret.

"Do you remember my asking about your dinner plans that night? I think that was in the back of my mind."

Dr. Larsen nodded. "I can understand that, Chris. I'm greatly concerned by the notion that one of my brethren may be capable of orchestrating this. This is a small community, and the odds of my knowing the person are high. But I can tell you that right now no one obvious is leaping out at me. Is there any other information to go on?"

"I'm not yet convinced that there's someone else," Jase said. "The people who were there wield a great deal of power in this area. It isn't necessary for the story to have someone even more devious pulling the strings. But we, meaning all of us, city, county, feds, will be leaning on everyone associated with this case for some time. If there's another person, a leader, I expect that one of the people we have in custody will rollover on him or her. It's just a matter of time.

"Plus, we've got the FBI on the case now, as well as the federal EPA for the dumping aspect. There's going to be a great deal of heat coming down on this area for the foreseeable future. I can't imagine that this anonymous leader, if there is one, will be able to remain anonymous indefinitely."

54

Twenty-four hours later, Chris was released from the hospital in the afternoon with the cautionary note that he shouldn't be doing much for several days. His wounds were healing well, but the head trauma he'd experienced was significant, meaning, he supposed, that he was lucky his head was still attached.

He'd clearly been the beneficiary of fairly high-quality medical treatment immediately following the accident, however, where that treatment had occurred was still unclear. His cast and the dressings on his head were now part of evidence, though it was unlikely that they would yield any critical insights.

The room where he'd awakened at the ranch was the only one in that building configured to support human habitation. After a little more than twenty-four hours on site, the authorities concluded that his treatment hadn't been delivered on the property. He'd been treated elsewhere then transported to the Tuscan villa.

Hendrix and the SEAL team had stopped by Chris's room before departing for places unknown. "We'll be in touch with you, Black. This consultancy we've got set up is generating more business than we could have imagined. And not just tough guy work, but some fairly sophisticated and interesting stuff. Johnson seems to be hesitant to man up and join us, but you seem different. Plus, having a Ph.D. around would class up the joint. Probably even bring in *more* business. We'll be in touch."

"I'm always appreciative of anyone who recognizes my manliness over Mac's," Chris said, to general laughter in the room, except from Mac, who had sauntered into the room in the middle of the conversation.

"Wasn't it Rodney Dangerfield who said, 'I refuse to join any club that would have me as a member?'" Mac asked.

"Actually, it was Groucho Marx, but we understand the sentiment," Chris said.

Peter Lloyd had also stopped by the hospital to encourage Chris to get out of the hospital as soon as possible and get back to work. Margaret happened to drop by the room at the same time as Peter. They hit it off famously, as usual. Chris was simultaneously intrigued and paralyzed by the image of Margaret and Peter seeing each other socially. It hadn't yet been suggested by anyone, and since Steven Larsen was in the picture now, his concerns were likely unfounded.

On paper the two of them were perfect for one another; high strung, high functioning, high intelligence, and highly idiosyncratic. But the reality of their potential coupling might be anything but harmonious. Chris laughed aloud, drawing quick looks from both of them, as he envisioned them competing to prove who was the more independent of the two. While most couples sought increasing unity, it was unlikely that any relationship they might have would take that course. But one never knew.

Chris walked in the front door for the first time in what seemed like weeks to find himself slightly unbalanced by the scene. Less than a week had passed, and nothing had changed, yet everything had changed.

Everything was where he'd left it, some of it were things he'd considered important. But at that moment, returning to all this stuff, Chris felt as though he were returning to someone else's life—to the personal infrastructure of a completely different human being.

There was an obvious familiarity with some things. The kitchen was populated with dishes he'd used to make dinners for Abby, back when the prospect of a long and rewarding relationship with her stretched out before him. The living room was where he, Mac, and Gretchen had spent many an evening playing games or watching movies. His brain briefly entertained the reality that such activities were never going to be possible again, before it tried, by necessity, to move on to other more mundane and less painful preoccupations.

The end result of these mixed messages was a feeling of distance from the architecture of his former life. He'd felt this way before, after returning home from long international trips, and the feeling had invariably passed. But there was something different this time.

Chris went out through the screen door to the kitchen and onto the porch. Mac would, no doubt, find great amusement from the fact that his porch furniture also came from IKEA. But what the hell? It was comfortable, fairly bullet proof, and never required cleaning.

As Chris leaned back in the outdoor lounger and looked up at the gnarled oak branches framed against the backdrop of a steel blue sky, he let the sum total of the past few weeks wash over him in a way he'd actively avoided prior to this point. The immediacy of the omnipresent threat posed by Kevin and Darrell had prevented Chris from stepping back and taking the long view. Now, freed from that threat, the crushing pain of losing Gretchen and the incredible frustration of having let that happen washed over him.

Watching a squirrel overhead nimbly work its way along impossibly narrow branches, jumping from tree to tree, Chris realized the poignancy of what Abby had been telling him in the hospital. He did live a dangerous life. Not that he went looking for trouble, but if trouble was in the vicinity, he didn't shy away from confronting it.

Where this instinct came from was unclear. Growing up, he'd certainly had an abundance of opinionated guidance foisted on him by both Margaret and Andrew. That helped, he was sure. But to blame this righteous engagement with danger on his parents alone seemed to oversimplify the matter. They hadn't been uniformly responsible for anything in Chris's life for twenty years.

No, there was something else at work here, something less convenient. Were Margaret not his mother, he would have been comfortable seeking her advice. But Chris knew from experience that dealing with the issues of her own family knocked her off her game a bit. She wouldn't be "on," as she liked to say.

So, what would others have done when confronted by Vans and Acid? Run? How would many of his scientific colleagues have dealt with an intruder trying to kidnap their mothers? His suspicion was that a few would've put up a good fight and the vast majority would have either, literally or figuratively, rolled over. Was this the appropriate response in modern society? Perhaps. Perhaps it was the better part of valor to walk away from danger to live another day.

Would Gretchen still be alive if he'd acted differently? The answer was unambiguous from the very long view. If Chris hadn't engaged Gretchen to the extent that he did, had he not pushed her to come west and work in California, she would likely be alive now. Gretchen's death was directly attributable to his actions. He nearly vomited the hospital food remaining in his stomach at that thought.

The biggest fuck up had to have been their collective failure to understand the threat against them and to take even the most rudimentary steps to protect everyone involved in the project. What if everyone had been placed under guard after the initial attack against Chris? What if Chris hadn't asked Gretchen to come out and relieve him so that he could attend the dog and pony show in Pebble Beach?

While Chris knew that the multitude of "what ifs?" would get him nowhere, he could feel his general attitude circling the drain. Still, despite all his self-destructive impulses, Chris honestly couldn't see how he could have changed anything else once the shit hit the fan. Indeed, several others close to him might have been hurt, or worse, had he and Mac not gotten the upper hand on English and his boys before the game was up.

But then again, maybe that was pure rationalization from someone not prepared to render an objective perspective on something he was so close to.

He grabbed the half empty glass of orange juice that Margaret had poured for him before she left to pick up Thig and threw it hard against the side of the house. It shattered, sending glass and juice raining down on the deck.

"Is everything okay back here?" Chris's next-door neighbor, Mary, poked her head around the corner of the house. She had approached the back porch via side yard. "I saw you come earlier and thought I'd drop this off." She held up a *FedEx* envelope.

"Hi Mary. Sorry for the drama. It's been a rough few days."

"Margaret told me some of the highlights. I'm just glad you're okay. We can talk later."

Mary stepped around the orange juice and shattered glass to place the envelope on the table in front of Chris.

"This was delivered to Joan's house across the street last week. But she's away until January. I went over yesterday to water her plants and found it on the front porch."

Chris lifted the large envelope. The cardboard was slightly wrinkled, likely the result of having sat outside for multiple consecutive foggy nights. "Thanks, Mary. I'm sorry I'm not in much of a mood to talk just now."

"I understand completely. But please let me know if you need anything."

Chris flipped the envelope over and the sender information caught his eye immediately. Joe Rothberg.

"Chris?"

"I'm sorry. Thanks, Mary."

As his neighbor disappeared back around the corner of the house and into her own yard, Chris rested his cast on the envelope while using his good hand to rip open the end. He extracted six pages; the first two a handwritten letter from Joe, and the other four a list of what had to be the barrels that were dumped in the Carmel canyon and their contents.

The letter rambled, but eventually Chris found mentions of both Kevin O'Grady and Darrell English. Joe was pretty clear about Kevin, while his information about Darrell was less specific. He leaned back and closed his eyes at the recognition of how useful this information would have been had he received it on time.

Reading further, the last paragraph drew Chris to a standing position.

"You have *got* to be kidding me," he said to empty deck.

55

A week after Chris was out of the hospital, he found himself standing on the bow of the *MacGreggor* off the coast of Point Lobos. The tangerine sun was setting into a fog bank hovering several miles offshore. The air temperature was a seasonable sixty-five degrees with no wind.

His head no longer hurt, and the hair had begun to grow back around the areas that had been shaved. It helped that he'd cut his hair close, to deceive the untutored eye. The cast had largely become an afterthought, though there were the occasional unscratchable itches, and it smelled like some kind of exotic locker room fungus if one got too close.

The entirety of CMEx, including faculty, staff, and many students, as well as Jase Hamilton, Margaret, and the Clarks, had come to say goodbye to Gretchen and to disburse her ashes at sea.

The intervening week had been alternately unbearably sad and strangely celebratory as Chris had worked with the Clarks to plan the type of memorial that Gretchen would've liked. Gretchen's parents had settled on spreading her ashes at sea in an area she loved. There had been some procedural issues to work through regarding the legal disposal of ashes in state waters, but Peter Lloyd had stepped in to provide some assistance in that regard.

The *MacGreggor* had left the dock in the late afternoon and made its way south in calm seas to the waters off Point Lobos. The evening's wind had reversed itself from its standard onshore assault to a pleasant offshore breeze that carried with it the slightest scent of pine from the nearby headland.

As the sun set, the Clarks, together, poured Gretchen's ashes over the bow. The ashes briefly formed a mystical blueish-white cloud that hovered just below the surface before slowly dispersing into the environment that Gretchen had dedicated most of her young life studying.

One by one, each of the people in attendance quietly dropped a single white calla lily into the ocean.

Peter had chosen to ignore the standard prohibition of alcohol on the ship, so the assembled group retreated to the main salon for drinks. Chris nearly choked as he watched Peter take Margaret by the elbow and lead her back inside.

The sun had set behind the approaching fogbank, and the air temperature was dropping precipitously. Chris, Abby, and Mac remained behind on the bow watching the orange glow of the sinking sun plunge toward the horizon through the fog.

"Into a canyon deep," Mac said, "one last time."

"I really miss her." Abby looked down at the calla lilies as the current slowly drew them away from the ship's hull and out toward Japan.

"Me, too." Mac was slowly massaging the shoulder where Darrell had shot him.

Watching Mac work on his shoulder, Chris reflexively wiggled the fingers protruding from his cast. His hand was definitely feeling better.

"What happened to the two of you during that trip to SoCal all those years ago?" Chris asked his friend. "You went down there in a huff, but came back having crossed some threshold, the best of friends."

Mac was first taken aback at the question, but then he smiled. "Well, we headed south in the CMEx truck. We hit L.A. traffic at precisely the wrong time and ended up spending nine and a half hours getting to San Diego.

"We exchanged some small talk for a while, but eventually I just tuned out and drove while Gretchen put in her earphones and listened to something on her iPod.

"Somewhere near LAX we pulled off the highway to get something to eat. We opted for this small, authentic-looking burrito joint. By the time we got down to San Diego I was sick as a dog. Something I'd eaten hadn't agreed with me, and the lower GI problems were incapacitating. It was an all-around shitty situation, if you know what I mean."

"We got you." Chris chuckled despite the situation.

"I'd set up a bunch of meetings for the first day with a variety of vendors to start putting together the new ROV. The next two days were planned as sea trials with different vehicles.

"I was feeling so crappy in the early morning that I forgot to be angry with Gretchen and gave her all the materials I'd prepared for the meetings and went back to lie down in the bathroom. I figured she was going to cancel the meetings and hang out by the pool.

"By 5:00 p.m. that day I'd begun to return to the land of the living, and we'd arranged to meet downstairs at the hotel restaurant for an attempt at dinner.

"I arrived to find her holding materials from each of the eight meetings I'd arranged. She'd not only *not* cancelled the meetings but had attended each and apparently been on top of things. I don't know how she did it on such short notice, but she'd asked good questions and apparently used her feminine wiles to extract all kinds of deals out of the reps that I would've never been able to get."

"Feminine wiles?" Abby asked, feigning exasperation.

"Misogynist bastard," Chris offered.

"You know what I mean," Mac said, obviously nonplussed by either comment. "The next day we went to sea with the reps. It was a classic Charlie Foxtrot. Everyone, everyone that is except Gretchen, me, and the captain, was violently ill for the duration of the trip. Not just sick, but lying on the deck sick, praying-for-someone-to-end-their-lives sick. Not one of the reps provided useful information for the entire day.

"Once again, Gretchen stepped up and volunteered to work on the equipment with me. The two of us spent the day learning the new ROV systems on the fly, with no input from the reps."

Mac smiled. "By the end of the third day we were finishing each other's sentences while on the boat and drinking beers in the bar back at the dock. I'd heard you talking so highly of her all the time that I was skeptical. Plus, I'd just never had any experience with someone being so capable, yet so pleasant. Not a lot of positive female interaction in the SEALs or in engineering school, you know."

Chris just nodded.

"It would've sounded idiotic to suggest that she felt like my long-lost sister, but that's what it felt like. I just didn't feel like talking about it when we returned."

Abby nodded but didn't say anything. She appeared to be a captive of her own thoughts. When Chris realized that Abby had caught him looking at her, he quickly redirected his gaze out over the rapidly darkening water. A couple of sea lions had found their way out to the ship from the interior of Carmel Bay and were frolicking directly off the bow, leaping over one another. With the wind this calm, he could hear every exhalation the sea lions made at the surface before they playfully dove below the surface again.

Somewhere out there right now was a man, who had orchestrated all the nastiness that he and his friends had experienced these past few weeks. While most of their wounds would heal, Gretchen wasn't coming back. Her parents would never again hear her laugh. He, Abby, and Mac would never again be able to lie around with her and watch a movie or laugh at her well-timed jabs.

No, law enforcement wasn't going to resolve this satisfactorily. It was going to have to be settled a different way. But not today.

He put his arms around the shoulders of Abby and Mac and looked out at the fog-enshrouded Point Lobos. "I miss her, too."

56

Chris Black deployed the mainsail of the *Hippocrates* as the hull of the ketch steered into the three-foot swells. The sun had set, and a nearly full moon was rising in its absence. It was 9:00 p.m. on a calm, late-August evening. The grey gloom that characterized the weather on the Peninsula for the last couple of months had finally dissipated, leaving the evening sky a radiant show of heavenly bodies, perfect for a short evening cruise.

The yacht's running lights were on and as Chris walked back to the stern to join Henry Morris, he could hear a Beethoven violin concerto begin playing quietly over the sound system.

"No complaints about this weather," said Chris as he joined Morris in the yacht's cockpit.

"I agree completely," said Morris. "There's nothing like an evening sail to put things right on the day. Once we clear the mile marker, we'll tack our way north-northwest out into the bay and return with the seas. Should be peacefully uneventful."

Chris looked back over the stern at the harbor as it slowly receded. Only one other vessel was visible in the moonlight; it too was leaving the harbor. He stretched out his recently broken arm, clasping and unclasping his fist several times.

The physical therapy had gone quickly, and his arm was nearing full capacity.

"Thanks so much for the invitation to join you for a sail, Dr. Morris," Chris said. "This is much more enjoyable than a meeting in your office, or any office for that matter. Makes even a conversation about funding enjoyable to a scientist like me."

"My pleasure, Chris. I know it's been quite a summer for you, particularly all that nasty business back in June. I've been eager to meet with you and hear what you've come up with."

Chris leaned back and ran his hand over the polished teak deck. "The rhythm of a sailboat is so different than what I'm used to. I've spent probably forty days offshore in the past couple of months but always on a large oceanographic vessel. You get used to the diesel engines, I guess, and forget they're there most of the time. But at night, here under sail, it's truly remarkable how absolutely peaceful it can be out here. I feel a much closer connection to the sea on this yacht."

"This, my friend, is the primal connection that humans have had with the sea for millennia. There's no purer way to know the ocean and its depths," Morris said. "When you sail you literally travel in the wake of the ages."

"I must go down to the seas again, to the lonely sea and the sky," Chris muttered.

"And all I ask is a tall ship and a star to steer her by," Morris continued. "Exactly, my good man. I knew you were someone worth looking into."

Chris laughed and finished John Masefield's verse. "And the wheel's kick and the wind's song and the white sail's shaking; And a grey mist on the sea's face, and a grey dawn breaking."

"Hear, hear!" Morris enthused while Chris made a ceremonial bow.

The two men sat quietly watching the bow bounce against the barely visible horizon and listening to the waves lap against the hull. Every few seconds a splash could be heard, one of any number of nocturnally active sea creatures in the bay coming to take a closer look at the *Hippocrates*.

Eventually, Dr. Morris turned to Chris. "It's a pity that your Michelle Tierney couldn't join us tonight. I know that she likes to be involved in these little get-togethers."

"True. The Development Office likes to keep an iron grasp on you donors. But the potential for sea sickness is quite a deterrent. No one wants to get sick in front of a valued contributor. We'll have to soldier on in her absence."

"Indeed. So how can I help you and your team, Chris?"

"Well, Dr. Morris, I had a great plan in mind after we met that day at the Lodge—a plan that leveraged all the work we already have going at CMEx but that would lead us off in new and important directions. But I have to tell you, the events in June have altered my thinking these past couple of months."

"How so? What's changed for you?"

"As a simple marine biologist, I'm not convinced that I have anything to offer in terms of fighting the evil that men do. I'm not trained to deal with those situations nor am I vested with any authority in that regard."

"Be that as it may," Morris interrupted, "it's my understanding that you comported yourself quite admirably considering the attacks launched against you."

Chris waved his hand. "Sure, I did okay, but one does what one can when confronted by uninvited violence. It's a different thing altogether to invite violence."

"Hmmm."

"Anyway, I was also not prepared for my visceral response to the dumping of waste in Carmel Canyon. Seeing that field of barrels covering the seafloor made me sick."

INTO A CANYON DEEP

"Interesting."

"It sickens me further when I realize that nothing will be done about it."

"I hear you. So how can I help with this?"

Chris looked back over the stern and saw the running lights of a vessel gradually overtaking the *Hippocrates*. Time to finish the performance.

"Well, I'd like to launch my own clean-up effort, and I'd like you to pay for it, Dr. Morris. I think, if we do this right, we can clean up the mess and maybe even determine the culprit behind the dumping."

Morris raised an eyebrow. "But it's my understanding that the criminals have already been brought to justice or have met their maker, as it were."

"Several of those involved were arrested or killed. That's true. But the ringleader, the man behind it all, has remained elusive."

"Fascinating. This wasn't in the press."

"Yes, we kept it largely out of the press. We don't want 'Mr. Big,' as I've taken to calling him, aware that we're on to him until we're ready to act and act definitively."

"But Chris, what do you expect to find that would lead you to this 'Mr. Big?' And as you yourself said, as a marine scientist, what would you hope to gain with that information? Isn't this something better left to the authorities?"

Chris looked astern again. The other vessel, which had been slowly gaining on the *Hippocrates* as he and Morris talked, was close enough that he could hear its motor on the calm night. For the first time, Morris followed Chris's gaze and saw the boat closing on them. He looked at Chris, then back at the approaching vessel.

Chris watched as Morris went through some kind of transformation. A veil of darkness descended over Morris's eyes. He reached behind the cushion he was sitting on and pulled out a revolver.

Chris didn't react.

"Who's that back there, do you think?" Morris asked. "The authorities? Your friends from special operations?"

Feeling the weight of the wire taped to his chest, Chris knew that Jase and Mac were coming up in the boat behind him, but they were about a half mile back. Staring down the barrel of a revolver, Chris was beginning to wonder if this had been the best plan.

"I don't know what you mean by 'my friends in the navy,' but I guess if we wait a few minutes, we'll find out."

"No. I don't think *we'll* find out anything. You've outlived your usefulness, Dr. Black, and your SEAL friends are too far away to save you this time. I won't let them shoot up my boat the way they shot up my house." He pulled the trigger.

Morris's face contorted into a mixture of confusion and rage as he looked at the gun, baffled as to why it wasn't doing his bidding. He pulled the trigger three more times. Again, the hammer fell on an empty chamber.

"Bummer!" Chris said.

Morris shifted in his seat and quickly looked astern. This time Chris leaned forward and unleashed a vicious punch to Morris's face, breaking his nose and showering blood down the front of his shirt. Morris's head jerked backward from the blow, hitting the rail with a thud. But he was a strong man, and Chris knew that. He followed up with two more jabs before Morris had a chance to recover.

Chris then pulled a pair of handcuffs from his back pocket and quickly locked Morris's right wrist to the wheel, grabbing the gun from Morris and punching him one more time with it for good measure.

Through a bloody mouth, wiping more blood away from his broken nose, Morris shrieked, "What's the meaning of this? Why, I'll have you—."

"You'll have me what?" Chris injected, pulling a handful of bullets out of his pocket and jiggling them a bit in his open palm. "Beaten? Shot? Killed? Good luck with that. You haven't had much success so far."

Morris shook his right wrist violently. Gone was the amiable but rough-edged old man. The eyes that looked at Chris now were those of a violent predator. How this man had made a living doctoring to children was beyond Chris at that moment. The thought terrified him, but Morris didn't. He wanted to beat the hell out of the old bastard.

"I'll fucking bury you, Black. You, your little whore, and your bitch of a mother, too," he growled. "You're all fucking dead." Chris laughed.

"Who's that back there? The police? Excellent. I'll be out in a couple of hours, right about the time your house bursts into flame. When they find your bodies, there won't be much left to mourn. Nor will there be anybody left to mourn you because I'll kill them, too. I'll see them all buried."

"I'm glad you mention burial, you demented bastard. This all began because of the waste you tried to bury offshore. A rich cocktail of waste from your various businesses as well as the body parts of people who evidently ran afoul of your activities. It's perhaps the least imaginative criminal plan I've ever heard of and a huge ecological disaster right in your own back yard. I think you should have stuck to doctoring."

Morris yelled, "You think you know anything about me? About my activities? You have no idea how far my reach extends."

"I'm sure. 'And it all would've worked if it weren't for you meddling kids.' Right?" Chris looked astern and reached back under his fleece jacket and unplugged the small microphone that Jase had outfitted him with from the battery pack mounted in the small of his back.

After reading Joe Rothberg's letter, Chris's initial impulse had been to confront Morris directly. But Mac had convinced him that it wouldn't be wise to take on Morris until they were both healthy. Preparation for taking Morris down had given Chris new impetus to recover, and he'd worked feverishly to rebuild the strength in his arm. By August, both he and Mac had been back in action and had decided to bring Jase into the picture once they had a plan.

Predictably, Jase was unhappy that they had kept Joe's letter to themselves rather than turn it over to the authorities.

But sitting in Morris's presence, having just had a gun pulled on him, Chris decided that the plan was about to take a bit of a departure. It was time to settle Morris's account, as it were.

"Of course, I'm offended as a scientist and a citizen that you would dump that stuff into the ocean. But it takes a special kind of asshole to dump waste into one of the most beautiful spots on the planet."

Chris searched Morris's eyes for any sign of recognition, for any sign of guilt or regret. There was nothing.

"But the dumping was just the first act for you. Next you had your minions go on a killing spree. First, they killed Joe Rothberg. Then they mistakenly thought that we were onto the dumping scheme, and they focused on us. They killed one of the nicest people I've ever known and tried to kidnap my mom.

"Finally, you realize what a colossal fuck up your entire operation has become, so you had the cops kill Kevin O'Grady, and you tried to have Darrell English killed, as well. I finished that job for you, by the way. That wasn't in the papers, either."

Morris shook his wrist again, a feral primate unaccustomed to being constrained.

"What'd you do, see an opportunity in a young and tortured English that you could exploit? You'd seen Joe Rothberg, too. What about

O'Grady? How many more like Darrell are there out there, I wonder?
God help us.

"Finally, *you're* the one who fixed my injuries after the car accident,
which I'm sure you caused. Why was that, by the way? Why save me?"
The other boat was almost directly astern now.

"I thought you might be useful. And if you killed English, then I
see that I was correct." Morris was calming his breathing, preparing
himself for dealing with the authorities. "None of this matters. You can't
prove anything, and you won't touch me in court. Though you won't live
long enough to find that out."

"Oh, you think that's the authorities behind us? Wrong, fucko,"
Chris said. "No such luck. You killed my friend, Gretchen, and now I'm
going to kill you. No cops. No jail. No trial. You're history. You and this
piece of shit cork we're riding on are going to join all the waste you've
dumped at the bottom of the sea."

Morris moved to say something.

"Save it. You're taking a ride. Straight down. I figure, if you hold
your breath, you might make it a hundred feet or so at the rate this boat
will sink. But after that, curtains." Chris stood up.

"I'm just going down below for a minute and pull the plug on this
piece of shit boat of yours and send you on your way." Chris turned his
back on Morris and descended the four stairs to the salon. He could hear
Mac and Jase approaching.

Morris screamed and ripped again at the handcuffs binding him to
the boat with feral intensity. The handcuffs held, but the yacht's helm
broke under Morris's assault. From the bottom of the stairs Chris heard
the metal snap. He spun around to see Morris in mid-leap over the
starboard gunwale. Before he could do anything, Morris was gone over
the side and into the deep black water. Mac secured the small cabin
cruiser to the *Hippocrates* on the port side and Jase jumped across. Chris

bent over the rail, searching for any sign of Morris, but could see none. The black water betrayed nothing other than foam wake generated by the movement of the *Hippocrates*.

A deputy shined a bright searchlight from the rear of Mac's boat, scanning the water looking for Morris. The roving cone of white-hot light found only a calm surface; no evidence of Morris.

"What happened?" Jase yelled, shining a larger halogen light astern of the boat. "How did he get away from you? Why did your wire shut off?"

Chris answered Jase but didn't take his eyes off the roving searchlight. "I handcuffed him to the helm. Morris snapped it off somehow and jumped overboard before I could stop him." He paused. "I'm not sure what happened to the wire."

"We had him," Jase said. "You got enough on the wire to put him away for a long time."

Mac stepped onto the back deck of the sailboat and said, "Fuck him. We're at least ten miles out. It's dark, and the water temp is fifty-eight degrees at best. Morris isn't getting out of this one. He's shark bait."

Jase looked hard at Chris, willing him to say more, to admit more. Chris returned the look but remained silent.

Jase then moved back over to Mac's boat to confer with the deputy and call for a search helicopter. Beethoven still played quietly in the background.

"Sounded on the microphone like it was getting fairly heated over here," Mac observed.

Chris took a deep breath, then exhaled. "I pushed him, you know. Morris. I told him I was going to sink his boat with him on it. I went down into the salon pretending to pull the plug, and he freaked out. Broke the helm right off and jumped over the side."

Mac snorted and looked out into the dark.

"I have to admit, I really wanted to do it," Chris said. "Sink him, that is. I wanted to kill that fucker more than I've wanted anything in a long time. Ph.D.s aren't supposed to do that kind of thing. Good people don't do that kind of thing. But it would've been satisfying."

"And now you're wondering what? If that makes you a bad person?" Mac asked, sounding as though he was worried for his friend's state of mind.

"Think about what we've been through, who we've had to fight," Chris replied. "O'Grady. English. And finally, Morris. These guys were all either abused themselves, abusing others, or both. And this had been going on for decades."

Mac looked down and sighed.

"You, Jase, and I were playing Dungeons and Dragons right about the age where English was getting cigarette burns on his arms from dear old dad and trips to the emergency room where he was probably treated by Morris, of all people, if Joe Rothberg was correct. Think about how deeply that kind of pain and suffering cuts and how many more people there are out there just like O'Grady."

Chris looked at the black water and reached down to scoop out a handful. "Abby seems to think trouble finds me. But how can I possibly avoid it when so many people are messed up?"

Mac had nothing to add to that. The two stood at the rail for several minutes, each lost in their respective thoughts.

Chris bent down and once again scooped some water from the surface. He looked over the stern and off to the lights of Monterey twinkling on the horizon. The fifty-eight degree water was four thousand feet deep underneath them, and the nearest land was ten miles away. He knew that was the last anyone would ever see of Morris.

Following Chris's gaze, Mac asked, "Where to next, boss?"

"Home," Chris replied, but he was thinking of someplace far beyond Carmel.

For Further Discussion

1. What drew you to this novel?
2. Do you feel the story is plot- or character-driven, or both?
3. Chris Black faces a number of challenging situations in the story. What is your assessment of the choices he made? And what, if anything, would you have done differently?
4. Chris is assisted by several friends that he's known since his childhood. Who do you know from your childhood years and could you imagine them providing assistance to you in the event of such challenging situations?
5. What was your favorite scene/line? Why?
6. What would you consider the theme of this novel?
7. The ocean was once thought to be limitless, capable of absorbing everything that humans threw into it. Recent revelations around the world suggest that is no longer the case. What do you know about debris in the ocean? Where does it collect?
8. What are some things individuals could do to help clean up our oceans?
9. Because humans are not well-adapted to breathing underwater, the study of undersea marine life requires the use of various technologies. What technology is used in the story, and what other types of technologies are you familiar with? How does each type of technology help us understand the underwater world?
10. The Center for Marine Exploration (CMEx), where Chris Black works in Monterey, California, is fictional. What do you know about research institutes dedicated to studying the ocean? Where is the nearest such institution to where you live?

Acknowledgments

Field scientists are, as a rule, an irreverent and sarcastic group of hardcore human beings. If you don't currently know any such people, I strongly encourage you to seek them out. I've been extraordinarily lucky to work with many such people over the course of my career, and *Into a Canyon Deep* would not have been possible without the generous support of several of them, including Peter Auster, Carrie Bretz, and Andrew DeVogelaere.

About the Author

Dr. James Lindholm is an author who dives deep for his inspiration. His novels stem from a foundation of direct, personal experience with the undersea world. He has lived underwater for multiple 10-day missions to the world's only undersea laboratory and has found himself alone on the seafloor staring into the eyes of a hungry great white shark. He has drafted text for an executive order for the White House and has briefed members of the House and Senate on issues of marine science and policy. James Lindholm's diverse writing portfolio includes textbooks, peer-reviewed scientific journal articles, and action/adventure novels.

For more information, please visit www.jameslindholm.com.

An Excerpt from *Blood Cold*,

Chris Black's Second Adventure

1

Bile, mixed with the remnants of some distant meal, erupted from Michael de Klerk's mouth as he was wrenched back into consciousness. His face slammed into the gritty, non-slip back deck of the small boat on to which he'd been dumped. The rhythmic hum of the twin diesel engines vibrated through the thin, vomit-covered deck plates, and de Klerk could feel the boat steaming quickly over the undulating swells. With every third or fourth swell, his body lifted off the deck and hovered briefly before the Earth's gravity drew him back into its massive embrace.

Relief that he was awake swept over him for about ten seconds, but that feeling was quickly replaced by pain, then fright, and then a mixture of the two. In addition to the scratches on de Klerk's face, pain emanated from the back of his head where someone had hit him. There was also the extreme discomfort of his bound limbs—his arms were tied behind his back and, judging from his inability to feel much of his left arm, he had apparently been lying on his left side for quite some time. His ankles were also bound, though this caused less outright agony.

He recalled leaving the office in downtown Cape Town in a hurry; there'd been something important going on, but he couldn't remember what that was. What had he been doing there? He crossed the street to enter the parking structure. Okay. And then he approached his car. Someone must've hit him from behind.

The next thing he knew, he was on this boat. Where was his stuff? His computer?

De Klerk was lying such that his face was directed toward the stern of the boat with his head nestled under the lip of the rear gunwale. He couldn't see anything. As the boat launched off the next swell, de Klerk took advantage of his status to shift his body. When he landed, he was facing toward the cabin of the small boat. The door to the wheelhouse was closed, and he couldn't see over it, so there was no way for him to guess at the number of people inside.

The gradually increasing ambient light around the boat told him it was near dawn, though he couldn't be sure precisely which day was dawning. He could see things more clearly now. There were two five-gallon buckets sitting against the gunwale to his left, each had five or six very large hooks hanging around its perimeter. He thought he could smell an odor of fish coming from the buckets.

Though he was a genius with mapping software, de Klerk was not particularly good with introspection. If his mind was busy with a mapping problem, he was happy. But if he was left alone to his thoughts, well, that didn't usually go very well.

The fact that no one had taken even a moment to check on him heightened his belief that he was in big trouble. Valuable hostages would receive good care. People who were not valuable would not. He'd also watched enough American TV shows to know that if the kidnappers let you see their faces, you were "toast." He'd always liked that phrase.

This latter point taxed his young heart when the boat abruptly cut its engines and drifted quietly on the undulating swells. The door of the cabin opened, and three large men emerged, none of whom was wearing any kind of mask to obscure his identity.

De Klerk knew he was toast.

The men wore knee-high rubber boots under Farmer John foul-weather pants. Each sported a sweater of some kind, and all donned knit hats. Only one of his captors looked at de Klerk before joining the other two at the boat's rail. There'd been no compassion in that glance. The other two were pointing at something away to the right and nodding their heads. No one said anything.

That is not to say that it was quiet. The aural void produced by cutting the boat's engines had been filled rapidly with what sounded like a loud cocktail party. De Klerk could hear hundreds or more voices arguing loudly. Overhead, dozens of common seagulls soared, and a penetrating stench was coming from a source de Klerk could not see. The pieces of this puzzle did not fit together well, and he did not understand what was happening.

The men conferred among themselves for a moment, and then two of them began working with the hooks. They each carefully strung three of the large hooks on a line. Next, they reached into the bucket and baited each of the hooks with a large fish head. With all six of the hooks baited, the men tied the lines off at either side of the stern and threw the heads into the water.

Perplexed by this activity, de Klerk's anxiety was temporarily abated as he tried to figure out what these men were doing.

The blue-eyed man came over to him. He squatted down, resting his large arms on his even larger thighs. When he exhaled, his breath smelled of bologna and old cheese.

"Well now, my little friend, you didn't honor our deal and now it doesn't look too good for you. Nope. Not too good at all." He shook his head in a world-weary way that almost made de Klerk believe that the man was on his side, that he didn't want to do whatever it was that he was going to do.

"Please. Please!" de Klerk exclaimed, now in a full-blown panic. "I don't know who you are and I won't say anything. I promise. Please just don't hurt me." He was crying now.

"Now, now. Don't make this any harder than it has to be, my little friend. We are just being paid to do a job, right? We have families, too, right? Won't do for us to come back without having done our jobs, right?"

"Just let me off somewhere and I'll disappear. I'll never tell anyone what happened," de Klerk begged.

"Did you hear that, boys?" the man said, looking back over his shoulders. "He wants to be dropped off somewhere!"

Looking back at de Klerk, the man said, "We can do that, my little friend. We can do that." His tone gave de Klerk no confidence.

One of the other men extracted a coil of line from a compartment in the starboard gunwale. At one end of the line there was a carabiner and a large Styrofoam float.

De Klerk was not a good swimmer. If they were going to put him in the water with his hands tied he might drown.

"Please. Please don't put me in the water. I can't swim! I'll give all the money back! I will do anything. Please." He paused. "At least cut my legs free. Please!"

The blue-eyed man grabbed de Klerk by his two wrists and hefted him up on to the stern gunwale. Momentarily disoriented by the move, it took de Klerk several seconds to get his bearings.

He was seated on the stern with his legs dangling over the back of the gunwale. In front of him, perhaps seventy-five feet away, was a very small island. More like a large rock pile than a proper island. It was covered with what looked like some kind of seals. There were literally thousands of them. The din of sound that earlier had reminded him of a party was their near-continuous vocalizations, kind of a barking yelp. The stench, even at this distance, was overwhelming.

Seals were coming and going from the island; leaping off the rocks into the water and jumping about in small groups. A small huddle of penguins watched from the water's edge.

A new panic erupted in de Klerk, a panic like nothing he'd ever experienced before. He shook violently and tried to rock his way back into the boat. Large hands clasped down on both his shoulders and prevented him from moving.

He knew he was staring out at Seal Island, a small rocky outcrop located a few kilometers offshore in False Bay. It was known to Cape Town residents, as well as much of the TV-watching world, as the home of South Africa's famous "flying" great white sharks.

De Klerk's mind involuntarily reviewed the last nature special he had seen on TV. This was the spot where one-ton sharks literally leapt from the water at 25 mph in pursuit of their Cape fur seal prey, a behavior rarely seen elsewhere in the world. Erupting from the water, the sharks would split the small fur seals in half. They would then thrash about at the surface in a frothy red mix of seal blood and seawater as they finished off the meal. Sea birds would swarm on the kill spot, grabbing loose seal innards and fighting over them in the air above as the shark thrashed about below. Occasionally, an unlucky seabird would stray too close to the gaping maw of the white shark and become dessert to an already satisfying meal.

Perhaps the most disturbing aspect of these predatory attacks was the incredible speed with which they took place. If you sneezed, you missed it.

THE LEGACY OF A FAILED REGIME RISES FROM THE DEEP.

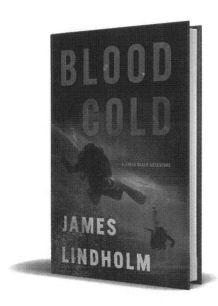

Indomitable marine biologist Chris Black is looking forward to six quiet months of scientific research off the coast of Cape Town, South Africa. But when on a routine dive Chris discovers the wreck of a fishing vessel that disappeared during a storm decades earlier, he inadvertently clashes with the ghost of South Africa's Apartheid. Thousands of gold Krugerrand provide powerful motivation for treachery everywhere, and Chris is forced to take a careful look at those he trusts most. Racing against time, he must find out who is providing critical information to the criminals . . . before too much innocent blood is shed.

"Opening this book is like diving with sharks. Big sharks. At night. In a hurricane. What next?"

—*Stephen Palumbi, scientist and author of The Death and Life of Monterey Bay*

Available now wherever books are sold.

An Excerpt from *Dead Men's Silence*,

Chris Black's Third Adventure

1

Damien Wood died first. In the dwindling twilight of a Colombian sunset, a pirate cut his throat from ear to ear as he sat at the helm of his father's sixty-foot cabin cruiser *Innovator*. The entire incident took less than twenty seconds. One instant he was leisurely staring out the cruiser's front windshield, smiling as he thought about the last *Game of Thrones* episode he'd watched, the next he was dying. Damien's last conscious act was to look down at the blood pouring over his tanned-but-skinny torso and wonder, "What the hell?"

The *Innovator* had left Newport Beach two months prior and slowly worked its way down the length of Baja California and along the Mexican mainland in four weeks' time. Investment banker Jared Wood had been initially hesitant to loan out the *Innovator* to his son Damian and his friends. He'd only owned the boat for a year and had hardly spent any time on it himself.

Wood had ordered the crew, via satellite phone, to steer clear of Honduras, El Salvador, and Nicaragua for fear that they might run afoul of "bad people." But it was at the last stop the *Innovator* made in Colombia that the boat had caught the attention of four men lurking in a small converted fishing boat at the partying crowd's perimeter. The crew of the *Langosta Espinosa* were nondescript enough to move freely among the boats moored around the island without attracting attention. The boat itself was unremarkable, and the five Hispanic males that operated it could have fit in anywhere along the Central American coast. If anyone had looked closely, they would have seen that the wooden-hulled boat had not been doing any actual lobster fishing for some time; with traps irreparably broken and fouled on the back in a way no active fisherman would ever allow. But in a crowd more concerned with merriment than potential dangers, no one gave the boat or the crew a second look. And the lagging Colombian economy had left the already under-funded coast guard with very few assets to patrol the extensive coastline.

Late in the morning, the *Innovator* had crossed into Colombian waters and sought refuge in the first cove the captain could find. The last week of partying had taken its toll on all passengers aboard, and the group required rest. As life-long, unrepentant nerds, Damien and his friend Stephen Long had survived this far with minimal experience at this type of alcohol-fueled merriment. Damien's other friend, Mike Hanson, had done his share of partying during his football days, but not in recent years. Though all three guys had warmed quickly to the opportunities for celebration among their international boating community, endurance wasn't their strength.

Cracks had begun to form in the façade holding the three young men together. As roommates during freshman and sophomore year at the University of Southern California, Damien and Mike quickly worked out the challenges of living in close quarters together. Stephen had no such training. He'd lived at home in his parent's basement for what little of college he'd attended before departing USC for the glory of the movie business. His career as third assistant to the director had lasted merely six months. The film for which he'd quit school was canceled mid-production due to financial issues. By the time the *Innovator* had reached Colombia, Stephen was complaining more frequently about Mike's nightly snoring. Mike, in turn, noted that Stephen rarely cleaned up after himself, leaving "his shit all over the place" while he played games on his smartphone. Damien had simply been frustrated by how stupid he'd thought these complaints were as he tried to keep the peace.

As the *Innovator's* first day in Colombian waters came to a close, the three friends were as far apart as the boat allowed, each lost in his own thoughts. That made them easy targets.

After Damian, Stephen Long died next; and just as quickly. He was stretched out on the *Innovator's* bow playing a driving game called *Asphalt 8* on his smartphone. Stephen was so immersed in the game that he didn't sense the pirate's presence until his attention was redirected to the handle of the eight-inch ka-bar knife sticking out of his chest.

For every pound that Damien had been missing from his torso, Stephen had made up for on his own. He looked down at his chubbiness for the last time and wondered where his mom and dad were. *Asphalt 8* continued on its own for another two minutes until the phone's battery went as dead as Stephen.

Mike Hanson put up a fight. He was down in the galley, making his second sandwich for the evening, when the third pirate came through the main hatch to get to him. At six-foot-four inches and two-hundred-and-fifty pounds, Mike looked at the smaller man wielding a knife and smiled.

Mike decided to resolve the situation quickly in his favor. Growing up in south-central Los Angeles as the only child of a single African-American mother, Mike had learned early to solve problems before they came back to 'bite him in the ass.' He grabbed the wooden cutting board on which his second sandwich rested and struck at the pirate, crushing the man's nose with a single strike. Mike then retracted the board and quickly struck again at the pirate's windpipe, forcing a guttural cough from the man as he collapsed.

Satisfied that he'd ended the incident, Mike paused to listen for other trouble. Hearing no immediate threats, he leaned over to pick up the pirate's knife, thinking he'd better check on his two less physically capable friends right away. The pirate could have already attacked one of them before coming down to the galley, he thought.

Rising back to nearly his full height, slumping slightly, so his head didn't hit the galley ceiling, Mike heard a metallic click that he didn't recognize. Before he had a moment to consider it further, a gunshot from the fourth pirate hit him in his left shoulder.

The impact of the bullet spun Mike around, so he was now facing the pirate who'd just shot him. Neither of them moved as the gun's loud report still wrung in their ears.

Mike glanced down at the wound on his shoulder and then peered through narrowed eyes at the pirate. As the man raised his weapon again, Mike used the cutting board, which was still in this right hand, to swipe upward, across his body. The force of the blow dislodged the gun from the pirate's hand and broke the cutting board in half.

Not waiting to give the pirate another chance, Mike hurled his large body up the steps toward the back deck. "Damien! Watch out—." His warning caught in his throat as he found Damien's body slumped in the chair at the helm, a gaping hole where his neck used to be, and his chest covered in blood.

Grabbing his bleeding shoulder, Mike stepped around the edge of the wheelhouse and moved as quickly as the narrow walkway would allow toward the bow. The shock of seeing his friend dead was briefly tempered by the adrenaline surging through his body. Perhaps if he could get to Stephen in time, they could escape together. He could hear someone coming behind him, but before he could turn around, Mike had arrived at the portion of the walkway that opened onto the *Innovator's* bow, revealing Stephen's lifeless body lying against a hatch. "Oh, my god."

Briefly stymied by the realization that his friends were no longer with him, Mike hesitated. At that moment, a pirate appeared around the edge of the wheelhouse. The man expertly tossed a large knife in the air, caught it by the blade, and then threw it directly at Mike's chest.

Mike frantically deflected the knife with his right forearm, the blade slicing deeply into his muscle before dropping to the deck and sliding over the side.

Now nursing two wounds, Mike determined that his best course of action in the increasing darkness was to flee. He grabbed the rail with his bloodied right hand and launched himself over the side.

Plunging deep into the warm Pacific water, Mike surfaced away from the *Innovator* and began stroking toward the shore, leaving blood in his wake. He could see lights shimmering at multiple spots along the edge of the large cove from what he hoped were houses or hotels. Someone there would be able to help him.

It was a long swim for Mike, at least the length of a football field. He was not a natural swimmer, and with both arms impeded by injuries, his progress was slow. Approximately halfway to shore, he heard what he thought was the sound of a small outboard motor. Pausing to listen over his labored breathing, it sounded to Mike as though the small boat was headed away from him. Maybe this plan was going to work.

Struggling with declining mobility in his limbs and significant blood loss, Mike continued to make progress toward land. He could see the silhouetted shapes of people walking along the shore, but he was too tired to produce a coherent cry for help. Pausing again to catch his breath, new hope swelled in Mike as his feet drifted down to touch the sandy bottom below. He'd made it!

His feet touching the bottom, he could now use both his legs and arms to make progress toward shore, which he began to do with great effort. Exhausted and delirious, Mike failed to process the tugging he sensed down by his right leg. When it persisted, he started to wonder if he'd become tangled in something.

Reaching down to remove whatever was holding him back, Mike was briefly shocked back into lucidity by the realization that his right leg was gone below his mid-thigh. His hand brushed against the end of what must have been his femur, surrounded by strands of tissue dangling in the water.

"What the f—?" Mike exclaimed, just before he was pulled underwater. He could feel the rough skin of the shark's nose on the underside of his right arm as it clenched its jaws around his torso.

Seconds after the attack began, it was over.

Twelve minutes later, the *Innovator* was once again underway, this time alongside the *Langosta Espinosa*. Neither the simultaneous departure of the two vessels nor Mike's struggle for survival had registered among the partying crowd in nearby boats or along the shore. As the boats disappeared over the horizon, the bodies of Damien and Stephen joined Mike one last time as the pirates tossed them over the side, wrapped in an old fishnet and anchored down by the dive weights that Jared Wood would never have the chance to use.

CamCat
Books

Visit Us Online for More Books to Live In:
camcatbooks.com

Follow Us:

CamCatBooks   @CamCatBooks   @CamCat_Books

Made in the USA
Columbia, SC
21 October 2023

24761933R00167